Copyright © 2023 by Chloe Ruffennach

All rights reserved.

Identifiers: LCCN 2023916110 | ISBN 979-8-9890390-0-5 (paperback) |

ISBN 979-8-9890390-1-2 (eBook)

No portion of this book may be reproduced in any form without written permission from the publisher or author, except as permitted by U.S. copyright law.

For the women in my life and all of the women I've never met.

A Note to Readers

This story contains content that might be troubling to some readers, including references to death and suicide. Please be mindful of these possible triggers as you continue reading.

1

Michael

The weather outside was just the way Michael Ken liked it the night that he met the girl in his head. Michael could taste the cold outside like it had a flavor. It was the kind of evening chill that froze the air in his lungs.

But she did more to take his breath away.

Michael walked into the dim bar, letting the stark change in temperature embrace him. He basked in the incredibly vivid rush and in the way the smells seemed sharp and focused. His vision even felt crisper despite the poor lighting.

It was the type of bar he might've found himself in on a Wednesday night a few years ago, back in college before there was work and responsibilities to tend to. The music blaring was far too raunchy for the number of patrons. No one was dancing yet, but it was still early. There was plenty of time for things to liven up. A group of girls in a tight cluster near the end of the bar swayed to the beat, shifting their weight between their feet, too afraid to dance until they were too shit-faced to care.

Michael approached the bar feeling vulnerable. Admittedly, he had never been to one alone. He had always believed that most people didn't venture into bars stag unless times were tough, but there he was.

He felt an acute sense of nervousness prick at him as he walked to get his drink, and self-consciousness gnawed at him like a teething dog. Michael knew better than anyone that under normal circumstances a beer or two in his belly would erase his anxiety, though he suspected that they wouldn't do the trick that night. This uneasiness was fresh and unyielding. No one was looking, but he had convinced himself that he could feel their eyes. He felt like a fool. A lonely failure.

And then he saw her.

It was as if the people around him had parted to give him an unobstructed view. The first thing he noticed about her was her blouse. It was lacy, white, and almost sheer. From behind, he could see the black straps of her bra beneath it. He knew that she wanted him to see it. She wanted him to be curious. Her jeans were light blue and styled to appear overworn. Even as he looked at her back, Michael could tell that she was slim, that she cared about her appearance, and that she was his type.

As though he hadn't been nervous enough before, Michael felt his mouth become sandy and his hands grow clammy. A lot was riding on how those next few minutes unfolded.

What the fuck is wrong with me? he thought. *I have nothing to lose, nothing to worry about. Get. It. Together.*

Michael approached the bar with cumbersome movements, his heart pounding with both worry and excitement. It was a potent concoction that made him feel alive.

If he thought the back of her was nerve-racking, the front of her nearly paralyzed him. She had big blue eyes, a small nose, and rosy lips.

Her face was angular, unique, interesting, and unfairly symmetrical. Just a glimpse at her made Michael hold his breath.

When she looked up, her eyes were nearly reflective in the dull orange glow of the bar's lights. For a moment Michael feared that she had caught him trying to see more of that black bra, but she smiled a warm, pleasant grin that eased that worry.

"You're new here," she observed.

Michael reflected on her voice. It was small and pleasant, almost musical, and not at all what he had expected. He'd almost hoped her voice would be nasally to ease her jarring appearance. But of course it wasn't.

"Is it obvious?" he asked.

She brushed her finger across the rim of her emptied glass. Her nails were polished in a burgundy coating of paint. "I come here often," she said and gestured toward the group of girls at the end of the bar. One woman's drinks were setting in, and she kept turning around to try to dance up against her friend. "We come here most nights."

"Why aren't you hanging out with them, then?" But even he could see why. Those girls were in it for the long haul. They were looking forward to hours and hours of drunken mistakes with strangers until each of them punctuated their nights with their heads in toilets.

"Guess I thought I'd try my luck at getting another Corona. The sex on the beach they bought me is not quite what I was looking for."

"Corona's my favorite, actually," Michael said.

Bella smiled even wider. It seemed like she wanted to say something important, then she simply said, "Yeah? Mine too. It's my go-to when I want to relax. I always keep a case in my apartment."

Michael smiled. *I should have assumed that already,* he thought as he slid down onto the stool beside her. Perhaps it was bold to assume that she would want to talk to him for longer, but she didn't seem to mind.

"Those drinks remind me of college," he said. "Sitting out on the porch sipping them when it was hot."

She leaned in and giggled girlishly. "Shirt undone, shades on, hanging with the frat boys?" she asked.

He did not let that lean toward him go unnoticed. His heart was pounding so violently in his chest that he was afraid she could hear it.

"Maybe," he said before mentally cursing himself. That one-word response gave her nothing to work with.

Before either of them could speak, a bartender approached. The man briefly regarded Michael's new companion with unrestrained awe. Then, he raised an eyebrow expectantly.

Poor bastard can't even ask her for her order, Michael thought to himself.

"Two Coronas," she said, holding up her fingers in a V for emphasis.

The bartender nodded. "Of course."

Briefly, he looked at Michael and shook his head slightly, a goofy grin playing on his lips. He tried to hide it as he hustled to get their beers, but Michael had seen it still.

He thinks she'll eat me alive, he thought. He looked back at her and noticed that she was staring at him eagerly. *And she just might.*

The Coronas landed in front of her, and she handed one to him with a smirk. When he took a sip of it, he had never tasted anything so pleasant. No Corona had ever been so refreshing. Then he turned back to her, prepared to get lost in the moment. To get lost in this girl.

And he did. As he talked to her, he found that he couldn't look away even if he tried. Her eyes trapped him; they were so rich and blue that they looked artificial. They were made to hook him.

She's perfect, he thought.

"Big frat boy, then?" she asked at one point, just before she finished her second beer. She was holding her liquor well. He could only tell it was affecting her when she laughed.

"Ah, not really," Michael said. "I was in one for a bit. I only stayed for two years."

"So, you got past the pledging and everything?"

"Yeah, my frat was cool about things," he said. "They weren't too harsh."

"I see," she said. "So why did you leave, then?"

"I didn't like the party atmosphere," he answered.

"And look who finds themselves in a bar on a Wednesday," she teased. She finished her beer and placed the bottle back on the table with a small, triumphant *bang*.

"Same can be said for you," he noted.

"I at least came with some friends," she said, giving a soft grin. "Did you come here alone tonight looking to pick up girls?"

Michael returned her smile. "I came here for you."

"Took you long enough," she said as she laughed, tucking a strand of hair behind her ear.

His eyes caught the dull screen of her smartwatch. He felt his stomach dip when he noticed the time was creeping toward eleven o'clock. It was getting late, and he had work in the morning, but Bella was still sitting before him, more intoxicating than any drink. He wanted to cement himself to the barstool and stay there for days.

"Can I know your name?" he finally asked.

"Oh, yeah! Duh." She held out her hand, and the golden bracelets on her wrists jangled. "Bella."

"Bella," he repeated as he gave her hand a shake. "I'm Michael."

"It's very nice to meet you, Michael." Bella beamed. Her rose-colored lips seemed to dare him momentarily. It made him swallow hard.

"It's getting late. I need to get going," Michael announced. He was pleased to see her pout at this.

"So early?"

"I have work in the morning," he said as he grabbed his jacket.

"Where do you work?" she asked, watching him begin to gather his things. She seemed disappointed that he was leaving but did not ready herself to follow him.

"RightMark," Michael answered. "It's a tech company. We make games, mostly. Video games."

"Fun," she said. "Will I be seeing you here soon?"

"I can be back tomorrow." Michael slipped on his coat. "Will you and your friends be venturing back here too?"

Her girlfriends had left about an hour ago without even telling her goodbye. Michael had been thankful that they had left the two of them alone. He almost offered to walk her home but thought better of it. He knew the implications that came with his offer. Besides, it didn't really matter. Not yet at least.

"We weren't planning on it," she said. "But I can come back tomorrow if you'll be here."

Michael couldn't help but grin sheepishly. "It's a date," he said. It was a bold assertion that made his stomach jump as he waited for her to react.

She only giggled sweetly. "It's a date. See you tomorrow, Michael."

"And you, Bella."

He tossed down a handful of cash onto the bar for good measure. It was enough to cover her tab, and he turned to leave quickly before she could protest about paying her half. He hoped it had made him seem mysterious, perhaps even giving her the false illusion of wealth.

As he walked toward the exit, he could feel her eyes trained on him. Was he walking normally? How did his hair look from the back? Did his jeans look okay from behind?

Yet when he had retreated into the chilled night air, the cold washed these anxieties from him. He was free from her gaze outside, where the only people around him were oblivious women in clusters, gorgeous and long-legged, their laughter loud and drunken. It was an odd thing, to be both relieved of the pressure and to want to be under it again. Bella was like a thrill, a hit of adrenaline that he could see himself getting hooked on quite easily.

And he would be seeing her again the next day.

He smiled to himself at the thought of being near her again.

The wind that rushed around him brought gooseflesh to his skin even under the many layers he wore, and his exhales were clouds. It had all been so exhilarating, so lively.

Michael stood alone in the cold, feeling very proud of himself.

If only it all had been real.

2

Michael

Every day that Michael came to work, he first noticed the bold and bitter scent of burnt coffee. He didn't know why his coworkers had yet to learn how to make a decent brew, but the bitter smell remained his morning greeting. What was worse was that he went to work with some of the brightest people in Pennsylvania, maybe even the nation. They were all incredibly intelligent but still couldn't manage to brew a good cup for shit.

Michael found his desk with ease, methodically, the way he always did. His desk was set in a small office room, blessedly separated from the rest by a wall of glass. He was proud of his little corner, even if it was just a tiny space. Michael had earned that desk and the privacy it came with. After only a short period of bright ideas and consistent work, he had gained a place that only senior and exemplary workers occupied.

He closed the glass door behind him and tossed his bag onto the small plush chair in the corner. Around him, the office space was sparsely decorated yet it was a welcome sight. It was a refuge of sorts from the other people of RightMark who never ceased to pester him and who always seemed to find a way to disappoint him. So even if the office wasn't much to look at, he thoroughly enjoyed its confines.

In reality, he felt that the barren layout was an apt reflection of himself. He had never cared much for frivolous things, and Michael liked to have his office space look clean, with a few photographs here and there, and black stationery sets displayed on his desk. That was all he needed.

Michael sat down in his seat with a huff. He was two coffees into his morning already and still felt exhausted. He hadn't slept well the night before with his mind wandering to thoughts of Bella. Her name was like an echo in his mind all night, her smile seared behind his eyelids. *Bella, Bella, Bella.* The idea of seeing her again felt like a dream. He peeked at his watch and sighed again. The day had just begun, and he was already counting it down. Michael knew then, with utter certainty, that he was going to need another coffee to get through it all. The mundanity of a day at work threatened to suffocate him when the prospect of *Bella* lingered so near.

He glanced outside absently. The city of Pittsburgh was sprawled out before him. He was eight stories above ground, and the cars whizzing by on the city's streets below looked small enough to fit in his hand. Large towers punctured the sky as the UPMC building stood above them all like a powerful father overseeing his children.

Michael cracked the window open, letting the warm September air breathe new life into his office space. Below him, the city was alive with its chorus of car horns, shouting pedestrians, and laboring buses. Those sounds were beautiful and familiar to him like the voice of an old friend. The way his office window framed Pittsburgh was perhaps his favorite part of going to work.

He was debating getting up to preemptively get his third cup of—unfortunately burnt—coffee when there was a knock at the door.

Michael sighed loudly. He did not need to turn to see who had dared to intrude on his little glass sanctuary.

Jon Way stood on the other side of the transparent wall, looking inward bashfully. He knew better than to disturb Michael so early. And yet there he was. It was common knowledge that Michael had never exactly been a morning person. So despite the inconvenience, Michael assumed that whatever Jon was there for must've been important. Or at least he hoped so.

Michael let out a small groan for his ears only and motioned for Jon to come in. Jon was a shorter man who liked to make up for his smaller stature by widening his build with muscles. Despite his broad appearance, he had incredibly feminine features and was known to paint his nails on occasion. He cared greatly about his style, and sometimes he wore tight button-downs that seemed ready to burst with the muscles beneath. Michael simply could not make sense of the man, nor could he fathom why he put so much effort into his appearance, especially when he was already happily married. It was an enigma he often found he did not have the energy to begin to untangle.

The two weren't exactly friends but Michael allowed Jon leniencies that he did not grant to most. This early morning visit, for instance, being a prime example. Michael owed Jon for his occasional useful breakthroughs, but Jon had yet to finish a large project on his own, and for that, Michael regarded him as a slacker. But for the assistance he had given Michael in the past, Jon was spared Michael's more abrasive morning crankiness.

Jon shuffled in with a thin manila envelope under his arm.

"What is it?" Michael asked before Jon was even in the middle of the room.

"Paperwork," Jon said. "Again."

Jon tossed the envelope onto Michael's desk. Michael opened it and flipped through its contents quickly, his eyes crawling over the words but not really reading them.

"What is all of this for, exactly?"

"Some bullshit they want you to sign away," Jon said. "They want to make sure that you're okay giving up your right to have a say in the cover art for your game. It's all crap if you ask me. And they want a status report by the end of the week. They're talking about pushing the deadline up."

"Up?" Michael couldn't hide the outrage in his voice. "To when?"

"The last Wednesday of September," Jon said. "The twenty-sixth."

"And they're just telling me now?" Michael ran a hand through his already-ruffled hair in exasperation.

"I don't know," Jon said. "I'm just the messenger."

"I know." Michael flipped the folder closed dramatically all the same. He rubbed his temples. "Do they know how hard it has been to write this game from scratch? With their standards, too? I'm busting my ass here."

"I get it. They're just saying they want it by the end of September instead of early October now."

It was doable but an absurd thing to ask of him still. He was in the final testing stages of the game, and from what he had seen, it was running perfectly. But they didn't necessarily need to know that it wasn't a massive inconvenience all the same.

"Again, it's all bullshit, man. I'm sorry. The offer's still open if you need help," Jon said.

Jon was a nice man, but his portfolio lacked luster. He hardly had the experience to tackle anything close to Michael's responsibilities. At the moment, Jon was working on a kiddy game about taking care of pets. It was the type of idea that Michael scoffed at behind closed doors.

"I'm fine. I just need to buckle down. Christ, they want me dead, huh?"

Jon laughed. "Well, again, let me know if you need anything."

"Uh-huh." Michael pulled a pen from his black pencil cup and clicked it, ready to work on the new paperwork before him. He hunched over, preparing to sign away his creativity, his work, and his life. "Thanks, Jon."

"No problem."

Jon looked around awkwardly, moving his feet about before deciding that Michael had dismissed him. He turned and left quietly, picking at his nails, which were painted in a chipping coat of purple polish. Michael didn't look up until Jon was out of sight.

"Motherfucker," he huffed as he stared down at the open folder. The papers were splayed out, promising pages and pages of tiny font and legal jargon.

He had gotten into this business to avoid the messiness of paperwork. The gaming industry was meant to be a world of creativity, filled with endless adventures and desires met, not the strait-laced corporation it had turned out to be. Sure, there was some creativity, and he had been granted a lot of freedom with his recent project, but the manila folder before him reminded Michael of everything he hated about the job. He was expected to sign away a bit of his artistic freedom, and he couldn't help but feel like it muzzled him.

The paperwork was finished quickly enough, though. Michael had long since learned that it could be speedy work if you chose not to read the fine print. He signed his signature on the dotted line, granting the people of RightMark the ability to make whatever shitty cover design they decided best fit his game. Michael also signed off on a few promises and clarified that, yes, the aspects of his game that he had pitched to them nearly two years ago would indeed be present when he turned in the product on the due date they insisted upon.

Michael leaned back into his chair, still seething even with the paperwork finished before him. Admittedly, he had set a precedent for himself in the past of finishing his projects well ahead of schedule. He wondered if they were frightened by his hesitance now, his inching closer to the deadline when he normally would have submitted the completed work by then. Yet something about this game was making him work slowly, forcing him really think his decisions through. And now they were moving up the deadline...

He was lucky he was already trying it out for himself. It was nearly done, and he just needed to play the game a little longer and test it for some kinks. But the moving goalpost frustrated him all the same.

Victoria knocked on the door at around ten o'clock to break up Michael's wandering thoughts. She stood outside of the glass, smiling too widely, showing off perfect white teeth that she had probably paid too much for. Michael motioned her in absently, but Victoria looked pleased with the approval all the same.

She was a curvy woman who loved for everyone to know it. Her skirts and pants were almost always a size too small, and her tops were typically unbuttoned one button too low for what was expected in an office setting. But no one complained, and Michael certainly wasn't going to. Today, she wore a gray blazer and matching skirt with a plunging pink top.

"Hi, Mike," she said. The grin on her face seemed to start at one ear and end at the other.

"Morning," he answered.

She almost bounced into each step with the eagerness of a puppy.

"Working hard or hardly working?"

Michael tried not to cringe. "A bit of both."

"I'm runnin' out to get some coffee in a second. I'm taking orders and wanted to see if you needed anything."

It was a near-daily task of hers that she enjoyed very much. Going from office to office allowed her to talk endlessly with everyone. She was fed on whatever fresh gossip the others so willingly gave her, and everyone got their coffee an hour after they ordered it. Michael supposed it was a fair trade.

"Yeah, actually," Michael said. He wasn't exactly eager to have any of that burnt office brew. "Can I just get a black coffee?"

"Definitely!" she said. "How very masculine of you."

"I try," he answered, mustering a smile. Victoria's flirting never did anything for him. Most women's advances fell short of his interests, in fact. But that had been before *Bella*.

"So, one black coffee for you... Anything else?"

"Nah," he said, shaking his head for good measure. "I need to get to work anyways."

"Oh, of course." She straightened, seeming to remember then that she was talking to Michael Ken and not one of her pals.

"While you're here," Michael added, "can you give this to Jon?" He held up the manila folder, filled with freshly signed documents. "I figured if you were heading that way…"

"Yeah, for sure!" she eagerly snatched it from his hands. She could be a bit annoying and awkward, but at least she was ambitious and a hard worker. Michael respected that. It was more than he could say about Jon.

"I'll be back in a bit with your — oops!"

As she was turning to leave, she dropped the folder, causing all of the papers it held to flutter messily to the floor.

"Darn it!" she said, never one for swearing. As she bent to scoop up the papers, her blazer and top slid up her back ever so slightly, revealing a bright red thong beneath. It was lacy and stuck out in a whale's tail, pulled up high as if she had hoped someone would notice. It almost seemed like she had hoped something like this might happen when she dressed that morning, and with a color so vibrant, it was hard to miss.

Once she had gathered her mess, the shirt and blazer slid back into place, concealing their little secret. It was a fleeting moment, yet it was the most action Michael had admittedly gotten in years. After diving into his work, he had very little time to meet women in real life.

"See ya soon!" She left with a pleasant smile, apparently unaware of what he had just seen.

He grinned a bit painfully in response and watched her walk away. How was he supposed to work after *that?* At least it would give him a bit of inspiration.

Michael turned to his computer, a rather massive heap of machinery amidst a room of such scarcity, and unlocked it for the first time that day. Once inside, he worked with the notes he had scribbled down in haste once he had left Bella the night before. His handwriting was downright sloppy, almost illegible. His thoughts after seeing Bella had been jumbled, and his poor handwriting reflected that well. He had never met a woman who made him so careless and clumsy.

Before Bella, there had only been Cindy, a college girlfriend who had not liked Michael enough to stop entertaining other men. Though Cindy had started out like a dream, she had snapped Michael back into reality quickly enough. It made him fear for Bella.

But Bella was more striking than Cindy could have ever even dreamed of being. Bella was far more confident in herself too. She had been the one who had ordered the beers and opened the tab, even if Michael had ended up paying for it to be chivalrous. Michael was beginning to think that he perhaps liked that better. Maybe he liked it when the woman led, so long as she was not leading him down a path of deception. She would know exactly what Michael wanted with those keen blue eyes reading him like his skin was translucent.

Seeing those blue eyes was the only thing that would get him through the day. That and coffee.

Speaking of, where is Victoria? he thought, a little angrily. It felt like it had been hours, but when he looked down at the tiny clock in the corner of his screen, it showed that a mere half-hour had been killed since she had left. *Fuck.*

So, Michael worked away, applying his scribbles to the game, pausing for several minutes every once and a while to squint and read his handwriting. Here at RightMark, they were on the cutting edge of technology, ahead of the competition by miles, and he was reading off of a yellow notepad, trying to force himself into productivity.

Victoria came back after another forty minutes balancing two trays. He was glad to have an excuse to break from his work, and he eagerly stopped coding to receive her delivery.

"One coffee for Mr. Ken," Victoria called into his office.

"Thanks, Victoria."

"No problem!" she said, handing him the small cup, which was warm rather than hot when he grabbed it. His smile faded instantly.

"Let me know if there's anything else I can get you!" Victoria said cheerily. She hadn't seemed to notice his displeasure.

"I'm good for now, thanks," Michael said.

Michael waited until she had finally disappeared down the hallway before he took a sip. Just as he had suspected, it was lukewarm. Worse, it tasted burnt anyway. He sighed and tossed the full cup into the garbage can beside his desk. It landed with a loud *thud*.

Another instance of a woman disappointing him. It looked like it was going to be a long, boring, laborious wait until the next time he saw *Bella*.

3

Jon

The sky looked like it was on fire. Jon Way sat on his back porch in a wooden rocking chair and stared at the expanse of red and orange above and before him as the sun finished its arc in the sky.

Sitting on his porch in the evening was a favorite pastime for Jon. He was a man of simple interests, but what he loved above all else was to end his days with a joint and some fresh air. September had granted him an abnormally warm evening, as the temperature hung in the high sixties. As Jon lit his joint, he couldn't remember a September night being so fine.

He used a white BIC lighter to set his joint ablaze, and the smell that followed was instant and warm. The state of Pennsylvania had recently legalized recreational cannabis, and Jon had gladly taken full advantage of it. He smoked almost every night to get himself to relax and to sleep, but his wife, Shayna, didn't have the same appreciation for the stuff. It was one of the very few things in life that she hadn't completely made up her mind about. Usually, she was set and determined in her decisions, but in this, she was flimsy and prone to her moods. Sometimes she joined Jon on the porch, and they passed a joint between the two of them until the sun had dipped below the stretch of trees behind their house. Other times she scrunched her nose at it and called the smell "skunky."

Regardless, she always made him do it outside. Their home was still treated as if it was newly purchased with the way they cautiously handled it. Shayna had said that she wouldn't have what little furniture they owned smell like a frat house if she could help it. Jon respected that, but he sure did plan to complain about it when the months grew cold again.

That day had been long and arduous for Jon, so the familiar scent of burning weed put him at ease at once. It was like smoking brought him back to center. Earlier, he had scrapped a game he had been making for two and a half months. It had been a hasty decision to throw the entire thing away. In an act of exasperation, he had decided to start fresh. In retrospect, he should not have reacted so brashly, but he had become so frustrated in the heat of the moment that he had deleted it all. Fresh ground. Yet when he left work that evening, he felt more like a fool than anything. Now, he was starting from square one, disillusioning him even more.

The game he had been working on allowed users to have and dote on a virtual pet. It had been highly interactive and was written with the same code that Jon had made for Michael's newest game months ago when Michael still felt the need to call upon Jon for help. The code tapped into a person's brain, pulling out subconscious preferences, and then *voila!* Your ideal dog or house cat became your companion. People could seek therapeutic comfort from pets without the real-life responsibilities of keeping them alive and well. There would be no need for scooping litter boxes or worrying about your pet's vaccinations in the game. The animals in there lived to serve. Or at least, that was the intention.

The mockup version had been horribly dull and the drive behind it had been far too similar to Michael's project. On top of it all, there was not much to do after removing the responsibilities of tending to the animal's basic needs. One dip into the skeleton of the world that he was working on was enough to dismay him entirely. Right-click, delete.

Now, Jon was left with nothing. He had wasted his own time, and he had wasted RightMark's resources. Jon had signed off on getting them a ready-to-sell product by next June, and he felt like he had been fucking around, kicking the can further down the street.

Jon took a long drag from the joint, letting it fill his lungs. He held it in for a few seconds before he exhaled, letting the large cloud of smoke briefly obscure his view of the sunset. He heard the glass door slide behind him and turned to see his wife step out onto the porch to join him. Shayna had a pleasant smile on her face. Her arms were crossed over her chest against the night air, and she wore nothing but a thick pink bathrobe that was tied tightly around her thin waist. It seemed tonight she didn't mind the skunky smell.

Shayna was a woman of average height and ebony skin. Even after several years together, she could make Jon's breath catch in his throat without trying. She simply had that effect on a person. Not a day passed that Jon didn't note how lucky he was that she had agreed to settle for him.

"Can you spare a few puffs?" she asked.

Jon held out the joint, and she grabbed it eagerly. She took an impressively long drag that made her cough afterward.

"Beautiful night," she commented, falling into the rocking chair beside him. The red sunlight glowed beautifully off her skin.

"One of the last warm ones," Jon observed before taking another greedy hit.

They sat in silence, watching the seemingly stagnant sky striped with colors so beautiful that they looked almost artificial.

As they both slipped into their highs, staring out at their property, Shayna observed, "We bought ourselves a damn good view, Mr. Way."

Jon nodded his agreement. They lived at the end of a cul-de-sac, and their backyard was almost entirely isolated from their neighbors. Their property had been fenced off by large pine trees that bordered their backyard like a green wall and blocked out their neighbors during any season. The woods behind their house cradled the sun and stretched on for miles, leaving them a large expanse of solitude.

"Yes, we did," he agreed.

The large house had been purchased partially through his undeservedly generous salary from RightMark, which had seen a pleasant increase as compensation for his earlier breakthrough work with coding. The other contribution had been from Shayna's nursing income, but the largest portion had been taken care of by Shayna's mom. She had given some of the money that she had received from her husband's death to Shayna as a loan so that they could buy the house of their dreams as newlyweds. Shayna's mom had always been one to value the traditional family, so she had been eager to give them the large house to encourage their marriage. She had also been frequently expressing that she was eager to get paid back.

"Living large," Shayna said with a tired giggle. She held out her hand for the joint again and Jon passed it, feeling sluggish in the blur of his growing high.

"Can only go up," Jon added, putting aside his thoughts of their debt.

"Speaking of only going up, what's the mood at RightMark? Are you starting to get nervous?" Shayna asked. As she took a hit, she stared at Jon with big brown eyes that briefly distracted him.

Jon had told her earlier that evening that the deadline was moved up for the company's next highly anticipated virtual experience. Right-Mark wanted the game to be out and ready for purchase by Christmas, and they expected a lot more testing would be necessary where Jon's new code had been applied. He had explained all of this to Shayna by way of venting but found it odd that she would bring it up unprompted. It wasn't like her. She had decided long ago that she found Michael's game horribly distasteful and often liked to avoid the subject.

"Nah," he said. "It's not my game."

"Yes, but RightMark's reputation is on the line." She passed the joint back to him. "A lot of money hangs in the balance. More than I care to know of if I'm being honest."

Jon ashed the joint and stared down at his feet. The topic of money was one of the few subjects that was tender to them. Neither could fathom much use for it beyond paying back Shayna's mom or ridding themselves of their mountain of student loan debt. They already had the house, the privacy, and two hand-me-down cars.

They had everything except what they really wanted.

"It's okay to be nervous," Shayna said.

Jon took a long hit. He felt his thoughts swirl and put out the joint on the cement patio. That was enough for the night. He was pleasantly sedated.

"I'm not," he said.

"You seem off, babe," Shayna noted. "I don't want to pry, but if you want to talk about it, we can."

He looked at her and felt like his mind was swimming. It took some time for his thoughts to come to the surface.

"I just fucked up today," he admitted. "I deleted my game."

"What? Why?" Shayna looked shocked. She was much more sober than he was.

"I didn't like it," Jon said with a shrug. "It didn't seem fun."

"I thought it was a great idea," Shayna said. Of course, she thought it was great. She would've loved it if Jon created anything besides Michael's detestable virtual reality.

"It was a boring idea," Jon said. "There's only so much you can do with a puppy that lives in your brain."

"So flesh it out," she suggested. "Introduce more animals. Create challenges. Make the animals compete in a competition."

Despite himself, Jon laughed. "You should be making it for me."

"If I had a techy brain I would," she said.

"Your job is a little more important," he noted. While Jon was coding puppies and kittens into an artificial existence, Shayna was busying herself trying to keep people alive. The juxtaposition of their careers was never lost on him.

"Maybe on the surface," she said. "But people need entertainment too. They need to escape."

Jon looked at her dreamily. The sun had nearly set by then, and in his high, he felt he had been sitting out there with her for a whole day. He believed he could stare at her forever, though. As night settled in, her features became muted, and her eyelids were growing heavy from the smoke. He often reflected on how he couldn't believe that she had agreed to marry him. Not many women would have supported their husbands as they messed around in a newly established gaming company. Certainly, women who looked and acted the way Shayna did settled down for that even less often. Longevity was unlikely in his career and yet she still sat beside him telling him that his job was worthy.

"I love you," Jon said.

This made her laugh. Her giggle briefly filled the night and was carried off on a gentle breeze.

"You're such a sap," she teased.

"Is that a bad thing?" he asked.

"No," she said. "I like it. That's why I married you. I like a sappy man."

She leaned forward and kissed him. Somehow, she didn't taste of weed but of strawberries, the sweet artificial taste of her lip balm.

They kissed for what could have been minutes or hours. She was the present, *his* present, and nothing else mattered beyond that sweet taste of her lips and the feeling of her so close to him. After years of marriage, they were still able to get lost in one another, touching and kissing like it was the first time. Two became one whole. Shayna could burn his stress and self-loathing away and blow them into the breeze like the smoke from his joint.

"I love you too," she said when they pulled away for air. "But it's getting chilly. Let's get inside and warm each other up. What do you say?"

He kissed her again in agreement.

4

Michael

They met at the bar at eight o'clock, as promised. Michael entered and was greeted by the warmth of the building, the crisp smell of drying spilled beer, and Bella's earnest smile. She was perched on the same stool she had sat on last time, her long legs dangling nearly to the floor. Her hair was wavy and styled in a cool, effortless way. She was wearing black ripped jeans, a flowy white blouse, and bright red lipstick.

"You came back," she said pleasantly. Her voice was almost a purr.

"Did you think I would skip out on you?" Michael asked as he removed his coat.

"I had my worries." Her finger traced the edge of her glass. Tonight, her knuckles were decorated with golden rings, and bright gold bracelets bounced and clattered around her slim wrists noisily with each movement.

"That was your first mistake," he said. He raised his fingers lazily, trying to get the bartender's attention while still staring at her, never letting his eyes wander. She looked unbelievable. Michael's heart was hammering away in his chest again, but he tried his best to appear outwardly at ease.

"Mm?" she hummed through her pursed red lips. "And what exactly was my error?"

"Doubting me," he answered. The bartender approached him then, and before he could ask for their orders, Michael said, "Two Coronas. Thanks."

Bella giggled softly and shook her head, taking a sip of whatever cocktail she was about to finish off. Her pregame, he supposed. He liked to think it was to take the edge off. He wondered how long she had sat there, waiting for him while sipping away at some concoction to pass the time until he arrived.

"So, how was your day?" Michael asked.

Bella pouted playfully. "Boring." She nearly sang the word. "I have nothing interesting to report. Hopefully, yours was better than mine."

Bella downed the rest of her cocktail as Michael spoke. "Actually, it was pretty much the same," he said. "Just paperwork and tweaks."

"And your job is? I know you said that you work at RightMark, but what do you do there?"

"I'm a game developer. I'm working on a game right now." He couldn't help but smile. "I think it's going well if I do say so myself."

Bella smiled too. There was a twinkle in her eye that was a bit mischievous. "So, I really am talking to a big tech guy, huh?"

"It would seem like it."

The bartender returned with the two beers, and Michael opened a tab.

As they drank, they discussed the normal first-date checklist. Where are you from? Who is your favorite musician? Do you like to read? Favorite food? Color? Place? Song? It was a meaningless conversation, really. Just posturing to test the waters and make Michael feel more comfortable.

He learned many things about the girl in front of him, though, all of which satisfied his desire to know her intimately, deeply, and personally. Most significantly, she told him that she had been born and raised in that very city, while Michael hailed from Philadelphia. RightMark had brought him to the Steel City.

"I heard of RightMark and had to move," Michael told her. "I had to. What they're doing is phenomenal. It is the next step in gaming tech. And my game... I don't want to sound too cocky, but I think it's going to really push things forward."

"So, from Philadelphia to Pittsburgh," Bella said. "A downgrade, if you ask me."

"Not at all!" Michael exclaimed. "I love it here. It's the perfect kind of city. Not too congested, but there's life on every corner."

"That's a good way to look at it," she said. "I suppose you like cold weather then?"

She gestured to the window behind them, which revealed that a flurry of snow was slowly falling in delicate clumps.

"I love it," he repeated.

Bella smiled with shared humor. "I knew you would."

"My birth mom used to live in Florida, and I never understood how she could bear it down there. She actually left her old house to me in her will, but I never go down and use it. It's always too hot. Always."

"I hate it when it's too hot," Bella said. "I only like to get sweaty when it's voluntary."

Michael laughed at that and took a long sip.

By the time their beers had been finished off, the conversation turned to the grittier details of each other's families, and Michael felt comfortable enough divulging to her that his aunt, Mary, had been the one who raised him and had been in a retirement home for two years.

"I'm so sorry," Bella said.

"Don't be. I think she likes being waited on."

Bella had little to report about her own family. Michael had predicted as much. It was not hard to expect certain things about Bella. Michael did not think that this was an inherently negative thing. Predictability could be good, he supposed.

The checklist had been checked, and around a half hour after their conversation about family, they agreed to leave without any more drinks. They both had work the next day, after all. Michael closed the tab rather hesitantly, not truly wanting to leave. It was all too good.

As they gathered their things, Michael watched Bella slip her coat over her shoulders. She stood almost at eye level with him but seemed to fall short by a mere inch. Her leanness and height made her appear overpowering like she was demanding the room's attention. Michael was acutely aware of a few lingering eyes from the bar watching her slip her arms through the sleeves of her jacket.

Michael led her outside, the way a gentleman would, and she smiled at him graciously. She grabbed his forearm lightly as they walked, letting him take the lead and visibly showing the rest of the bar's patrons that she was claimed. It pleased him to watch the surrounding men avert their gazes, pretending as if they hadn't been staring with hope just moments before.

The night air was cold, yet the chill was pleasant, the kind that awakened you instantly, striking you back into the present. Bella leaned into him, seeking his warmth as she continued to hold onto his forearm.

"Another cold one," she observed. Her breath came out in gentle clouds.

"It's not so bad," Michael said. "I like this type of weather, remember?"

"Me too," she agreed.

They huddled together as they walked. Michael was glad that they both were shameless about touching. The cold was forcing them together, making them appreciate the other's warmth.

People passed as they strolled by, and Michael was only mildly aware of them. They seemed out of focus, utterly unimportant when compared to the woman hanging off his arm. Yet Michael did notice a group of teens huddled together at a street corner, passing around a cigarette. It was probably the only one that they could get their hands on, stolen from a parent's pack no doubt, and they were trying to make the most of it.

Bella scrunched her nose slightly. She leaned further into Michael as they walked past, seeming to want to put distance between herself and the group.

"What's wrong?" Michael asked.

She looked up at him, perhaps a bit embarrassed. Then she motioned toward the teens who were now several feet behind them.

"Cancer sticks," she said. She gave a little shrug. "I just don't get it."

"I know right!" he nearly exclaimed.

"I'm assuming that means you don't smoke," she said. She looked up at him again, her eyes searching, but he chose to continue training his gaze forward. If he looked at her, he was afraid he would fall into her stare.

"Never," he said. "I think it's so gross."

Michael could still remember when Mary had dragged him to his grandmother's vacant house weeks after her death. The memory of the way he had had to wipe down the walls was still so vivid he could smell the aged scent of cigarettes even there on the street with Bella. They had been cleaning the house to sell it, and they needed to restore the white paint to make it look presentable. The walls had yellowed with nicotine, and he would never forget the way the brown water would run down the wall when he would swipe at it with a wet towel.

Bella stopped suddenly and her rhythmic footfalls came to a dramatic halt. When he finally looked at her, her cheeks were flushed from the night's chill. She looked as though she were blushing, and small flakes of snow had fallen into her hair and were glistening like white crystals.

"That's good to hear," she said.

They stared at each other for a while, both smiling. Then she tucked her hair behind her ear and looked down at the sidewalk.

"Are you walking home then?" she asked.

"Yeah, I mean..." he stumbled over his answer, trying to determine how to word it best. "Yeah, I guess."

"I was thinking..." She was still avoiding eye contact. "Do you have anything you need to go home for right now?"

Michael gave a small laugh, suddenly nervous as he realized what she was suggesting. Bella bit her lip and raised her eyebrow as she finally looked at him.

"Not really, no."

"Well... My apartment is just a block away. If you wanted, you could come hang out at my place."

His heart felt like it could cut through his ribs at the speed it was racing.

"Um, yeah." Now it was his turn to look at his feet. "Yeah, that sounds lovely."

They both giggled, awkwardly filling the quaint night with the excited, mildly uncomfortable laughter of new lovers.

The walk back was blessedly short, and they made small conversations about silly things that didn't truly matter. Michael's mind was elsewhere the entire time.

When they finally got to her apartment, Bella flicked on the switch and said a ceremonious "Ta-da!"

As the lights went up, her apartment unveiled itself in a wave of neutral colors. Michael walked into the hall and took in the sight. Her apartment was small but chic. Everything was tidy as if she were selling the place and had prepared it to be shown. There were no dishes in the sink, no letters on the table, and no blankets or clothes strewn about. Her home was fixed to perfection. Minimalist, just how Michael liked it.

"Welcome," she said from behind him as she closed the door.

He had a sudden urge to take off his shoes. As he was slipping them from his feet, Bella chuckled.

"You don't need to do that," she said.

"It's just really nice in here," he said as he kicked his shoes to the side.

"Why thank you. I've been thinking about moving out. It's a little big for just me."

She was beginning to walk toward a hallway that was glowing dully with a faint golden light. "How about you make yourself comfortable?" she said. "There's beer in the fridge with your name on it. I'll be back in a second. I just want to take my shoes and coat off and put them away."

"All right," he said. The idea of rummaging through her refrigerator felt suddenly odd, almost intrusive. "What type of beer do you have?"

"Just Corona, of course," she said, turning back briefly with a smile. "There's lime in there too if you want to add a slice."

"My favorite."

Bella beamed again in response. "I'll just be a few minutes," she said and then continued down the hallway, presumably toward her bedroom. Michael waited until the door clicked shut softly before he gravitated toward the refrigerator.

He opened it to see nearly an entire shelf packed with Coronas. The rest of the refrigerator's contents seemed to be made up of healthy foods, staples that Michael would have liked to keep his refrigerator stocked with if he wasn't too busy to make proper meals most nights. It was filled with leafy greens, juices, berries, and raw meats waiting to be cooked.

He grabbed a beer before prying further and closed the doors.

Michael took a few small sips as he admired Bella's apartment, weaving his way through her furniture and toward the couch. It was expertly decorated in different shades of well-kept white and beige. In a vase on the counter was a bouquet of snowy-colored flowers. He smiled. Lilies of the valley were his favorite.

He found his way to the couch and plopped down with a small grunt. Michael continued to drink his beer, looking around intently at whatever little insights he could find out about Bella from his seat without actively snooping. On the table beneath her large, mounted television was a set of framed photographs that Michael squinted at to try to make out. They all looked too blurry from where he sat, but he could tell they were likely family pictures, memories from vacations and other events that might have held some sense of consequence under different circumstances.

Set on the coffee table in front of him were black square coasters and a spread of flimsy magazines. There were some issues of *Vogue*, a couple of *Sports Illustrated* magazines, and one curious copy of

Playboy. He was leaning forward to get a better look when he heard the light clicking of heeled shoes growing nearer.

"I thought you were taking your shoes..." his words trailed off as he turned to see her.

Bella paused in the doorway, leaning lightly against the frame, wearing only a set of lacy red lingerie. Her skin was glowing in the faint light, looking clear, pale, and delicate. The bra she was wearing was constructed of only lace, so thin he could see everything beneath it.

"...off." He finished his sentence and then swallowed hard. "Christ."

"You like it?" she asked, but it wasn't really a question, just a statement posed as one. She knew she looked good, but she wanted to hear it.

"Yeah. Yes!" He was fumbling over his words, unable to string together a sentence to accurately convey his thoughts.

Bella approached him then, sauntering like a cat. She did so with a fierce look in her eyes like she wanted to consume him.

"I got it for you," she said. Her voice was soft and silky.

When she stood before him in his seat on her couch, she towered over him. He felt pleasantly overshadowed. Michael unthinkingly reached out and touched her waist.

"Red is my favorite color," he said, stupidly.

Bella's smoldering demeanor broke for a moment as she cracked a small smile. "I know."

She took him to her bedroom and straddled him almost immediately.

Bella was masterful. She was pleased by the things that pleased him, happy only when he was.

Of course, she was. That was how he had designed her.

After he finished his second round, he logged off, leaving Bella alone in her bedroom and her world, and returning back to his.

5

Michael

Sirens was going well, Michael concluded with great satisfaction. He knew—with more certainty now than he had expected to experience—that others would feel the same once they gave his game a try. Bella was a dream, both figuratively and in reality. She was the perfect woman, a manifestation of all of the characteristics Michael desired in a partner, plucked from his own head and projected back to him like a customized film. Bella was the result of a man soured by his experiences seeking to find what he deserved.

And after tonight he fully believed he had found just that.

Michael put his Emissux to the side. He was glad to be free of the tight metal collar that was used to plug into the Sirens game. The device harbored the Sirens cartridge on the front, which could be credited for the many sleepless nights of coding it had taken to create. The collar was cold when you first put it on and rather tight, making it feel sometimes as if there were metallic hands wrapped around his throat. He had to respect its efficiency, though. RightMark was the first to think of its intuitive design, to tap into the potential of the human nervous system and elevate the gaming experience. There was no working around it, but Michael still despised the feel of the contraption.

In Bella's world, though, he hadn't felt the cold metal bite of the system. It was nonexistent; the only sensations he felt were those his head projected to him, the ones that his brain wanted him to feel.

He was still a bit in awe of it all. Michael had expected it to feel real—after all, he had designed it to be as true to life as possible. But everything about it—from her skin and her lips to her touch and her kiss—felt almost eerily authentic. Most of the time, he found himself forgetting that he was even plugged into a game at all.

He had done it.

Michael wiped a hand down his face in disbelief, chuckling to himself in the quiet darkness of his bedroom. He had *really* done it.

His bosses would be pleased, of course. The people on the floor above him would see the financial benefits of it all. James Sherrod, RightMark's president, had shown a personal interest in the Sirens game, and Michael was sure that he would be thrilled to see just how real it all seemed.

Bella was all his, though, completely designed to his interests. She changed depending on the person who plugged into Sirens. Thanks to Jon Way's line of code, the Emissux tapped into the user's nervous system and read their brain like a book. It took all of the desires the player wasn't even fully aware of and built the perfect partner out of them. And for Michael, that partner was *Bella*.

Strangely, Michael longed to get back inside the game with her, to dawn the uncomfortable Emissux collar again and plug in for just a few more hours. The urge reminded him of when Cindy and he used to part ways back when they had first started dating. Something in him craved to see her again, to dip back into Bella's world and her apartment. It was an odd sensation, like an itch that he was dying to scratch, and Michael chalked it up to a sign of unbelievable success.

However, he resolved to wait until the next evening to slip back into Sirens and continue testing and looking for flaws, though he doubted he would find any. So far, there had only been small errors, like the smell of the bar being too overpowering and the streets being too cold for comfort.

So, he concluded that he would treat Bella like his nightcap for the time being. He would visit her in the evenings to finish off his day. Strangely, it made him eager to get through tomorrow, the way good plans always had a way of doing.

Michael stood up from the cushioned chair he was sitting in at the edge of his room. As he walked toward his large bed, he realized just how tired he was. He felt exhausted and droopy, the same way he usually felt when he came in real life.

Another good sign, he thought.

Before he could succumb to sleep, he cleaned up the mess he had made. It seemed that the feelings of pleasure and completion translated identically into reality, which was another success. After Michael changed, he climbed into bed, and it took him mere minutes to fall asleep.

As he began to slip from consciousness, his thoughts were wrapped up in Bella. She played in his mind like a recording on a loop. Her face, her eyes, her legs, her voice saying, *you're amazing* after they both came simultaneously for a second time. Those words were a purr in his ear that kneaded at his insides while she spoke so softly, sweetly, and truly.

You're amazing.

He smiled softly as sleep took him. Maybe he was.

6

Shayna

Shayna Way watched as a little girl of no more than seven years old pedaled on her bike so slowly that it was hard for her to steer it forward.

It was a bright and particularly sunny day, and Shayna had been walking through town dressed head-to-toe in blue scrubs with her purse weighing down her left shoulder. She was in the process of running errands and enjoying the pleasant warmth of the day while dwelling on the knowledge that there would likely be snow on the sidewalks within a few short weeks. Soon, walking from store to store would be miserable work, but because the sun was still brilliant and the air was warm, Shayna enjoyed running her errands on foot.

She was on her way to CVS when the little girl staggered by her, nearly cutting her off as she wobbled along. The girl's eyes were wide with knowing panic, and she zigzagged her bike to overcompensate for its inability to continue.

As she watched, Shayna bit her lip in understanding. She tried to divert her gaze and focus on her errands, but in her stomach, she felt the same feeling of forthcoming failure that the girl undoubtedly did.

Everyone had been there before, steering something that seemed out of control so far past the brink of saving that you just had to wait for the crash.

When it came, the noise was spectacular. There was the unmistakable sound of flesh hitting the pavement, followed by a metallic clanging as her bike fell after her. The cacophony was punctuated by a small *thud* as her plastic helmet bounced off the street.

Now, there was no ignoring the girl. Shayna looked up to see her tiny features screwed up in pain and unspecific anger. The girl tipped her head back to face the sky and let loose a horrible wail, her face instantly flushing a deep red.

Without thinking, Shayna rushed toward her, instinct taking over. From somewhere to her right, a slender blonde woman also began to run in the same direction, clutching her bag tightly to her shoulder with one hand and covering her shocked, agape mouth with the other.

Shayna got to her first, though, and she bent down with some hesitance. The girl's eyes were squeezed shut with terrible fury, and she screamed at the sky with such unabashed and raw emotion that it was startling.

"You're okay," Shayna told her softly.

Her words parted the girl's eyelids. The girl's eyes bulged, and the surprise cut her cries short as if someone had hit mute.

"You just have a few little scratches." Shayna pointed to the scrapes on her bare knees and calves. The girl had been wearing capris that exposed skin, and her right calf was now oozing with bright red blood from where she had fallen. The cuts were large and angry, bleeding rather profusely despite seeming fortunately shallow.

As Shayna turned her attention toward her bag in search of a bandage, the other woman came up behind her.

"Honey!" the woman exclaimed. She knelt beside the girl, pulling her into her arms in an aggressive way that visibly discomforted the child.

Shayna pulled out a large bandage, roughly the size of her palm, and handed it to the thin woman who was now holding the girl. Shayna assumed that she was the girl's mother. Otherwise, the possessive show would have been incredibly inappropriate.

"I think it's just a scratch," Shayna told her.

"Thank you," the woman responded. She tore open the packaging and put the bandage on her daughter with a swift, practiced hand. Shayna felt useless as she watched the mother console her child.

The girl was sniffling in her mother's arms, staring up at Shayna with big, wonderous eyes. There was an ache that overcame Shayna as she looked down at the girl, and she felt the desperate urge to hold her as well.

"Her daddy," the mother huffed, "he keeps buying her all of this garbage." She gestured toward the bike, splayed out in the sun on its side. "All he does is buy her S-H-I-T," she said, spelling the word out so her daughter wouldn't understand. "I keep telling her she's too young, but she still keeps trying to show us she's a big girl, huh?"

The girl nodded, still staring up at Shayna with a moony gaze.

"Kids fall." Shayna shrugged. "No biggie."

"We were lucky there was a nurse around," the woman said. She raised an eyebrow at Shayna's scrubs.

"You don't need to be a nurse to have a bandage," Shayna said.

"Yes," the mother agreed. "I suppose you're right. Lesson learned."

The mother's stare followed Shayna as she rose to her feet. Something about the woman's unbreaking attention made Shayna feel uneasy. It was as if the mother was angered that Shayna had gotten to her first, as though Shayna had screwed her out of being a good mom.

This mother had countless times to make up for it, though. Shayna didn't have any.

"I have to go finish my errands," Shayna said. "Do you need anything else?"

"No," the woman answered. "Thank you."

Shayna nodded, not sure how else to respond. She thought about telling the little girl that pedaling faster would help with the steering but thought better of it. That was for her mom to say. Shayna pressed her lips together to keep from speaking.

As she walked away, Shayna could still feel the mother and daughter's gazes on her, the girl's in wide O-like eyes and the woman's in narrow, measuring slits.

When she was far enough to not feel their stares boring into her, she dropped her shoulders. She had been maintaining a stiff posture as she walked away. Now, she saw no need to uphold it. Her shoulders slouched, and her body slackened from its stiff composure.

She turned the corner and entered their small, local CVS, feeling strange and suddenly drained. The store was a tiny thing, packed with all of CVS's normal conveniences in its limited space.

As she walked into the store, she noticed that the shelves were already filled with holiday treats. The bright red and green candies were displayed up at the front, striking Shayna as funny. She could never understand everyone's eagerness to skip the fall season and go right into wintertime. Everyone rushed toward Christmas and New Year's, and the preparation was continuously starting earlier and earlier.

Shayna had no interest in skipping to December. Winter was a time for all of the dreary things in the world: darkness, cold, and seasonal depression. She had tried to convince her husband, Jon, several times to move somewhere warmer when they had first begun searching for a house, but he had been stubborn about keeping his job at RightMark, which didn't have any locations in sunny Florida or California. It annoyed her that she kept losing the argument, but she was ultimately glad her husband was doing something that he enjoyed.

She had learned early on that marriage was about compromise, but she had always been an inherently stubborn woman. Besides California, she didn't give in to many arguments. She let Jon fold, and most of the time he was happy to give in just to be rid of the discussion. Perhaps she liked that about him.

Jon was a different breed of man, to her at least. Shayna supposed that almost every wife felt that way about their husband, but she truly believed that Jon was unique. After all, he had been the one to make stubborn old Shayna bend and finally fold for once.

Shayna was a woman who had never cared much for men. They had all bored her. She had figured men out a year after her breasts had started to bud, and she had determined rather quickly that the old saying was right: they only ever wanted one thing.

That was not to say that she hated men. No, she just hadn't been quite as interested in them as her friends had been. They were like solved puzzles, and she wanted to move on to the next thing. This is why from fourteen to college she had determined that she liked women exclusively. For a while, as she huddled in a closet of her creation, she considered herself a lesbian. Throughout those formative years, she had kissed girls and dated women, not bothering to try out her male courters. Men were fun to flirt with but nothing beyond that. They were entertaining to tease and to paw at, but she had never cared to commit herself to one.

It was that way until she met Jon. They had both been at a college party, the kind where everyone around them was belligerent by eleven, and anyone less than blacked out wasn't having a great time. She was one of the handful of people with some sanity left in her. So she had placed herself at the back wall of the host's overcrowded living room and twisted her hips unenthusiastically to the beat.

That was when Jon had slid up next to her, smooth as maple syrup. He had sipped his drink slowly, buying his time while calculating how to approach her. She found it funny that he was so cautious when she had been groped by men by way of greeting in the past. Shayna had let him take his time, patiently waiting to see the pickup line he settled on.

Finally, he said, "This party sucks."

Shayna couldn't help but laugh. It was a short giggle, produced purely from him not meeting her expectations.

That's what he came up with? she thought.

"Then you should drink more," she suggested.

"You just want to see me drunk enough to bust moves like that guy over there." He pointed toward a man in the center of the room. The kid looked young enough to be a freshman, and he was letting the beat control him entirely as he moved jerkily to the blaring song.

"I would, actually," she said, laughing again.

"You're going to have to get me more than this horrible jungle juice then." He motioned toward the red solo cup that he was holding in his left hand. Inside, the drink was almost gone and was tinted a bright blue.

"I think he's on more than juice," Shayna said.

Jon looked back at the man thrusting his body off-time now. "Yeah, you're probably right."

Shayna felt a warmth with Jon instantly. It was as if an old friend of hers had approached her. But she was guarded, of course. She was a lover of true crime and had heard one too many stories about college-aged women going home with strange men.

And she only liked girls, didn't she?

"So, why aren't you dancing?" Jon asked.

"Not drunk enough," Shayna answered.

"Then you should drink more," he suggested.

Shayna cracked a smile. She held up her solo cup and they clinked their plastic drinkware in cheers before taking deep swallows.

They didn't dance that night. In fact, Shayna's friends had spotted her talking to Jon from across the room and had drunkenly pulled her away, assuming the worst.

Shayna didn't talk to guys.

But the two of them had exchanged phone numbers before her friends stumbled to her rescue, and suddenly Shayna was talking to a guy. A *cute* guy, for that matter.

She liked the way he didn't push. Their conversations started intentionally slow. Shayna would give him an inch to see whether he would push for a mile. She had texted him three times a day, short little blurbs to see if he was still curious. The last thing she wanted was for her first man to be some drunken frat dude who had seen her with beer goggles and wanted to cut to the chase.

But Jon had matched her three texts, sometimes sending four, but never five. She liked that. And she was beginning to think that she liked him too. So she began to text him more than she normally did until, despite her better judgment, she was texting him about almost everything.

Their first date had been at a donut shop, where they both got vegan donuts. She had proudly announced that she was a vegan, and he didn't cringe when she told him. Instead, he had gotten a vegan sweet himself, and declared, "This stuff isn't half bad!" Two years later, he was a vegan as well.

She couldn't deny that she strung him along when it came to sleeping with him. Though she wasn't particularly proud of it, she wanted to test him. Part of her thought he was aware of the constant trial, but if he did, he didn't seem to mind. He was the type of guy who would wait for what he wanted. He must've truly desired her because she didn't undress in front of him until the sixth date. By that point, she had been giddy with excitement.

They had gotten married shortly afterward.

Never in her life had she ever seen herself partnered with a man, but Jon was kind and open and not as concerned with masculine standards as other men tended to be. Sure, he liked his muscles and his hair cropped short, but he also didn't mind it when she painted his nails shades of pink and purple, and he always gravitated toward traditionally girly prints for his work shirts.

And she loved him for bending her a bit.

Shayna found herself staring down at the racks of sugary candy in front of her, searching for Jon's favorite vegan jellybeans. Oddly, they didn't sell them anywhere else nearby, so on pleasant Fridays like that one, she would swing by and pick up a pack to treat him.

It made her feel good to make him feel good.

Shayna was smitten, perhaps even domesticated when compared to her college days. But she didn't mind. Jon wasn't forcing it, and she was comfortable. He was unwaveringly loyal, and she was almost entirely sure that he didn't have it in him to hurt her.

Shayna picked up two bags of jellybeans, and, before leaving, she finished the rest of her shopping list. As she walked toward the back of the store, her eyes fell on the pharmacy, and she tensed. Beside the pharmacy were little purple boxes of pregnancy tests, lined up and on display like they were mocking her.

She turned from the shelves sharply, feeling unnerved. As she hurried away, she felt the draw of them behind her as if they were watching her just as the mother and daughter had minutes before.

The last thing Shayna picked up was a box of large bandages to replenish the supply she carried around. She had given the little girl her last one.

The clerk checked her out as her mind wandered, dreaming up images of a Jon, a bike, and a daughter of her own, pedaling hard and straight.

7

Michael

Work was horribly boring, as it always was now that Sirens was in its final stages. Michael was mostly beyond the creative aspects of the game, and recently, there seemed to be no purpose to coming into the office, especially now that he could conclude that Sirens would soon be undeniably successful. Michael was blinded by exceeding his own expectations.

He had liked Bella just the way she was and didn't want to think about changing her in the slightest. If he had a gun pressed to his head, he still wouldn't be able to think of an edit to make to her.

So, Michael sat there twiddling his thumbs and killing time. He planned to run out the clock shamelessly by playing on his computer and pulling up images of celebrities to find the women who had inspired Bella. He wondered what elements of previous women his subconscious had chosen and preferred. Perhaps it had been the lips of some model, the hair of an actress, the hips of a random musician that pieced together the woman that Bella had manifested as. But as he searched for similarities, all he found were differences. Everyone's lips lacked the same appeal, their hair wasn't as silky, and all of their hips looked less inviting. Bella was an intoxicating creation of personal perfection. Though she was his subjective preference, he couldn't fathom the idea of anyone considering her less than flawless.

Throughout the day, her voice echoed in his head like a shout down a vacant tunnel. *You're amazing*. He couldn't get the luscious way she had said it out of his mind. Those two words were running through his head at all hours. It was inebriating, making it hard to concentrate, and he itched to plug back in and hear it fall from her mouth again.

The game had left him with a strange urge he had never had when he finished playing games on the Emissux before. It was like a craving, a constant yearning in his mind to return to that makeshift universe. Though it was strange and strong, it left him rather pleased overall. If the creator couldn't get enough of his own game, he couldn't imagine the eagerness that consumers would approach it with.

He had been sitting at his desk, pondering this earlier in the day when Victoria had come into his office to visit him around ten, asking for his coffee order.

"Coffee?" she had asked, poking her head in.

"Nah, I'm okay," Michael answered. He barely looked up from his computer screen, which was swimming with pictures of some lingerie model. *No, still not like Bella's legs.*

"Are you sure?" Victoria leaned in a little further. "You look a little bit... tired. Did you sleep all right?"

Michael looked up then, regarding her rather angrily. She was in another tight skirt, but Michael was particularly focused on how the fabric was excessively wrinkled as if she didn't own an iron. He also could not help but notice how the sleeves of her blazer were far too long for her, so much so that they nearly came up to her knuckles.

"Just working on the game last night." It came out like a snap though he hadn't intended for it to seem so abrasive. Perhaps he truly was that tired. "I don't need any coffee."

"Oh." Victoria was a bit taken aback but she smiled softly, trying to still appear pleasant. "Well, I'm sorry you had a late night. I'm sure it'll be worth it in the end. Everyone here can't wait to see it once it's finished."

"Thanks," Michael said shortly. His eyes fell back to the screen, and he waited for Victoria to leave. She did after a beat, looking as though she had wanted to say more. Michael was grateful when she didn't.

He was relieved to see her go. It was not like he needed to concentrate; he simply didn't want to talk. Michael was comfortable in his own little world, the impression of Bella still on his mind to put him at ease.

The truth was, he probably did seem visibly tired. Only after unplugging the night before did Michael realize how long he had been in Bella's world. It had all felt so quick, yet it had apparently unfolded over the better part of the night. Michael wasn't sure he had even slept for three hours altogether, but he felt fine. It was like he was running on the caffeinated feeling of adrenaline, though he hadn't dared to look in a mirror at his reflection since he woke. He knew his fatigue would be staring back, and perhaps he couldn't blame Victoria for acknowledging it.

The scrolling felt endless. He continued until his eyes felt strained and dry. When it was past noon, he closed the tab and deleted his history. He knew that if anyone at RightMark really wanted to check in on him, they could subpoena his search history, but he was ready to excuse the copious searches as research for Sirens. And it was research, wasn't it? He was trying to make sense of how Jon's code could be so excellent and could read him better than he could read himself.

He strolled down the hallway thoughtfully. There was little visible commotion in the office at any given time. In fact, RightMark was almost always silent. Any stress or anger was directed toward screens, lost in a world of code. Most of the employees plugged in at eight and unplugged at five, leaving little room for conversation among each other in between. RightMark allowed most of its employees to work with minimal oversight until their game's delivery day, and most of the employees in front of him were hard at work on their own individual projects, plugged in to perfect their creations. Michael had always found the silence that came with this unique environment uninviting in a way that sometimes put him on edge, and he doubted he would ever become used to it.

Michael got a Snickers from the vending machine down the hall. It wasn't much, but his stomach was nearly empty, and he hadn't brought a lunch, so it would do. He was so hungry that he unwrapped it seconds after pulling it from the machine, and he had finished it before he even returned to his desk.

On the way back, he couldn't help but peer into Jon's office. He was two offices down from Michael, and Jon had been given a glassed-in room as well. This had been a reward for Jon's loyalty to RightMark, as he had been with the company since it had essentially been a small startup with a dream. Michael also suspected that it had to do with the coding he had done for Sirens. He had been given the office around the same time Michael had successfully been able to apply Jon's idea to the game. He didn't see the two events as a coincidence.

Michael peered through the glass wall and saw Jon plugged into his Emissux, lying virtually unconscious. His office was a mess, posing a perfect juxtaposition to Michael's. His desk was littered with seemingly unorganized forms and papers. Despite being emptied by the janitor every night, his trash can was filled to the brim with crumpled papers, bottles, and cans. The wall behind his desk was almost completely covered in a collage of photographs. There were pictures of Jon and his friends, photos from college and high school, and snaps of past pets. Mostly, though, they were pictures of him and his wife, Shayna, in various places, always smiling as if they couldn't be happier.

Under the watchful gaze of a thousand stagnant eyes, Jon's body was slack in his reclined chair, mouth slightly agape. Jon appeared utterly relaxed, almost as though he were asleep, yet his green eyes were open and vacant, staring up at a ceiling he couldn't see.

He should've closed his eyes, Michael thought. *They'll dry out if he's in too long.* It was a rookie mistake, one that Michael hadn't expected from someone as experienced as Jon. For this reason, Michael could only assume that he would be plugged in for just a few minutes, maybe even moments.

As if being called into the present, Jon began to blink rapidly, coming to. As his mind settled back into the real world, a frown pulled down the corners of his mouth. He unlocked the collar around his neck and tossed it carelessly on top of the mountain of mess on his desk. With a huff that Michael could hear even with the glass partitioning them, Jon tore a page from one of his many notebooks and crumbled it in his fist. He threw it toward the trash can, but it missed, falling among the other discarded papers scattered on the floor. He didn't seem to notice.

Michael hurried away before Jon could return his stare.

When the two of them began working together years ago, they both had the same drive to them, the same hunger and eagerness to create. Jon was a man of wild thoughts, the artist behind a lot of RightMark's most creative decisions. He was always thinking outside of the box, sometimes impractically. But that fuse fizzled out quickly. Jon was not made for longevity. He was a sprinter. He provided some of the best insights and small ideas that RightMark could have, but he had never created a game entirely by himself. He couldn't write a story, only scenes.

Sometimes Michael suspected that Jon was a bit jealous of him. While Jon was made for the dash, Michael was built for the marathon. He could create a tale from beginning to end if given the time. Sirens had been the longest and most thorough one he had ever created, yet he had found success despite it being his first game designed for the Emissux.

Sirens had been Jon's idea at first, though. In truth, it had been his little nugget of wisdom on a drunken night, and Michael had run with it. But without Jon allowing Michael to take the reins, Sirens would've never been born.

Despite the revolutionary feeling that now accompanied Michael's thoughts of Sirens, he knew that it would be met with pushback. There were already protestors who didn't like the invasive nature of the Emissux. They were repulsed by how it hooked into your nervous system and temporarily highjacked it. This criticism would only flourish with the release of Sirens, which was the first game to read its players instead of the other way around. It would likely only revitalize the fears the release of Locked and Loaded, RightMark's first game, had worked so hard to squash.

Locked and Loaded hit shelves and changed the gaming industry entirely. It was a battle game meant to simulate actual warfare, from the recoil of a fired gun to the dusty sand of deserts. The players were amazed. They could feel the wind on their skin, smell the environment they chose to play in, and even feel light injuries. This was all because of the Emissux turning the key into their nervous system, making them hallucinate these sensations.

On the eighth floor of their building, at least a dozen new Right-Mark games were in production, possibly more, that utilized the Emissux device. Only one took full advantage of it, though.

The thought of people seeing his finished product initially made Michael very nervous, so much so that his anxiety was almost paralyzing. But he was instantly put at ease when he dived in and saw Bella. He hadn't wasted over a year for nothing. It would sell, some lonely men would get their rocks off to it, and Michael would walk away from the deal as a very, very wealthy man.

Now, instead of fear, he was eager.

Michael thought of Bella the night before, her voice echoing those two familiar words in his mind yet again, and he felt as if there was no way to fail.

8

Jon

Jon was sitting in his living room with the lights off and growing particularly aware of the way the large house around him had settled into stillness. When he was home, he spent almost every minute with Shayna, enjoying the way they could laugh away each other's tough days, yet she had turned in early that evening, leaving Jon to his own devices.

He often didn't like being left alone, and he was currently trying—and failing—to distract himself by brainstorming ways to improve the game he was trying to remake over a bag of vegan jellybeans. But it did little to ease things for him. Nothing brought him comfort the way Shayna did.

When she was off doing something else, he craved her company, finding that every second with her was well spent. She was just behind their bedroom door warming her side of the bed while Jon sat in the quiet and procrastinated his work while he reflected.

Jon was consumed with a worry that had blossomed in the pit of his stomach an hour before and had only continued to bloom. Perhaps Shayna had been right to assume that he was nervous about

Sirens. He couldn't help but think about it on occasion, wondering what Michael had done with Jon's idea. Sometimes he found himself fretting over it, worrying that it would be a failed attempt, one that would only lead to embarrassment. That night he had pitched the idea to Michael had been the first time Jon had really put himself out there since he had proposed to Shayna. Months later, his stomach twisted at the thought of Sirens with the same worry that had festered in him the day he had presented her with that diamond ring.

Other times, Jon felt a flutter of excitement in his belly, warm and sparkling like the first sip from a champagne flute. These dueling emotions fought for dominance in him at times like this when he was alone with his thoughts. It was why he so often preferred to seek refuge in Shayna's company.

Sirens was in the odd position of being both highly anticipated while also being considered a sin by some. Jon leaned more toward the wonderous approach. He thought it was a natural thing and that it was a human curiosity to want to know the naughty details. He believed that it was even more natural to want to play out those fantasies than it was to resort to graphic violence for entertainment like Locked and Loaded had allowed users to do. As far as Jon could tell, Sirens would be a gift to curious people who didn't know how to experiment or who to do it with.

Jon had to hope that it did well. He was anticipating his cut, and while it would be a fraction of a fraction of a fraction of what Michael would get—which was a fraction of a fraction of a fraction of what RightMark would rake in—it was only fair that Jon was still paid handsomely for the stroke of genius that had set the whole project in motion. Sirens would be the third game he had had a say in, but this game had been Jon's idea as much as Michael's. Jon was particularly proud of the creativity of his concept even if it had started from a drunken thought.

Jon could still remember the night that Sirens was conceived in the dim light of a bar. Michael had been utterly lost trying to perfect the concept for his game. Before Sirens was what it had eventually become, it was a sexless game about finding a companionship more like friendship, not unlike the scrapped therapy pet game Jon was currently working on.

Michael had been visibly distraught over it, so Jon had invited him to grab drinks for happy hour at a restaurant called Mal's just down the street from their building. Through the booze in their system, the two men had opened up to each other in a way they had never before and hadn't since. Michael had talked about his arthritic, in-home aunt and the way his mother had been killed when he was just a small child. In return, Jon had discussed his secret worry about paying back his loans and debts, which lingered over him like a heavy, dark raincloud at all times.

That night had been strangely rich with conversation and opportunity as the drinks had loosened their tongues. By eight that evening they were happily drunk. Michael's cheeks had been flushed, and his usually unkempt hair had been even more tousled. Through laughter, he had said, "I have no fucking clue what I'm doing, man."

This had been particularly jarring to Jon. Michael had always seemed so in control of his work and his life. Up until that point, Jon had perceived Michael as a man of no-nonsense, strictly looking to complete his job efficiently and then go home in the evening promptly at five o'clock. Perhaps it was the cold way he sometimes approached people or the way he spent most of his time hiding in his office, giving unhappy looks to anyone who dared to disrupt his workflow.

"What do you mean?" Jon asked.

"The fucking game," Michael said. "It's horrible. I don't know where to go with it. The characters are so dull they feel like caricatures. I wouldn't talk to them if I didn't have to. I feel like I've stalled out in the middle of the fucking road."

Michael looked down at his drink as he spoke. He had talked about his dead mother, but this was truly hard for him. He was admitting defeat.

Jon reflected, looking at the busty woman behind the bar who had been serving them all night. She looked back reproachfully, likely not intending to appear disgusted, but she gave them a glance that said it all. They were sloppily drunk, and she wanted them gone. Fair enough.

Jon lowered his voice. "What if you could like... okay, hear me out." Jon laughed, glancing back at the busty bartender, thinking about what he was going to say next and weighing Michael's reaction. "What if the characters were customizable?"

"They already are," Michael said. He looked at Jon a little confused, trying to find the humor in what he was saying.

"Yeah," Jon began. "Manually. What if there was a way to tap into what we *really* want, though."

Michael's eyebrows had knitted together. "I'm not following," he said.

"The Emissux taps into our nervous system directly," Jon said. "It puts out signals and creates sensations. But what if we programmed it to take in signals too? Like, what if we *reversed* the code? What if we made the game so that it learned as well instead of just transmitting?"

Michael did not relax. Instead, his face grew even tenser with thought. He sipped his drink slowly as he turned over the idea. "I'm not sure that's even possible."

"It wouldn't be easy," Jon admitted. "But I don't think it's *impossible*. It's got all of the little elements we need already; it just needs to be reversed."

There was a moment of silence as Michael visibly weighed his options. "Do you know how to do it?" he finally asked.

"I have a crumb of an idea," Jon said. "But it's worth a shot poking around at it, I think."

Michael nodded, appearing to become surer of something with each bob of his head.

"Yeah, all right," he said. "Code it up for me. I like the idea of it. I think—if it's successful—incorporating something like that could be big, man."

"And, I know this is a tall order," Jon said. "But you need to spice it up, and I think you know how. Don't make it just a game about talking, you know."

Michael flashed him a look that was both amused and surprised. "Oh? Are you suggesting what I think you are?"

"I think it's just the next step," Jon said. He took a long sip from his drink, finishing it. "Sex sells."

"Do you think people would seriously buy a porno game?" Michael asked with his voice hushed.

"People buy porn, man, and people pay for the real deal. If you give them a space where they can be free to do whatever—especially with the promise of no data collection—I think it would sell millions."

"Really?" Michael asked. "I just... don't know how to make that tasteful."

"Let that be something that's driven by the user too. They can decide how 'tasteful' they want it to be."

Michael thought about this for an especially long time before giving one last curt nod.

"All right," he said. "I'll try it out. But if I don't like it when I'm testing it, I'm cutting it out. My intent was always to make this about companionship, first and foremost."

"Fuck yeah." Jon let out a slurred, drunken laugh before raising his drink. "I'm sure you'll have fun coding that bit. Cheers!"

Yet Jon's intoxicated thought had turned out to be a lot more difficult than he had planned. It had taken Jon months to code what he wanted, and it had taken Michael even longer to add such a widely varying element to his project. It was the hardest Jon had worked in his life on something and it was the most consistent he had ever been on an assignment. He could taste the rewards as he went along, and with each hour he felt increasingly accomplished.

The board at RightMark had practically drooled over Jon's creation. The code he had shown them had earned him his very own glass office and the promise of a small fortune once Sirens was out for sale. For the first time since he had started the job, he was truly, deeply excited, and for perhaps the first time in his life, he was genuinely proud of himself.

It was as if that week in early spring when he had given Michael the code and was gifted his new office had been Jon's peak. The rest of the year crawled after that. His ideas beyond that one stroke of genius had been lackluster, tossed into the trash can with shame. He had promised RightMark a game by next June and was still having writer's block even as the months tore past him at an alarming speed.

Worst of all was that Jon's idea, and what was likely to propel him out of debt, was looked down upon by his wife. Shayna detested the concept of Sirens. He could see where she was coming from as it wasn't exactly built upon the idea of respect or female pleasure. Yet Shayna was vocally and aggressively against the game, unintentionally tearing at his confidence.

"It's just messed up, Jon," she said one time. "It's almost 2030 and they're still treating us like we're toys."

"I don't think the intent is to make you seem disposable, babe," he said.

"Maybe not." She didn't appear convinced. "But you have to see how bad it is, don't you? Imagine if it was a bunch of naked guys! Men would lose their minds."

"You're right," he said.

"Why aren't there any men in the game anyways?" she asked.

"We've discussed doing that for a second addition. You know, if the first version sells well."

"Of course," Shayna scoffed. "Equality as an afterthought."

He didn't like to argue with her about things like this. She almost always won those disagreements, but he could do nothing about it now. Though he vaguely understood her frustration after enduring so many of her rants, it was too late. They were mere weeks away from the delivery day.

In the end, he simply stopped talking about Sirens altogether with his wife. Jon felt he could never tell Shayna the truth. In the face of her disapproval, he had never admitted to her that he had contributed to Sirens. Jon couldn't stop things from moving forward, so he had concluded that he would collect his money for Sirens while sparing her the knowledge of how the money was truly made. It hurt to hide something so large from Shayna, but he figured what she didn't know wouldn't hurt her even if hiding it hurt *him*.

As Jon sat there in the quiet, he felt his stomach turn uneasily. Shayna was in the other room, separated from him by a thin wall. The thought of her not knowing everything was painful. It was the first time he had ever held a secret from her.

Jon put his jellybeans back in the pantry and walked to the large bedroom that he and Shayna shared. He found her already sleeping in their bed, lying on her stomach. Her arms were under the pillow, and she was wearing one of his oversized T-shirts. He admired her then, watching her back rise and fall with the rhythmic flow of her breathing.

Jon closed the door behind him and let darkness overcome his vision. Everything went black, but he found his way around the room by habit. He stripped to his briefs and climbed into bed beside his wife as soundlessly as he could. Shayna had always been a light sleeper, though, so she stirred despite his caution as she felt his weight dip the mattress toward him.

"Babe?" Shayna murmured, not opening her eyes.

"It's me," Jon said. His eyes had slowly begun to adjust to the darkness, and he found the silhouette of her head. He kissed her forehead lightly, and though he couldn't see it, he assumed she was smiling sleepily.

"Good," she whispered, still groggy.

She sighed loudly and rolled onto her other side, pulling some of the covers over with her. She was a blanket hog, but Jon didn't mind. "I love you," she said. Almost instantly, her breathing evened out again as she fell back asleep.

"Love you too," Jon said, so quietly it was barely audible.

As he turned over, he could feel the warmth of her body just inches from his. It was comforting and strangely reassuring. There was no feeling to replace the one that came with knowing that she was right by his side.

9

Michael

Bella's skin glowed brilliantly in the sunlight. The occasional breeze caught her hair, brushing it from her shoulders in an effortless cascade. In the light of day, Bella was even more breathtaking than ever; she was utterly ethereal.

Michael had willed the game to create a beautiful, cool day for the two of them to take a walk in. The cold winter weather he had started the game in had melted away overnight to fit his preferences, giving way to an intoxicating springtime scene of brightly colored flowers and breezy air. All of the colors surrounding them pierced the world with unfiltered vibrancy. It felt like seeing nature for the first time.

Bella held his hand as the two of them walked. They were on a bike path that snaked through fields of luscious grass. Purple, yellow, and red flowers dotted the green expanse of the field around them.

"We should have a picnic soon," Bella suggested. "We could bring wine and cheese and sandwiches. I think that would be so lovely."

"It would," Michael agreed. He pictured the two of them sprawled out in the field before them on a checkered blanket, sipping sweet wine thoughtfully before losing themselves in each other. "We should do that tomorrow."

"Oh, yay!" Bella exclaimed. "I've always wanted to try it!"

"What else would you want to try?" Michael asked.

Bella slowed and looked at him in confusion. She had evidently never expected to be asked this. Providing an opinion wasn't a primary function for her, but Michael wanted to try it anyway, to see what she would want to do when prompted.

There was a small crease in her forehead as she thought it over.

"I think..." she began as she pondered the question. "I think I want to walk like this. I want to be in the warmth like we are now. Really, I would be glad to do anything with you, but I think I love this, right here and now, most of all."

Michael nodded, pleased with her answer. "Is there anything you don't want to do?" he asked.

This seemed to confuse her even more. The line on her forehead deepened. It took her much longer to come up with an answer.

"I don't think I like playing in the snow," she said finally. "I don't think that I would want to make a snowman or something like that. It would be too cold on my hands."

Michael gave a light chuckle. Of course, she didn't. He didn't want to either, but the specificity of her answer struck him as funny all the same. It felt so juvenile.

"Don't laugh at me," she said before jabbing her finger playfully into his side.

"I'm not," he said. "I wouldn't make fun of you."

"Good," she said. "Because I can stop cooking meals whenever you visit, mister."

"You wouldn't."

"True," she agreed. "I'm sure your cooking would be awful by comparison. I have to save us both."

"That's very valiant of you," he said.

Bella stopped walking again. Her hand tightened around his and he turned to see that her face was very serious.

"Michael?" she asked. "Will you stay the night?"

"I always do," Michael said.

She shook her head. "Not like that. Not to just sleep *with* me. I mean I want you to sleep beside me. I want you to sleep over at my place. For real this time."

Michael hesitated. "I don't know if that would work," he said finally.

"We won't know until you try it," she said. "I just get so lonely without you. I want you beside me all the time."

Michael had never fathomed sleeping in her world. He needed to figure out what it entailed and if it was even possible. He was especially unsure as to whether that would mean he would be sleeping in reality if he was in Sirens.

Even if it meant he wasn't truly asleep in his world, he didn't have work the following day. It was a Friday, and he could afford a night of restlessness.

"All right," Michael agreed. "I'll give it a try."

Her face broke out into a beaming smile that consumed all of her features. The sunny day around them seemed dim compared to the way she looked.

"Oh, that's wonderful!" she exclaimed. She held his face between her soft hands and kissed him. "I'm so excited."

"Me too," Michael agreed, and he was. This element was unknown to him. He had never planned to go to bed in her world, and this was an unexplored factor of his own game. Testing out the repercussions of this agreement was important to know the full scope of Sirens' possibilities. Plus, he found himself eager to try out the idea. The thought of spending as much time with Bella as possible sent a jolt through him like electricity.

"We should hurry back," she said. "It's already late afternoon. I'll cook us up something special to celebrate."

That night, they ate Michael's favorite dish: rare steak, mashed potatoes drowning in gravy, seasoned asparagus, and a rich chocolate cake for dessert. Bella knew without asking what would hit the spot.

These meals meant nothing to him in reality. They would not sustain him, and they had no nutritional value to him in the real world. He had discovered this the hard way when merely rising from bed some mornings after plugging in made him feel frail and withered. It may have had no value to him, but the food in his world never tasted as delicious as it did in hers.

When evening settled in, they made love, and afterward, Michael turned over and tried to fall asleep. Later, he reflected that he had been surprised that sleep had found him so easily. In fact, he believed that it was easier for him to drift into slumber in Bella's world than in his. It was quick and painless, the process perhaps lasting only a handful of minutes.

Yet when morning came, and he finally left Bella to unplug, it felt as if he hadn't slept at all. Within moments of reemerging in reality, he concluded that sleep in Bella's world didn't count in his, just as the food she made did nothing to fill him. Michael felt just as exhausted as he would have if he had been actively awake the entire night before. He would have to remember this going forward.

So, he took a three-hour nap to recover, and then, realizing he had no other plans to occupy his day, Michael plugged back in. As soon as he had woken up from his nap his entire body seemed to be staticky with excitement to return. He spent that entire Saturday with Bella and when night rolled around, he couldn't help himself.

He fell asleep in Bella's world again, knowing that it wouldn't truly count.

It didn't matter.

10

Jon

Jon was quick to pick up on Michael's change. It had been subtle at first, starting after their return to work on Monday, but as the week progressed, it became more visible. It was in the slouch in his posture, the dark circles beneath his eyes, and the distance in his stare. He hadn't even bothered to tuck his shirt into his pants on most days, and his hair was growing unruly instead of stylishly unkempt. A shadow of facial hair had developed on his chin and cheeks.

Before long, everyone at RightMark had picked up on it as well.

Though Michael had been perhaps one of the least well-dressed people at work on a good day, his complete disregard for the RightMark dress code was an affront that all employees had noticed. They had begun to talk behind their palms to other coworkers, whispering noisily in the excessively quiet office. There was rarely anything to gossip about at their work, especially when they spent so much time plugged in, and Michael's appearance was some of the first material they had been given to discuss in months.

Jon had been meaning to check in on Michael throughout the week but knew better than to enter his office unprovoked and disrupt him.

So when on Thursday morning Jon found himself standing behind Michael as he filled up his cup with coffee, it seemed like the perfect opportunity.

When Michael turned to leave, Jon saw him up close for the first time that week and nearly jumped. Michael almost looked like a completely different person, a faint sketch of the man Jon knew. Yet with some effort, Jon composed himself and cleared his throat casually.

"How're things going, man?" Jon asked.

"They're going," Michael said. He yawned loudly and then held up his cup of coffee. "This thing smells especially wretched today. Doesn't anyone know how to make a decent brew?"

"Yeah, someone burnt it to high hell," Jon agreed. "You could always wait for Victoria's coffee run."

"I'd rather drink it burnt and hot than tasteless and lukewarm, I think. Besides, this one is free. I'll probably need more than just one today," Michael said.

"Not sleeping much?" Jon asked though the answer was hanging on his every feature.

"I've been spending a lot of time in Sirens," he said. A thin smile spread across his face that was both genuine and lacked energy. "It's wonderful. You've absolutely killed it with that code."

"Have I?" Jon was astonished. He had fully expected the code to need tweaks once Michael had started to test the game in its entirety.

"Fuck yeah." Michael grabbed Jon's shoulder, staring at him with serious eyes. The intensity in his gaze was paralyzing. "It's amazing. Really. If I could give you more than that little glass office I would."

Jon could feel his heart beating fast. This swelling sensation of pride was new and welcomed, making him temporarily forget about what he wanted to ask Michael in the first place.

"Why don't you then?" Jon joked.

Michael laughed a lethargic, short laugh. "I don't have the funds yet. Maybe when that Sirens money rolls in I'll find a way to thank you."

"I'm holding you to it," Jon said.

Michael laughed again and took his hand from Jon's shoulder. "You do that."

Michael sipped his steaming hot coffee as he walked away, and Jon watched him as he left, feeling that sweet sense of accomplishment bloom in his chest.

It was not lost on Jon that despite the rather disheveled appearance, Michael seemed to be in great spirits. He took it as a good sign that Michael was forgoing sleep and choosing to keep playing Sirens instead. Could he really blame him for enjoying the game he had created?

Jon smiled to himself as he turned back to the coffee pot. The realization sent a bolt of motivation through him. A zip of inspiration, an image of a dog with an Emissux collar on it, burst through his mind like a flashbulb. After Jon poured himself a cup of burnt coffee, he hurried back to his office.

Jon sat behind his desk and spent the rest of the day working—*really* working. If his previous project could impress Michael so much, then he could create more. That feeling was foreign to him and hit him like a special type of high. It made his fingers fly across the keyboard like they were piano keys and his head spin with a whirlwind of possibilities.

He would prove them wrong.

He would prove himself wrong.

Jon felt, for the first time, that the only way to go was up.

11

Michael

Michael always disliked visiting his aunt. It was nothing against her, but retirement homes had always felt sterile and unwelcoming to him. He had never appreciated their demure, gray appearance and had never felt particularly comfortable in a building that smelled vaguely like decay.

Even despite this, Michael tried to visit Mary once a month. Somewhere near the middle of every month, Michael would find himself driving an hour and a half out of the city to pay her a visit, figuring that the journey was the least he could do after she had put in so many years of work and time for him.

After he had checked in, he turned toward the lobby of stiff seats, prepared to wait and be called back. Even the plush chairs and sofa didn't have much give to them. They seemed to hold him in place, not giving way under his weight. All of the furniture was decorated in different floral patterns that had faded to gray or yellowed with age and use. The different colors and designs of their original prints were mismatched, as though they had decided on decorating with floral patterns but couldn't agree on which one to stay consistent with.

The lighting in the waiting room was also quite dim like the sun lost its strength on its way through the windows. It made everything look as though it had been painted from one uninspired, bleak palette.

He had only just sat down on a hard armchair when a pleasant-looking young woman came in. Strangely, she held a clipboard like a nurse. Michael briefly caught himself fearing that she was taking notes on something that had happened to Mary. But then he looked at the woman's genuine grin and let himself relax.

It's this place, he thought.

"Mr. Ken?" she called out. Her eyes were focused on him as if she already knew who to look for. There was only one other man seated in the far corner of the room.

Michael got up quickly and returned her smile awkwardly. "That's me."

"Your aunt is ready to see you now." She gestured for him to follow her.

A deep, despicable part of him was trying to resist pulling his gaze down and watching her hips swing beneath her uniform as she walked. But a louder, more stubborn part of him kept his gaze forward. Guilt bloomed in him like a flower, and he found his thoughts drifting to Bella as they so often did nowadays. She gave him what he needed, and he felt that he should not waste time staring at some random woman's ass. The best had already happened to him. She lived in his head, sweet and loyal and perfect. Bella would be waiting for him to return, and her hips would be more intoxicating than anything he could find in this world.

So, eyes forward.

The woman led him down a hallway he was familiar with. When they arrived at his aunt's room, the door was agape, leaving Mary open to any prying eyes.

Michael stepped in and was greeted by the familiar and overwhelming smell of Mary's perfume. Whatever nerves he still held from the waiting room seemed to vanish in a puff of rose-scented fragrance.

"I'll leave you two to it then," the woman said, pulling the door behind her. She left it cracked an inch, as though to ensure that if Mary croaked during his visit, they could hear any of Michael's yelling.

But Mary Ken was far too young to croak anytime soon. Though her arthritis had made her feeble, she was still one of the youngest residents in the building. At sixty-nine years old, she was still quick-witted and not quite the shriveled skeleton of some of her peers. Despite losing significant weight since moving in, she still appeared healthier than most other residents, and her face remained warm and kind even despite the dreary atmosphere around her.

Mary had been a mover and shaker since she was a teen. She had worked hard for all of her initial wealth and was very proud of it. Since Michael was old enough to care, he could recall how she had displayed this success on her wrists, knuckles, and throat, letting the world know that Mary was not of middling wealth in a gleam of gold and jewels. She had been enjoying a life of luxury when Michael had been dropped off at her door.

Mary's younger sister, Candice, had given birth to Michael three months before she was killed by a driver who had instantly snuffed out her life while she was crossing the street. Candice had died on impact when a driver, who had been reaching into her handbag to find her lip gloss, had sent Candice cartwheeling through the air.

Michael had been a surprise for Candice, but one that she had grown to appreciate during the nine months she carried him. For those first three months of his life, Michael had been her whole world.

When Candice died, three-month-old Michael had been passed off to Mary—Candice's closest relative despite the states' worth of distance placing them geographically at odds. So poor Mary Ken, with her career ahead of her and more riches to be had, put it all aside to raise her dead sister's surprise baby. She had filled the role of a mother nicely and had loved Michael as much as she could.

At times, however, she could be cold to Michael, as if she went through phases where she remembered that he hadn't come from her own womb. He was an unwavering reminder of the sister who had been taken too soon. It was only natural that she would grow frustrated with her situation occasionally and that Michael would feel the wrath of it. He hadn't held a grudge over her for those lapses. Michael felt he would have done much worse in her position.

Mary looked up at him with eyes that shone with pure happiness. Michael wasn't used to people approaching him so warmly outside of Sirens, and he felt a firework of delight in his chest.

"Michael!" she said.

"Hey," he greeted her, a little sheepishly. He suddenly thought about how he should've brought her some flowers. He always told himself to when he was in the retirement home but forgot to buy them every time he came back.

"Oh, Michael," Mary said. "You look so pale! Haven't you been going outside at all?"

Michael laughed. "I've always been pale. It's just more noticeable in here."

Mary nodded in agreement. "Yes, these damn lights! They really want their residents to be depressed, I swear."

"You're not getting all sad on me, are you?"

"Nah." She shook her head furiously. "Not me. I'm fit as ever in the head. It's these fucking hands that want me dead."

Mary had gotten a horrible case of rheumatoid arthritis in her late fifties. It had been genetic, and she had always told Michael that it was coming for her, even when he was just a boy. But when it hit her so early and so young, she was still taken by surprise. It was an angry disease that escalated quickly. After a little over a decade of navigating it independently, she was in a retirement home, unable to take care of herself. And admittedly, she wanted to be doted on. But retirement homes were expensive. This dismal place had been the best she could consistently pay for after Michael had drained her riches while she raised him. It was yet another reason Michael felt inclined to despise the building.

Mary had vigorously refused Michael's suggestion to let her live with him when he had offered it. She claimed that didn't want him to give up the young adulthood he had worked toward even though she had given hers up for him. Though he had pushed her on it—multiple times—she wouldn't give, even when he had proposed that it was payment for the time he had taken from her. That had made her cry, but she still didn't budge.

"How are your hands doing, anyway?" he asked, knowing the answer.

"They're spiteful bitches." She smiled. "But you knew that. Nothing new here, surprisingly. They're thinking about putting in a voice-activated remote. I say it's about time. Past time, really. But that's about all that's cracking over here." She leaned forward and put a stiff hand on his. "I want to know how you've been."

Michael fell into the seat that had been propped beside her bed. He sandwiched her cold, brittle hand between his two warm ones.

"I've been tired," he said.

"I can tell," she observed with a pitying grin. "I noticed your dark circles when you came in, but I didn't want to say you looked pale *and* tired."

Michael chuckled. "I appreciate the restraint."

"So, what's keeping you up?" she asked.

Michael sighed softly. "It's just work."

"Fuck that," she said. "You need your sleep."

"I need this thing to be done," Michael said. "I can sleep when it's over, but I'm so close. I just have a few more weeks."

"You know what I always said, though. You're no good without sleep. No one is."

"This is the homestretch," Michael explained. "It's just testing and tweaks now. And I busted my ass in the early stages to give myself this time to fix things."

He didn't have the heart to tell her the real reason why he wasn't sleeping.

Mary looked a bit confused. "Then what's keeping you up?"

He wasn't sure how to explain it to her in terms that wouldn't be mildly offensive. Even then, weeks away from the delivery date, she still wasn't even fully aware of what Sirens was. Sex was perhaps the one thing she still regarded as taboo. Mary had never been bothered by cursing. During Michael's teen years, she had ignored the smell of weed that wafted from his room and the bottles of liquor he had thrown in the recycling without much caution. But she had always been skittish around the topic of sex, and Michael often wondered if it was because of what happened to her sister. The reason he was there. Regardless, he couldn't bring himself to tell her that he had coded virtual pornography, that he had spent countless hours trying to make sure the anatomy of his female avatars was realistic, or that he had created something intended to feed the animal instinct of men who were not getting any in real life.

So instead, he had told her it was a game about romance, which was not entirely untrue. Sirens had been about companionship from the start.

"It just takes a lot of time to go through it all," Michael said. "I've actually kind of enjoyed it."

"Well, that's good!" she exclaimed. "If you're getting lost in it, I can't imagine how it's going to sell. Michael Ken will be living in a mansion by February!"

"Yeah, hopefully, people like it," he said. Then, he grew serious. "I'm going to get you a better place than this when the money starts coming in."

Mary's eyes grew wide. "Oh, no! You'll do no such thing!"

She was a proud woman who had worked for her early wealth without the help of a man, but she had settled for a poor retirement home to be realistic about her savings. Yet she still dressed in her old expensive loungewear, making sure to coat herself in what was left of her designer perfumes so that she proclaimed her status in any room. The only things she had surrendered entirely were her makeup and jewelry, which her arthritis had made nearly impossible to put on.

Michael had known that offering this would be another small punch to Mary's pride. But he had braced himself for it and the nervousness he had felt sitting in the waiting room had only strengthened his resolve to present her with an alternative.

"Please," he said, softly. "Let me do this."

Mary shook her head. "No. That's your money. You earned it."

"Yeah, I did," Michael agreed. "I earned it, so I choose how to spend it."

Michael gestured to the dim lighting, the aged curtains that framed her window, and the small, boxy television sitting across the room.

"You shouldn't live like this," he said. "You deserve better. And I want to give that to you."

"Michael, no," was all she could say.

"Let me," Michael said. "It will make these sleepless nights worth it."

Mary shook her head for a bit but didn't argue any further. There was nothing else to say. Michael had made up his mind anyway.

He changed the subject to smaller topics afterward to keep her talking. They discussed the new menu items at the café they used to go to when he was in middle school, summarized the new books they had recently read, and talked briefly about the news. Michael skirted around larger political topics as the conversation grew more serious.

He desperately wanted to tell her about Bella. He wanted to say *I made something great, and I met someone made of starlight,* but even he knew how that would sound. He would not risk Mary wincing at his admission, and he could not bear the thought of her dismissal. So he tucked Bella away, kept her to himself the way he always had.

In the end, the visit had been pleasant, and around lunchtime, Michael decided he should leave before her food was delivered. Most days she needed someone to help her eat, and Michael knew that she wouldn't want him to bear witness to that.

"You bring back some of that new chili from Café Laura when you visit next time," she said. "It does me no good to just hear about.

"Yeah, definitely," he said. *I'll bring that and flowers,* he made a mental note.

When he stood to leave, she grabbed at his wrist with stiff fingers that didn't quite close or hold him in place.

"Please, Michael," she said. "Reconsider how you spend that money. Treat yourself before you start throwing what you've earned at useless old ladies."

"Don't say that," he said. "You're not useless. Without you, who would I discuss Charlotte Lemon's new book with?"

"I'm not being funny, Michael," she said. "You deserve to pay yourself back before you start thinking of other people."

Do I? he asked himself.

"It's not up for discussion," he said. Then, he bent forward and kissed her on her forehead lightly. "I'll see you soon with some of that chili."

As he turned to leave, he pulled his wrist from her grasp easily. It was almost pitiful how her hands slipped away so feebly.

When he was out in the parking lot, his mind slid back to Bella as easily as sliding into bed after a long day. He let the memory of her wash over and soothe him. She seemed to push aside all of the concerns he had over his arthritic aunt and the chilly, unsettling atmosphere of the retirement home.

While it was pleasant to be quelled by the sheer image of her, part of him felt insecure about it. The thought started small in his mind, but he allowed himself to acknowledge that in a moment of uncertainty, he was turning to a fake woman that he had manifested in his head for a sense of reassurance.

Alone in his car, he allowed himself to admit that it was probably not the best way to cope.

12

Shayna

Shayna swiftly pulled into her driveway with a knot of excitement in her stomach. Hunched over the handlebars of her bike, she was grinning. She couldn't help it, and she didn't mind if the neighbors briefly saw her smiling to herself as she zipped by.

She parked her bike in their garage, beside the large black hand-me-down BMW her mother had given her. Shayna didn't like to drive, especially if the trip was merely down the street, as hers had just been. While the weather permitted at least, she preferred to use her bike.

Eagerly, she pulled her shopping bag from the bike's front basket. Its contents sent another spike of thrilled energy zipping through her. She clutched the hemp bag to her chest, feeling her rapid heartbeat beneath the fabric.

Hurriedly, she rushed into her home, nearly stumbling over her own feet in her haste. She locked the door behind her despite the vacant house and took in a deep inhale that felt sharp and exhilarating. Finally, she opened her reusable bag and looked at the lone object inside with sharp anticipation. Shayna pulled out the pregnancy test, noticing that it was light despite its heavy implications.

She took the test with swift familiarity. She had done this process three times before and felt she had a routine at this point. All had come back negative, of course, but Shayna could feel something different in the air this time. There was a sureness in her movements that made her certain. This one *had* to be it.

She was so jittery with excitement and nerves that it made her feel like she had drunk too much caffeine. To take her mind off of the what-ifs and to leave it to fate, she stripped until she was naked and hopped into the shower as she waited for the test to present its result.

Shayna let the water rush over her as she tried to ground herself into the moment and not lose herself in spiraling daydreams of a hypothetical future. As she rinsed off the slight sweat she accumulated from her bike ride, she let the water wash her mentally too. She tried her best to indulge in the present, but she found that the hot water only did so much to diverge her mind that day.

If the test came back negative, she would be devastated just as she had been three times before staring at that lonely line. She reflected that it was very much like a representation of the circumstances. One line for yourself, two lines for you and your child.

Jon didn't know that she was taking the test. Shayna hadn't told him because she didn't want to get his hopes up. Jon would never be able to wrap his head around her struggle. He wanted children but not to the same degree. He could live happily without them, smoking his weed on their back porch in the evenings and making love without having to worry about the kids hearing from down the hall.

Shayna had always known that children would be a part of her future, though. It was almost a primal urge, an instinct, one that she had sought to fulfill since she was young. Even when she thought she would never be with a man, she had always assumed that she would conceive in other ways. Shayna would have a baby even if she had to adopt. But first, she would muster up the funds to conceive on her own. If she could carry it, she would.

She washed her body quickly, too eager to take her time. Her scrubbing lingered over her lower belly, hopeful.

Please, Shayna thought. *Please, please, please.*

It was a quick shower, lasting maybe ten minutes at the most. Jon would be home soon, and she intended to read the results for herself before he was there to look over her shoulder. Perhaps she would throw it out without him knowing if the results were negative. The first test she had taken had been with him. They had sat together on the cold tile of the bathroom floor holding their breath, and when she saw that lonely, single line, she had felt embarrassed more than anything. She had taken the other tests alone, allowing herself to feel disappointed before passing the feeling on to her husband.

Shayna stepped out of the shower, feeling her muscles grow taut. She tied the towel around her body, letting the excess water drip onto the bathmat as she peeked at the stick laying on the counter.

The imprint was faint, and Shayna had to lean forward to really make it out. She was almost scared to touch it like it might be white-hot with the truth.

When she finally could see its verdict, her heart sank.

One line.

She could feel the disappointment rising from beneath her like a tide until she was under it, consumed by it, feeling nothing but its shame. The feeling was in every crevice of her body, overwhelming every inch. In disbelief, she snatched up the test and held it closer to her face. The single line only became clearer, still lingering with no companion.

Shayna tossed it in the trash furiously. She was beyond sadness at this point. After wallowing in her tears three times before, she knew well that they had done nothing to wash away the hollowness she felt. Now, the negative test felt almost like a cosmic joke. It was the one thing she had always wanted, even ahead of marriage. She had gotten the large home, the doting spouse, and her dream job. But her body was betraying her, refusing to catch despite years of trying.

It could easily have been Jon's fault. Maybe his sperm wasn't agile enough. But her anger wasn't directed at anyone in particular, not even really herself. It was blinding and all-consuming as if her resentment was spread evenly across everyone who could be involved.

She heard the garage door go up and felt her anger halt abruptly and her belly flip. In the trash can beside the toilet, the test was lying perfectly on top, face-up, for anyone with a curious eye to see. She debated burying it, hoping he wouldn't see it by hiding him from the truth. But with another flash of anger, she decided to let it lie on top.

Let him see it, she thought. *Let him be angry too. Let us be angry together.*

When she left the bathroom, a gust of steam billowed outward, following her into the comparatively chilly living room. Her husband was there, putting down his work bag and stripping off his coat.

Shayna took a deep inhale of cold air and then mustered a smile. She was vaguely aware that it might look strange and unnatural, but she also didn't care.

"How was work, honey?" she asked as pleasantly as she could.

"Ah, you know. Same old, same old."

She knew what that meant. Jon had an amazing way of fucking around all day at work. He had yet to complete a project of his own despite being one of the first employees that RightMark had taken on full-time. She was still in awe over how he got his big glass office without having completed a game.

His eyes lingered on her semi-nakedness. "Nice shower?" he asked.

"Ah, you know. Same old, same old," she said with a widened smile. The joke only fell on her. Jon simply looked confused by her humored grin.

He glanced at the kitchen, undoubtedly focusing on the lack of pots and pans cooking on the stove. She almost always made dinner for the two of them. It relaxed her after a day of tending to others' maladies. Over time, she had concluded that it was a good trade-off; she enjoyed cooking and he enjoyed eating. Jon appeared to note the absence of cooking food as another bad sign. But if he was curious, he didn't openly question it, most likely to not push her buttons.

"I was thinking about pizza tonight," Jon suggested. "Sound good?"

"Yeah," Shayna said with a few quick head nods. "That sounds nice."

"I'm just going to pee and then call for one," Jon said.

Shayna watched him dully as he approached the bathroom.

Let him be angry too, she repeated to herself as he closed the door behind him.

She knew he would find it. Its handle was bright pink, and he would practically be looking down at it as he pissed. She resigned to the inevitable as she sat down and folded her hands in her lap, waiting. Perhaps it was all in her head, but she felt that he was taking longer than usual.

There was a flush and the faint sound of running water followed by the slow, almost hesitant creak of the door opening. His eyes found Shayna immediately. For a moment, they just looked at each other.

Shayna could hear her heart beating in her ears as she waited for him to speak.

He cleared his throat. "Do you want to talk about it?" he asked.

Shayna shook her head. "I don't think so."

Jon nodded and straightened. It seemed like he wanted to say more but he didn't, and Shayna was grateful for it. Instead, he shoved his hands in his pockets, walked to his work bag, and then pulled out his phone.

"Vegan veggie?" he asked.

When their pizzas came, they ate them on the couch together. Shayna allowed her old rule of only smoking outside to bend just this once, and they smoked inside the house for the first time. She had earned a bit of leniency.

Once under the influence, the pizza tasted unreal. They watched the television absently, not really paying attention to any of the shows that flashed before their eyes. They were too consumed by how the pizza tasted and the simple thoughts flowing through their stoned minds.

Though the smoke had dulled her anger and feelings of embarrassment, they were still there, and they nipped at her like a small cat taking swipes at her ankles. As she finished her last pizza crust, she reflected on whether or not she should break their pleasant silence. It was better sooner than later, she decided.

"I want to save up for IVF," she finally said.

Jon looked at her strangely, processing what she had said slowly. "Oh."

"Is that a bad idea?" she asked.

Jon wiped his mouth with a napkin. "No," he said. "I figured you would eventually. You know, if things didn't work naturally."

"Can we?" she asked. "Or is that too much?"

"We'll have to be smart about it for sure," Jon said. "And we need to start putting away money. But if that's what you want, we can try to make it work."

"It is," Shayna said, solemnly. She knew that it was a hefty price, almost too much to ask. They hadn't even properly furnished their new home because they had been so frugal in the face of other financial obligations. But if it bothered Jon, he was very good at not showing it.

"I'll have more money coming in with Sirens," Jon said. "That should give us a boost."

He blushed as he said it, knowing that Shayna did not like to talk about the game.

"You would spend your money on that?" she asked.

"It's not my money," he said. "It's our money. And yeah, I want a little kiddo too, you know?"

Shayna smiled. It was exactly what she'd wanted to hear.

"Even if we have to tell my mom that we need to skip a payment or two, I think we should go for it," she said. "We should make it a priority."

"And she'll be fine with that?" Jon asked.

"Sure," Shayna said. "She wants a grandchild more than anything, and Kelly isn't showing any signs of slowing down. I think she'd be thrilled."

Shayna's mom had been constantly highlighting her lack of grandchildren since she and Jon had married hastily. In fact, her mom had suspected that Shayna was pregnant when she announced she was marrying her college sweetheart. Unlike most mothers, Shayna's had been thrilled by the idea of her daughter being knocked up. She was a woman with traditional views and out-of-date joys. For her daughters, she had always wanted the white picket fence and envisioned so many children that they overwhelmed their vast, fantastical properties. So when Shayna told her about their plans to marry, her mother had been delighted. A possible looming pregnancy and a marriage to a *man*, no less, was absolutely exciting and so positively normal that Shayna's mom had encouraged it.

But years had passed, and it was clear that Shayna's pregnancy would be no easy feat. She would often explain to her mom how they were trying, waiting for their time to be right, but her mother still didn't understand the issue.

"You think so?" Jon said though he looked uncertain. He had never cared for Shayna's mom since she had told him of the way she had turned her nose up at Shayna's interest in women. This division did not completely dismay her, though. Shayna and her mom had grown apart naturally throughout the years without Jon's help.

"Yeah," Shayna said. "She might crack a few jokes, but I think it's worth it, don't you?"

"Of course," Jon said. "If she's willing, that will definitely help a lot."

Shayna's chest felt like it was filled with butterflies. Jon was loyal and honest, protective yet lenient. Even as he laid before her, stoned and slouched, he was incredibly attractive to her. His support made him infuriatingly sexy.

With sudden urgency, she leaned in and kissed him, feeling the warmth of his body caress hers. It was then that she realized she had been holding a deep sorrow, her breath always bated. In Jon's embrace, it was released, like a satisfying exhale after coming up from being underwater.

Both of their hands were roaming, curious as though they were breaking new ground and discovering each other for the first time.

He broke from the kiss momentarily to smile and breathily say, "I guess we could still try the old-fashioned way first."

Shayna giggled. "Shut up."

They kissed again, and then her mouth wandered his body, kissing him up and down, lingering on the artistry of the tattoos he often covered with his button-down shirts. Her mouth touched the butterflies on his shoulders, the flowers on his arm, and the calligraphy on his chest that spelled out his favorite band's name.

Shayna got lost in Jon, and Jon was consumed by her. It may not have been fruitful, but it felt right.

13

Michael

Michael awoke to the smell of bacon. It made him salivate as soon as he recognized it. The scent reminded him of the way Mary had made it when he was little on the weekends, sizzling it in a pan so that Michael woke to the fragrance and was served once he came stumbling into the kitchen. The memory made him smile as he rolled over and stared at the ceiling.

It was a stucco white ceiling with a large black fan in the center, the blades spreading wide like a large bird in flight. Somehow this was comforting too. It looked like the one in his childhood bedroom, back before Mary's hands had gone stiff and before the bacon had stopped cooking in the skillet.

He sat up and the white sheets fell around his naked body, slipping from his torso and gathering around his waist. The air was cool on his skin but not uncomfortable. He stretched his back, feeling the light scratches on his skin produce a fiery prick. It was not so much painful as it was an occasional annoyance. But Michael wasn't mad at it. In fact, he quite liked that they were there, for the most part. It was like Bella had marked him, branded him as hers.

After gathering his clothing, which had been scattered throughout the room, he dressed in his boxers and a loose T-shirt. For a moment, a jabbing feeling of fatigue shot its way into his consciousness. It sometimes did that when he spent the night with Bella. Occasionally, this feeling of sleeplessness was so intense that it was able to puncture the veil of the Emissux. But Michael only slept with Bella on Friday and Saturday nights when rest wasn't necessary for work the next day, so this tiredness was inconsequential.

When he opened the door to the kitchen, sunlight poured in. It was so brilliant it was nearly blinding, setting the white kitchen into a seemingly reflective surface. Michael had to shade his eyes with his forearm lazily while they adjusted.

The sound of bacon sizzling filled his ears, along with Bella's sweet humming. She was humming a tune that he didn't know or at least didn't recognize through pursed lips. She swung her hips to the song in her head as she hovered over the skillet with a spatula in her hand.

He noticed that she was only wearing a white T-shirt and the rose-colored panties she had worn the night before. Her hips twisted in an absurdly mesmerizing way. Michael stopped shuffling across the room toward her to take in the scene. It was dazzling, awash in light and a strange sense of comfort, but Michael felt a pang of sorrow. A fleeting, unbidden thought appeared in his mind, reminding him that she was not real, that she was cooking bacon he would not be sustained by in sunlight that was merely a thought in his head.

But the feeling passed as soon as it had come, and when she turned, her blue eyes catching his, he felt any maladies wash from him.

"Morning, sunshine," she said.

"Good morning."

"Are pancakes and bacon okay?" she asked. There was a bowl of cut berries in front of her too, and she plucked half a strawberry out and put it on her tongue. She chewed it in a strangely seductive way.

"Yeah, that sounds great," he said.

"Get yourself something to drink," she said. "It should only be a few more minutes. I was hoping to be done before you woke up."

"Don't worry about it," he said. "Thanks for making it."

Her features were warm and pleased. "No problem. There's orange juice in the fridge. There should be some apple juice and water too. Or, fuck it, you can have one of the Coronas for all I care."

While the idea of beer for breakfast felt deliciously daring, he decided against it. Something about its heaviness so early made his stomach feel uneasy. So when he reached into the refrigerator, he took out a pitcher of orange juice and poured himself a glass. It was wonderfully fragrant and pulpy—just how he liked it. Michael briefly questioned if it was freshly squeezed.

Of course, it is, he thought. *I like fresh-squeezed orange juice so that's what she has in her refrigerator.*

He sipped it slowly as he watched her cook. It tasted delightful.

"You seemed to have slept well," Bella observed as she scraped some bacon out of the skillet and onto a plate.

"I did," Michael said, ignoring a wave of aching fatigue. "Everything was wonderful."

He took another swallow of the orange juice. He had never tasted anything so pleasant. At least not since he had drunk the Corona with Bella the first night they had met.

"Good," she said. "I'm glad. Sit down! I'll come to you."

Michael did as he was told, plopping down in a seat with place settings in front of it. There was a small custard cup filled with her cut berries and a cup of coffee steamed cozily in a white mug. He must've missed the smell over the scent of bacon, but as it wafted near his nose, the coffee smelled like it was the perfect amount of bitter, undoubtedly stirred with only two packets of sweetener, unsullied by creamer in the way that he preferred.

Bella put down the plate of bacon in front of him and he grabbed four strips eagerly. They crunched as he chewed. The bacon was dark and nearly burnt, devoid of the white chewy fat he cared little for.

"Pancakes will be a few more minutes," Bella said. "I made the batter, and it just takes a bit to make. I'm sorry. I thought you would sleep in later."

She was a bit pouty about it, like a child who had been scolded. It was strange to see her so distraught over uncooked pancakes, but Michael knew pleasing him was her only job and she felt that she was falling short.

How he reacted was a test. Should he choose to chastise her, he would reveal himself as someone more uptight, preferring loyalty and strict fawning over all else. Should he excuse it, Bella would assume relaxed submissiveness, one where she knew she would be accepted even if she made small errors. Every action they made together was a test intended to change her accordingly. She could be altered into the image he wanted, and how he reacted to the pancakes would help form her more fully.

Other players might assert dominance and give her a firm reprimand. They could rage against her. But Michael saw himself as more of a relaxed man, wanting a more relaxed woman. So he reacted accordingly.

"Don't worry about it," he said. "I'm good for now." He snapped a piece of bacon between his teeth happily.

Bella's downcast eyes found his face again.

"It'll be just a few minutes," she repeated before hurrying back to her cooking.

In the end, everything tasted fantastic. Every piece of bacon was like the best one he had ever eaten, and every sip of coffee or orange juice was like the first one he had ever drunk, exciting, new, and delicious.

Bella snacked on berries over a cup of coffee across from Michael as he ate, watching him blissfully. Michael scarfed down his food, perhaps unattractively. It didn't matter, though. Bella would still want him even with maple syrup dripping down his chin. The food didn't count anyway, so he could eat all he wanted. And he did. He finished all of the food Bella had prepared, never growing full. It seemed to only please her more to see him indulge so aggressively in her cooking.

In the back of Michael's mind, he knew that he had to unplug and eat a real meal soon. It would be a dull affair by comparison, entirely uninspired by the poor fixings Michael had laying around his dingey apartment. When the hunger—the true hunger—gnawed at him, he pushed it aside, wanting to enjoy the food before him in Bella's world first, even if it was only a figment of his imagination.

"What do you have planned for the day?" Bella asked.

"I have to go and get things ready for work tomorrow," he answered. "And I have to respond to a few emails to see what's happening."

It was a lie. He had nothing to do but eat and perhaps nap for real. Then, he had every intention of returning to the little slice of heaven he had coded to fit his mind.

"Boo." Bella pouted. She took a sip of her coffee. It was still warm and brought a slight color to her cheeks as she drank.

"I'll be back tonight, though," he said. "I promise."

"That's what I like to hear. I'll make you something special," she announced. "How do you feel about chicken marsala? I can make it with pasta or rice, whichever you prefer."

"That sounds wonderful. Surprise me," Michael said with a smile. He stuck the last strip of bacon in his mouth, chewing it happily. The moment he swallowed it, he missed the taste.

"We could do whatever you want to," she continued. "Or go wherever."

"I was thinking about another night indoors. Just you and me."

Bella raised an eyebrow knowingly. She flashed a coy grin, her cheeks still prettily flushed. "Oh? And what would we do with all of that free time tonight?"

"I think we could find some way to fill the void," Michael said.

"Filling my void, you mean?"

Another test. Did he like vulgar jokes? Would he approve of it with a laugh, or would he ignore it disapprovingly?

Michael chose the middle ground. It was fine but he didn't want to hear it all of the time. He breathed out of his nose sharply in a makeshift chuckle.

"Something like that," he said.

Bella's smile faded slightly, registering the response neutrally.

"What time do you have to leave?" she asked.

"Soon," he said. "Probably now, even."

"You'll come back in a bit, won't you? I get so lonely here without you."

"Of course," he said. "I get lonely without you too."

"Kiss me before you go," she said.

He stood and leaned across the table. She did the same, and they met in the middle, their lips connecting abruptly. It was sweet and closed-mouth at first. Her lips were soft and kind, and they slowly parted, inviting him in. He logged off before he could feel her tongue, knowing that if they began to kiss more deeply, he wouldn't be able to leave for a while.

The real world came back in a rush. It was like being sped down a tunnel and then coming to a crashing stop. Michael jerked forward in his seat and gasped. The air tasted stale, and it was significantly colder in his room than it had been in Bella's kitchen.

Shortly afterward, he felt a sudden pressure in his bladder. It had been twelve hours since he had taken a piss, and his body ached horribly as if in punishment. He lurched from his seat and rushed to the bathroom, hunched over in newfound pain.

When he reached the toilet, he slipped his underwear from around his waist and let it fall to the floor. He kicked it to the side as he relieved himself and was disgusted to feel the hardened fabric meet his toe momentarily. It was a small price to pay for the pleasure that came with Bella's world, but it still left him feeling rather pathetic.

He sighed with relief as he finished. After flushing, he disposed of his soiled boxers in a hamper and found himself a new pair of briefs. Then, he padded out into his own kitchen and couldn't help but frown at its juxtaposition.

Outside, the world was cloudy, and the pavement was wet from recent rainfall. The poor weather cast a dreary, dull light into his kitchen. It painted the room so dimly that Michael had to flip on the lights to properly see anything. The room lit up in faint gold.

He rubbed at his sore eyes, feeling the fatigue begin to make itself truly known. It was in his bones and his joints. The sinuses of his face felt puffy as well. He felt awful and creaky, wishing he could stay in his bed and take a small nap. Michael longed to take a real one this time, one without Bella by his side, warming the mattress to his right.

But the hunger roaring in his belly drove him deeper into the kitchen instead. He opened the refrigerator, listening to the few condiment bottles on the shelves clank and clatter noisily with his abrupt gesture. Inside, the refrigerator was sparsely filled. There was half of a cake wrapped in saran wrap that he had taken from the office leftovers three days ago. A bag of wilting spinach sat in one of the drawers alongside a half-eaten loaf of sliced bread, and leftover spaghetti and mashed potatoes had cooled in separate bowls. Ketchup, soy sauce, mustard, and peanut butter loaded the door's shelves. It was a dismal scene. There was no bacon ready to be cooked, no ingredients fit to make pancake batter, and not a single berry begging to be sliced in half and popped into his mouth. So he reached for the loaf of bread and the small tub of peanut butter, kicking himself for not picking up any jelly the last time he had gone shopping.

He made himself a makeshift sandwich out of the two ingredients and scarfed it down in four large bites. Michael then made himself another and devoured it as well. He was chewing away on his third sandwich and the last of his bread when he opened his pantry and took out a box of Oreos for his dessert. The peanut butter had stuck to the roof of his mouth and coated the back of his throat.

As he stuffed his mouth with the rest of his meal, he checked his phone and saw that he had only missed five messages. Two had been inconsequential. They were simply texts from Mary, asking to talk. The two of them hadn't spoken in a few days, and she wanted to catch up. Was six o'clock tonight okay?

Michael cringed slightly. Bella would be cooking up something special for him by then, creating a dinner that would put even Mary's cooking to shame.

"No," he texted her back. "But four o'clock works!"

Two of the other text messages were worse. He almost didn't respond to them either. They were from "Jon (Work)."

"How are things with Sirens?" the messages asked. "Can I get an update soon?"

Something about Jon's eagerness exhausted Michael. He was enjoying his time within the world in his head without any intruders. In fact, he was past looking for flaws. It was almost impossible to find any when he was so thoroughly distracted anyway. He was not, therefore, particularly eager to hear Jon's critical opinion. He wanted to bask in the idea that he had created a space of perfection—a personally tailored paradise—for just a bit longer.

Michael sighed deeply as if typing out the two words was overtaxing.

"Yeah," he texted. "Soon."

It was as if catching up on what he had missed had wiped out what little energy he was running on. He was not sure how sustainable the idea of sleeping in Bella's world was, but even while it left him feeling bitter and achy, he would have slept over again that very night if he didn't have work the next day.

Finally, he opened the last message. It was sent from one of his old college buddies. This text was a little bit more interesting, at least.

It was a screenshot from one of Cindy's social media pages.

The picture showed Cindy, beaming wider than Michael could remember, with her left hand shoved aggressively toward the camera. On her ring finger, a large diamond glistened, pairing well with her polished blue fingernails. A man with a dark beard and slick hair had buried his face in the side of hers, kissing her cheek.

The picture hit Michael like a punch to the stomach. He doubled over, bending forward like he had truly been hit.

Something about it made him feel sick. That smile most of all had unsettled him. It was one he could only compare to some from the deepest parts of their time together, way back at the beginning when they were new and seemingly in love.

Michael found himself wondering if she had been loyal to this man—her new fiancé—in the ways she should've been to him. Something about that sickeningly sweet smile made him think it was quite possible. She would be loyal so long as she was entertained, and Michael had failed her in that. He was a game developer, someone who was paid to keep people excited and on their toes, and he couldn't even do that with his own girlfriend.

Michael remembered a time when they had sat on the couch together, curled up close and watching a game. It could've been hockey, baseball, or football. They had watched them all together.

Her head was on his chest, and he was twirling her hair aimlessly. It had been soft and always smelled faintly of strawberries.

He was sitting with an odd pressure on him, the weight of that heavy question lying on him like an anvil. It was a question he had thought about for months. He felt that the two of them had been through it all. She had been caught cheating on him twice by then, and at the time Michael liked to think that it had brought them closer. They had made it through hell together, so he had to ask.

"Do you ever think of marriage?" He was embarrassed by how tight his voice had been, and he remembered being particularly thankful that her gaze was unwaveringly focused on the screen in front of them.

"No," she answered without hesitation.

"No?" It was not the response he had been hoping for but in retrospect, it was the one that he should have expected.

"No," she said again. "I think it's stupid. Mom and Dad did it and look how they turned out."

Her mom and dad had fought throughout her whole childhood, leaving her to seek attention elsewhere. When they had finally gotten a divorce, she had been just thirteen years old.

"I would like to," Michael said.

She finally turned to look at him. "Oh?"

"Yeah," he said, feeling fortified as he heard the increasing conviction in his voice. "It's like, if not for marriage, what is dating for?"

Cindy thought for a moment. He believed she didn't have an answer, not one that was planned out at least. "Love," she said. "And monogamous sex."

And you're so good at that, he had sarcastically thought.

"Maybe," he said. "But I like the idea of its finality."

"Well, I don't like the idea of the paperwork," she countered. And that had been it. She had turned back around, drifting into her own thoughts, eyes fixed on a game that had no consequence.

He reckoned she didn't mind the paperwork now. It had been daunting when she wasn't in love, but now it no longer seemed like a chore. The idea of the ring had once acted as a chain, but now it was a happy sort of branding, like shouting out at the world, "Look at me! I'm E-N-G-A-G-E-D!"

Michael couldn't even respond to the message. He didn't know how to. It occurred to him then that Cindy was still an open wound for him, not a scar. Sufficient time had passed, and he should've moved on like she had, but he had failed in that regard too. It still hurt, and after all that time, he simply didn't know what to say.

He felt sickened and stumbled aimlessly away from the kitchen. He left his phone awake on the counter, too tired and stricken to lock it.

Michael finished his Oreos and collapsed on the couch in his makeshift living room. He was too tired to go back to his bedroom, and the couch was close enough to a bed anyway.

He curled up in the fetal position, the way he had on his futon in college when he had been too hungover and exhausted from vomiting to crawl back up onto his bed. Even with the lights still on, Michael found himself drifting into sleep quickly. The gray life he lived in faded, darkening around the edges until it was consumed by sleep. In his dreams, he escaped back into a familiar world. One where the sun was bright, the air was warm, the kisses were soft, and the women were loyal.

14

Jon

Jon could not deny the negative change in Michael any longer. It was becoming increasingly clear that Michael was being kept awake all night by Sirens. Whether it was from stress or excessive testing, Jon did not know, but the evidence was in Michael's every movement. It was bent into his posture and audible in his tired tone.

Every day that week Michael had stumbled into the office looking more and more haggard, and each day, Jon would leave thinking that Michael could not regress further. Yet Jon would come in the following morning to see Michael taking another step in his decline. Though his hair had always appeared lightly tousled, it was now absolutely unkempt, standing out from his scalp at wild and unfathomable angles. His face was now starting to be consumed by the beginnings of a beard, and his eyes were ringed with purple circles that seemed to grow darker and deeper by the day.

He was becoming even more uncomfortable to look at each time he came into work. It wasn't easy to witness a man drowning. Jon couldn't deny that he felt a hollow pity for him. It was a helpless feeling, to see Michael floundering for aid.

That Friday, Jon had decided to throw Michael a life preserver.

Jon had walked into Michael's office with hunched shoulders, knowing that he was intruding on Michael's precious personal space. He felt like a kid on his way to the principal's office, bracing to be scolded during the walk there. But when he had asked if Michael wanted to go get a drink after work, Jon was surprised to see Michael appear inexplicably scared by the suggestion. Michael's eyes had popped wide, his mouth parting in surprise. His already pale complexion blanched until that was almost milky. Where Jon had assumed to be met with annoyance, Michael reacted almost with horror.

"I have work to do," Michael said. He had spoken so quickly, stumbling over his own words, and it took Jon a moment to even decipher what he had said.

"So do I," Jon replied, though that wasn't necessarily true. He should have been working to recreate his pet game idea from the ground up again, but he kept running into creative walls with it.

"I really shouldn't," Michael said but his voice was low. It was almost like he was talking to himself, convincing himself and not Jon.

"Come on!" Jon said. "It will only be an hour! Entertain me, man. Shayna is going to be out all night with some work friends. I really don't like the idea of drinking or smoking at home alone."

The prospect of being in that large, vacant house, with just his thoughts, made his stomach squeeze. He had never enjoyed being alone with his mind, without another person to bounce thoughts off of, or a joint to filter his wonderings.

Michael blinked hard as if bewildered but then cautiously agreed with a grimace. They had decided to meet at the restaurant where they had first formed the idea of Sirens. Mal's had been chosen out of a lack of other options.

Jon arrived at Mal's right in time to see Michael already sitting at the bar with a cold Corona in his fist. He was hunched over, staring blankly at the array of liquor displayed behind the bar. His clothes hung from him, looking like they were dripping from his body. Strangely, Jon noticed that Michael was wearing a loose turtleneck, which was a top that he had never pictured Michael wearing. He had been surprised to note that Michael even owned such a piece when he had first seen it earlier that day. It was quite oversized on him.

Michael didn't look over at Jon as he approached. He didn't seem aware of anything beyond the various liquor bottles right in front of him. He didn't acknowledge Jon until he clapped him on the shoulder, startling Michael so much that he jumped. The drink he clutched tightly in his fist splashed some of its contents onto the bar and his hand.

"Shit!" Michael said as he shook beer from his hand.

Jon laughed. "Sorry, man. I thought you would've seen me coming."

"No," Michael said. "I didn't." He was visibly unhappy, but Jon chalked it up to lack of sleep. He slid onto the stool beside Michael as he confronted the beer catalog.

"How have you been?" Jon asked as he made up his mind and dug in his pocket for some cash. He held it out, waiting for the bartender to take notice of the new patron.

"All right," Michael answered.

"If I'm being honest, man, it doesn't seem like it. You look worn out."

"Yeah, I am," Michael admitted. "I've been working. Testing."

"I figured," Jon said. "But it doesn't look like you've been sleeping at all."

Something flashed across Michael's eyes. It was a jarred look like he had been caught in something. He turned his gaze downward, staring at the small puddle his Corona had made on the bar.

"I haven't," Michael said. "Not much, at least. It's a small sacrifice, though."

"I think it's a big one," Jon said. "I may just be sort of a slacker when it comes to our projects—and yes, I can admit that—but sleep is important, especially if you're worried about getting the job done right. You can't work well without it."

Michael chuckled darkly. "I'll be okay."

Jon finally hailed the bartender's attention and ordered a draft beer. It was in front of him before Jon could even think of what to say next.

Michael raised his eyebrow when Jon opened a tab. "Plan on staying a while?"

"Just for a bit." Jon suddenly felt a pang of guilt. He had promised Michael it would only be an hour. But he didn't see the harm in pulling Michael away from his work for longer than anticipated. "Why?" Jon asked, half-joking, half-mocking. "Got somewhere to be?"

Michael took a sip of his beer. He was tapping his heel against the ground so quickly that his leg almost looked like it was vibrating. "I just want to get back to... to work," he said.

"First time I ever heard someone say that," Jon said with a laugh. "I get it, though. You're in the zone."

"Mhm," Michael hummed in agreement. "Yeah. I'm in the zone."

"I thought you could use a break, even if it's just for a short while," Jon said. "Everyone needs one, especially when they've been working as hard as you have. I've found that a drink is just what you need when you're in the trenches. It got me through college at least."

Michael's leg was jumping so violently that his beer sloshed in its bottle. "Thanks."

"I'm not going to lie to you," Jon began. "I drank like a fish when I was coding up that reversal stuff for Sirens. It was a *bitch*. If I didn't have weed and beer, I don't think it would've been possible."

"Interesting," Michael said, though it didn't seem like it was to him.

"What's your poison?" Jon asked, trying to keep the conversation going. "What's getting you through?"

Michael laughed. He tilted his head back and the laughter rose from his throat in a forceful surge. "You don't want to know," he said.

Jon stared at him for a beat incredulously. Michael was acting unhinged. Jon had never seen someone act so erratically. As he looked at Michael, with his jerky motions and stilted interactions, Jon couldn't help but feel a twinge of fear, but for whom, he wasn't sure. He shook his head slightly as if wishing to shake the impending feeling of discomfort from him.

"You're in the homestretch now, though," Jon said, trying to stay positive. He clapped Michael on the shoulder again in the hopes that the gesture would not let on that he was growing increasingly unnerved. "Almost to the finish line."

Michael looked at where Jon's hand had just touched his shoulder, then looked back at Jon with narrowed eyes. His leg had stopped moving.

"Did you invite me here just to talk about the game?" he asked.

"No, I wanted to break you away from your work. You've been a slave to it, and I wanted to give you an out," Jon said.

It was as though the air had frozen.

"I don't want to talk about it, Jon," Michael said. He held eye contact for a second longer, then downed the rest of his beer in one large and final swallow.

Jon was itching to ask why. A distant feeling of nervousness was growing closer, stalking toward him like a predator, and drawing Jon in. But Jon refrained from pushing the subject any further. He decided that it was time to ask the big question, the one everyone around the office was whispering behind their palms to one another.

"Are you okay?" Jon asked.

Michael placed his bottle back on the table with a hard *bang*. "I told you I'm all right," he said.

Though Michael had never been particularly warm, this outburst was new. Jon didn't know what to say. He knew then that he was trying to steer through dangerous waters.

For a moment, he only played with the napkin his glass was placed on, thinking of the right thing to respond with. It dawned on him that no words would calm Michael. There was no perfect way to respond because Michael would be angered by anything Jon said.

"I don't believe you," he told Michael, finally. "And I don't know why you're lying."

Michael scoffed.

"I'm here for you if you need anything," Jon continued. "I always have been. If it's my coding that's making the testing hard for you, I want to apologize. I shouldn't have made your project more complicated than it already was."

"It's not your coding," Michael said. "Your code is very good. Too good."

"I'm not going to press you, but if you want to talk..."

Michael cut him off. "I don't want to talk. I don't need to either. Let it go."

"Jesus, man." Jon put his hands up defensively. "I'm just trying to help."

"I know you are, but if I'm being honest, you're going about it all wrong. I don't need a beer, brotherly advice, and some slaps on the shoulder. I need to work."

"I know you're stressed but it will get done. You can afford to have an hour off."

Michael tensed. "You don't get it."

"I don't, but I'm trying to. I can't understand it until you tell me."

"I don't want to."

Jon shook his head. He couldn't help it. It was clear that this was more than sleep deprivation. It was something far worse. This was deeper, something that a full eight hours of sleep couldn't fix. There was no saving him with this friendly approach. Michael was too far in his head; he would have to save himself if he wanted to improve. These were decisions Jon couldn't make for him; they were changes only Michael could make.

"You don't have to be so cold. I was just trying to help," Jon said.

"I'm sure you were."

"If you can't break yourself away from coding for an hour, that's not on me," Jon said. "Good luck, though."

"It's more than coding!" Michael raised his voice. A few bargoers around them turned to look in their direction with judgmental glares. "It's more than that. Yes, it's fulfilling to create something. To watch it come to life before you is so... it's incredible. I want this to be perfect, but this is about more than just stringing lines of working code together. It's bigger than that, and I can't tell anyone why because... because, well, I'll look more like a crazy person."

Michael stood. He looked down at Jon with anger and distrust pulsing behind his tired, bloodshot eyes.

"It's hard to explain, and I wouldn't expect you to understand. I can't expect anyone to truly get it, especially not you. You haven't completed a project in your life, Jon!" Michael exclaimed. "I knew you wouldn't get it, no matter how many times I explained it or put it in different words. Now, if you'll excuse me, I have to get back."

The words hung in the air, heavy and thick. Jon's mind whirled with what to retort with. A million angry responses zipped around his head. He wanted to jab back at Michael, to pull something out that would hurt him, but he couldn't find the right words to. What stung the most was that Michael was right and that deep down Jon knew it.

Jon could only muster one word in response.

"Wow," he said.

Michael didn't appear to have even heard. He was too concentrated on leaving, springing with refreshed eagerness and energy. He put on his coat with haste, and Jon was surprised to see him looking just as astounded as Jon felt. Michael looked startled by the words that had come from his own mouth. Perhaps it had poured out of him, like some pent-up emotions straining against him had burst forth, unable to be contained once he had started.

It didn't make Jon feel any better to see Michael's shock. It only made him feel even more distraught.

Michael grabbed a fistful of cash from his pocket, not bothering to count out the total, and tossed it onto the bar by his glass.

"I'll... see you at work," Michael said, his eyes still gaping with disbelief. But there was no apology.

Michael left in a hurry, and Jon watched him hustle out of the bar in wordless discontent. He couldn't tell if it looked like Michael was running from him or toward Sirens.

15

Michael

When the beginning of a new week broke and Monday was in sight once again, Michael called off work. He had dialed up the general RightMark number on Sunday with his mind made up and said that he wouldn't be coming in. There had been no explanation, no justification. He simply wasn't going to be there.

On the other end of the call, there had been no protest or question. Though Michael had expected to leave a message, the receptionist who manned the ninth floor surprisingly answered his call despite it being a weekend. She took his request for a day off without a hint of curiosity. She didn't seem to find it odd and failed to press him for a reason, so he had given none.

Michael knew that he should have felt somewhat guilty, but he had no remorse for doing it. He had worked at RightMark for years and never called off once—not even when he was sick or severely hungover. Despite the clean record, it was as though his absence would go unnoticed like this wasn't an abnormality at all. They likely assumed he intended to work from home.

The truth was that Michael hadn't done anything work-related or productive in days. He was spending roughly twenty hours each day in Sirens, coming out only to eat, piss, and take a two- or three-hour nap before slipping in to see Bella again. His body was a network of various aches and pains, and he had noticeably lost weight. When he had brought it up to Bella after briefly worrying about the physical effects, she had simply rubbed his sunken stomach gently and said, "I like it. I think you look lean and sexy." Suddenly, it didn't matter anymore.

So, when Sunday faded away and Monday emerged quietly, he spent the day in Bella's world, drinking tasty Coronas, eating crispy bacon, and having unbelievable sex. It was a Monday well spent as far as he was concerned, and it was perhaps the best one he could remember. Thoughts about the deadline or his argument with Jon were far from his mind, almost like they had happened in a different galaxy.

Later in the afternoon, he decided one other day off wouldn't hurt. He had amassed many free passes from his spotless attendance over the years. So he called off again. This time, when he made the call, the receptionist on the other end had taken a deep inhale of air, and Michael knew that she was going to ask why. He had hung up before she could. It hadn't mattered the first time, so why did it matter now? Michael was far too tired to answer questions anyway.

After he had hung up, he slipped back into Sirens until midnight, when he left again to have a makeshift meal and briefly sleep in his world.

Michael woke from his nap to his alarm blaring around three on Tuesday morning. Though he was exhausted, there was a light excitement in his chest as he found himself eager to begin his day for the first time in perhaps years.

As he woke, he was acutely aware of the puffiness in his eyes and the soreness of his muscles. His world was filled with these pains. Unplugged, he was weak, easily succumbing to basic desires. He was feeble and useless, like an abandoned calf. But the escape from those troubles was always so easily accessible. All he needed to do to evade the maladies was to put on a collar and sit back.

Michael rolled onto his side with a groan and turned his alarm off. With the press of a button, everything was deadly silent, the quiet filling the room like a physical being, taking up space. Only faint crickets chirped on rare occasions like even they were tired by the hour. Michael felt a fleeting sense of loneliness as he navigated this still, sleeping world by himself, but the knowledge that he would not be alone within mere minutes gave him the assurance he needed to not fall into a fixation.

When he stood, he felt the weight of his body distribute itself on his frail legs. He was sure that atrophy was taking place, as he rarely stood anymore. For a searing second, he felt a sharp panic break through his hazy, half-awake mind. He was mildly aware that he was withering, but Bella's voice rose up involuntarily, reminding him that she liked him "lean and sexy."

Well, he certainly was growing leaner.

He also was getting an indent from the collar that wasn't fading as it normally would for people who plugged in for shorter periods of time. It was as if his flesh was forming around it, accepting its presence as semi-permanent. The collar had created long parallel lines across his throat from where the edges had dug into his skin. To avoid curious stares and prodding questions, he had started covering the marks with high-collared shirts during his few ventures out of his house.

Michael stumbled around his dark room to the familiar place where his plush seat was. Atop the cushion was his Emissux collar, nestled in the indent his body had created after hours of sitting. The cold metal pressed against his throat with its familiar bite as he eagerly secured it in place. Over time, Michael had grown almost fond of it. He welcomed the familiar clasping feel of the collar as he leaned into the chair, being swallowed by cushions and his subconscious as Sirens emerged around him.

Sirens pixelated itself into view, and within seconds Michael was in Bella's bedroom. She was lying on her bed asleep when he reentered. With her eyes closed, she seemed peaceful as she lay there quiet and unmoving until Michael was fully formed. Then, seeming to sense that he was finally back to her, she rolled over with a serene smile on her face.

"You're back," she observed in a sleepy voice.

She almost always greeted him this way, appearing surprised that he had returned.

"Of course I am," Michael said.

His fingers began to stroke down her bare back, tracing the indent of her spine. Her smile widened at his touch.

"I can go make some breakfast," she suggested. "Then we can go on a walk or something. It's going to be a beautiful day."

The sun was peeking through her window, golden and unfiltered. It never rained in Bella's world, and recently the weather was getting increasingly warmer. The world was coming awake around them. Birds were chirping happily, and the distant sound of crickets was far gone, lost in another universe.

"That sounds lovely," Michael said. "Maybe we can finally have that picnic we talked about a while ago."

Bella bit her lip and kicked off the sheets. She was wearing nothing but a pair of lacy red panties.

He watched her slip on a large T-shirt and then followed her into the kitchen. As she cooked, she yawned and talked quietly, still hazy from sleep. She pulled out ingredients swiftly, working with practiced ease.

"Anything new?" Bella asked casually.

"Not much," Michael said as he slid into his seat at her table. "I called off work again today."

"Did you!" Bella said with pleased shock. "What did you tell them?"

"Nothing," Michael said. "They don't need to know."

She looked at him with a devilish smirk. "No," she agreed. "You're right. It's our little secret."

"Anything new with you?" Michael asked.

Bella giggled as she put the batter she had just made onto the skillet in even dollops. Michael sometimes asked her this to break the ice, and it never failed to make at least one of them chuckle.

"Oh, you know, just sleeping," she said. "Should've been cooking, though. I didn't know you would come back so soon."

"I don't like to waste time on the other side," Michael admitted.

"I don't blame you," Bella said. "From what you've told me it sounds horribly boring."

"It is." It was like his own world was dulled, covered by a filter, whereas Bella's was crisp and realized. "It's like everything over there is clouded."

"Meaning?" She gave the pancakes in front of her a flip, and they came up a beautiful golden brown.

"For one thing, pancakes don't look like that over there," he said. "And women don't look like you."

Bella smirked. "Are you trying to flatter me, Michael?"

"That's not the intention." Michael shrugged. "Just telling the truth, but if the shoe fits."

"Well, at least you have an escape," Bella said.

Michael watched her cook, thinking. Finally, he admitted, "I'm starting to worry actually. Just a little bit."

Bella's eyes went wide. "Why's that?"

"I hate it there," Michael answered. "When I'm there I want to be here."

Bella considered what he said for a moment. "Well, you're a grown man. You can decide if you want to keep being in that world or not. It's up to you, but I certainly wouldn't complain if you wanted to make the move here permanent."

She talked about staying in Sirens as flippantly as someone discussing early plans to move into a new apartment.

"I have to keep going back, though. I can't stay here all the time even though I want to."

Bella smiled humorously. "What, are my pancakes not enough?"

"Unfortunately, no," Michael said. "And there's Mary to worry about." He thought about Mary, hardly able to do things unassisted, surrendering to her bed, and felt a pang in his chest.

Michael knew that Bella wouldn't truly argue with him. He knew she would listen and comment and question, but it was not in her to tell him to do one thing or the other. That was for him to decide and for her to listen to.

"Am I not good enough?" she ventured, biting her lip with worry.

"Don't say that," Michael said quickly. "Don't even think that. You're perfect. Absolutely perfect. It's just... family stuff. Life obligations."

He stared down at his plate, smelling the sweet and heavy scent of pancakes and syrup. *Mary deserves better,* Michael thought to himself. Bella seemed to sense his self-loathing because she abandoned the bacon she had just started to cook in a pan and went to him. She rubbed his shoulders gently and spoke soothingly.

"Mary loves you very much," Bella said in a hushed voice. "I don't think you need to worry about her. She will respect your decisions. From what you've said, she has in the past."

"I don't know how much she would respect me if I completely left."

He had to remind himself that leaving was not truly leaving, though. Michael greatly suspected that moving from one reality to the next would be moving from life into death. It was hard to remember sometimes that this decision was not as simple as it appeared. It had consequences that would affect people beyond him. The idea of living with Bella truly and forever felt so easy, almost mindless, like falling asleep. Yet he could never do it.

"You would know better than me," she said. "The only thing I can say is that I like it when you're here. I love it. And when you're gone, all I do is miss you and wait for you to return. You're always welcome. This your home too."

She punctuated her thoughts with a kiss on his right cheek. Then, she returned to the bacon and tended to it.

Michael paused and thought about what she had said. There was a pull toward her that was magnetic, from his head to his groin, a full-body and all-encompassing tug in her direction like some biological instinct. It was unbearable, and he was aware that it was also unnatural. But it felt so right and good and warm to be with her. She was beckoning him toward her without any explicit intention to.

"I can't leave Mary," Michael said in a whisper, mostly to himself.

"That makes sense. I'll support you in your decision either way."

"I know," Michael said, looking up to watch her slide the bacon onto a plate. Her eyes were downcast, and she was biting her lip as if holding back her thoughts.

"She took me in when so many others in her position would've turned me away. She raised me like her own when she didn't have to."

"I know," Bella said in a low voice still avoiding his gaze. He knew that she genuinely did.

"She used to drive me to school every morning. When I offered to take the bus, she would insist on driving me there before she went to work even though taking me left her with ten minutes to rush over to her job. But she still insisted. She'd pack my lunch bag in the morning and hustle me into her Range Rover, and we would listen to music she liked when she was younger. I caused her a lot of grief, but I think she liked taking care of someone. She liked the responsibility and the hustle of motherhood even if I wasn't her kid. Mary was a good mom. And I can't just leave her."

"I understand," Bella repeated. "I'm sorry you feel so torn. That wasn't my intention."

"I would never blame you for it," Michael said. He took a bite of bacon. It was flavorful, rich, and so crisp it cracked in his mouth, tasting like the best thing he had ever eaten all over again. "It's just bad circumstances," he said as he chewed.

"We can make them better, though." She took a strand of his long and increasingly unruly hair and twirled it between her fingers. When she finally looked at him, her eyes were expectant and asking.

He knew that this would be how he spent his day; it was how he had spent all of the days before too. They always began with Bella's good cooking. They would eat, take walks, drink beers, and have sex. Lots of sex. Sometimes, Michael would discuss harbored secrets with Bella, who would listen unwaveringly, absorbing his worries as if they were her own. The days were always similar and consistent, though they never seemed to grow tiresome or boring. Michael pushed that quiet, disapproving thought from his mind.

He took Bella's hand and kissed the palm. "I love you," he whispered into her hand, and he meant it.

"I love you, too," she said, her face glowing with happiness.

She wrapped her hand around his and pulled him gently in the direction of her bedroom—their bedroom—to consummate their love.

16

James

Dreary September nights like the one outside bored James Sherrod. He would rather the seasons stick to a strict binary: cold or hot. Pick one. That evening produced a middling temperature in the sixties, but a drizzle outside turned the world soggy.

He could see all of this from his penthouse window, overlooking the city of Pittsburgh. The towering buildings were still alive with lights that rarely seemed to turn off. He assessed them all as he sipped a late nightcap of whiskey from a glass.

Bravely, he stood before the window completely naked. In his bedroom, several feet from him, his secretary was fast asleep. He liked the cliché of having her there and the thrill of leading her on. Lizzie was far from the only woman he had taken to bed that month but making her think that she was special had a rush to it. He suspected that she knew what he told her was untrue deep down. She had to know that those little promises and exaggerated compliments were lies. Yet even if she chose to confront him, he was sure that she would eventually forgive him. That was the type of person she was, and he was the type of person who had so much success people were eager to look the other way from his faults.

Since becoming the president of the fastest-growing gaming company, RightMark, people fell to their knees before him and asked for forgiveness even if he was the one who had directly wronged them.

James took another sip of his drink. It was nearly three in the morning, and he had work the next day. There were meetings to attend, decisions to be made, and ideas he had to sign off on. The thought of the impending day made him sigh loudly. He hated his job if he was being truthful. The responsibility weighed on him heavily, but the power and wealth that came with it were fantastic and blinding. If he had to continue this misery to reap all of the rewards, so be it. As his mother had been so fond of saying, "Eat your vegetables, kid!"

James was kept awake that night with many thoughts, as he always seemed to be. Sleep had been one thing that had never come easily for him. But one specific irritant was especially bothersome that evening. All day he had been nagged by the idea that his star creator, The Next Big Thing, Michael Ken, had not come into work that week. The kid had always been ambitious, so some last-minute cramming on his project wasn't surprising. Yet when Lizzie told James about it and he asked for Michael's excuse, he received none.

"I forgot to ask him the day before but when I tried to ask today, he just said he couldn't and hung up on me," Lizzie had said, blushing prettily with embarrassment.

"Why didn't you ask the first day?" James had snapped. He had been tipsy, and the drink had lit a fire in his belly.

"I just, you know, I thought he was busy." She had turned completely scarlet by then.

"If he calls in again, I want to know why," James had said as he seethed with anger. How could she have been so stupid? With the deadline approaching on the last Wednesday of the month—just eight days away—James wanted accountability. He wanted to be able to see Michael working with his own eyes.

"Yes, I'll ask next time," Lizzie said. Her eyes were downcast.

James drained the last of his drink as he recalled this and continued to stare out at the expanse of Pittsburgh, dotted with all of its little lights and quirks, as he debated pouring himself another glass. He had never liked the city; he found it filthy, really. When he looked out at it, he was only reminded of the dirty streets, the foul scents that wafted sporadically, and those hazy gray days that hung over the city like someone had put a lid of dull clouds over them.

Michael was his hope of getting out.

After Sirens' release, he hoped to count off his successes and move somewhere nice, somewhere it was hot for most of the year and there were beaches where he could drink cocktails and admire women. Pittsburgh had never been his dream. It was merely a convenience. Pittsburgh was where he had grown up, where his family had rooted down and raised him, and still lived years later. He didn't want to be like them, stuck in the same corner of the world for his whole life. His dreams were down south, where the sun cleared the skies like it was parting a crowd and the weather was more certain of itself.

He needed Michael there, in his office, to ensure that this was a tangible dream.

James' vision would come to fruition if he could only get Sirens into his hands. There was no way a game about tits and ass didn't sell to the lonely men of America. Fuck, even James' interest was piqued by the idea.

That southern dream was within his reach, just days from being in his hands. If Michael could just do his job and do it well, they would all leave the deal very happy.

Should Michael come into work that day, James might just pay him a visit to chew him out. He was sure he could strike the fear of God into him if need be. There was serious money involved and stern expectations. This was not the sort of thing that could be hand-waved away or put off without a good excuse. Michael's inability to see that made James feel warm all over with frustration. Or maybe that was just the alcohol.

17

Shayna

There was a sharp pain in Shayna's throat. Whenever she biked this way, she would notice that familiar, piercing feeling and know that she was really working. It was not a pleasant sensation, but she often pursued it, seeking it as a way to prove that she was pushing herself.

The feeling was amplified by the morning air. It was the first definitively cool day of the year, promising autumn. September hadn't even passed before the warmth had been sucked from Pittsburgh. Soon, the cold would be unbearable, and she wouldn't be able to bike with all of the snow coating the sidewalks. It was the beginning of the end, and she wanted to take advantage of being able to bike while she still could.

Shayna zoomed through her neighborhood, down the street, and through another neighborhood of supple homes. Despite the colder temperature, the sky was a lovely, cloudless blue. Something about that clear day lifted her spirits, making her think that she could bike further than she normally did.

So, she found herself going well beyond the distance she habitually went and rode down another street. This was a busier area, one where cars carelessly tore down the road.

She biked to the sounds of heavy rock that she had listened to as a teen. They made her feel nostalgic as the discordant, yet musical screams of Vic Fuentes filled her ears, reminding her of a time when she felt angst over small things, things that didn't really matter. Despite herself, she longed for when her biggest fears were of a lack of parental attention, whether the girl in her biology class thought she was cute, and if her dress was short enough to be dress coded.

Now, she was consumed by adult concerns and real-world issues. Bills and a moody husband weighed on her mind instead of Katy from bio. These new worries were more serious, tangible, and unforgiving. It made her sad and angry to think that she was a settled adult.

So, she biked harder as if moving faster might allow her to flee those burdens.

She turned down Milmare Street, which let out onto a highway. She planned to bike to the edge, right where the sidewalk gave way to a daunting crosswalk that connected the two opposing ends of the road, and then turn back and head home. She could smell the scent of her sweat breaking through the sickly-sweet smell of her lavender vanilla deodorant. Despite the slight chill in the air, she was sweating hard. The thought of a shower sounded incredible at that moment.

The highway was in sight, with cars zipping by at speeds that nearly blurred them. At the edge of Milmare was a small beer shop filled with local brews that Jon often liked to buy. It grew closer as Shayna pedaled, tearing toward her halfway point. As the end of the sidewalk grew nearer and more visible, Shayna was becoming acutely aware of the dryness of her throat.

Her legs kept the momentum, carrying her to the end of the sidewalk. She was about to turn back when a great red rectangle in the sky caught her eye. She hit the brakes hard, stopping dead so that she could take a better look.

Hanging back and surrounded by a nestling of trees was an imposing billboard. It screamed for attention on the other side of the highway with its color blazing a red the shade of fire. It was no ordinary stagnant billboard either. It was cast in LED lights that were bright and intimidating, practically pleading for the fleeting awareness of highway drivers. Despite its grand appearance, it was a simple advertisement, one of few words.

It read:

SIRENS

FRIENDSHIP, INTIMACY, ROMANCE... SHE CAN DO IT ALL!

Shayna set her bike to the side, leaning on it like a crutch. She looked up at the letters stupidly, rereading them until they made sense. Jon hadn't told her that there would be a billboard just a bike ride down the street from their house. If he had known about it, he had hidden it from her.

Something about it made her stomach twist. The billboard hung over the highway like a watchful eye, looking foreboding among the trees. Its contents were minimal, merely writing on a bright canvas of red. She supposed she should be grateful that it wasn't an egregious photo of a naked woman.

She hadn't wanted to think about the game at all; Shayna was happy to forget that it was even in production. Yet a constant reminder now hung just minutes from their house, appearing obnoxious and greedy above the familiar stretch of road. Beneath it, she felt dwarfed, as if she were legitimately standing in the shadow of something bigger than she could comprehend.

Shayna was vaguely aware that she must have looked strange to those who were passing by. As she stood there, gaping up at the electric sign, she briefly pictured what she must look like to a passenger in one of the many cars. Self-consciously, she closed her agape mouth and began to steer her bike away, clutching the handlebars in fists.

Her buzzing phone snapped her from her deep thoughts about Sirens. Shayna's eyes jumped to her phone, which was tucked tightly into the small pocket of her leggings. When she pulled it out, her jaw dropped again, this time in pleasant surprise.

In bold letters, her sister's name, Kelly, was announced on the screen. Kelly hadn't called her in over a month. The last time they had checked in, her sister had been strolling through Europe, living in luxury hotels, and being paid to review her experience. It was rare that Shayna's sister called her.

"Hey!" Kelly's voice sprung from the phone almost the instant Shayna answered the call.

"Hey!" Shayna said. She found that her voice sounded odd and strained.

"Everything all right?" Kelly asked. Her tone had drastically dipped from its happy greeting.

Shayna cleared her throat. "Yeah," she said. "Just out biking. I'm thirsty."

"Look at you! It's fucking cold out this morning if you ask me. *Much* different from the warmth Brazil had a few days ago. That's some dedication," Kelly said. "Where are you biking?"

"Just close to our neighborhood," Shayna answered. "I'm out by the highway now, near that little beer store off of Milmare Street."

"Oh! Did you go to check out the new billboard?"

"No," Shayna said, holding the phone closer to her ear with fresh interest. "I didn't even know about it until a second ago."

"I can't lie to you," Kelly said. "It's obnoxious looking. The red is so bright it almost burned off my corneas."

"Jon didn't even tell me about it." Shayna gave the sign one more glance before she walked away. It still hovered over the trees like a neon light in a dark room. "It's horrible though."

"Only a man would be so bold about something so vulgar," Kelly added. "Sorry if that was rude. Last time I checked you didn't particularly like that game."

"Yeah," Shayna said. "That hasn't changed."

She forced her eyes to remain forward, fighting the instinct to turn around and take another glance. But she continued to hike back up the sidewalk she had ridden down just minutes before, using one hand to steer and the other to hold her phone to her ear.

Shayna cleared her throat, feeling the rawness from dehydration and overexertion setting in. She wanted nothing more than to go home to a nice cold drink and a hot shower. So long as her sister was on the phone, though, that dream would be out of reach as she shuffled her way back to her house.

"So, what's up? Is everything okay on your end?" Shayna asked, trying to be polite.

"Hell yeah!" Kelly said. "Better than okay, actually! Just wanted to catch up with my sister."

Shayna felt slightly irked at this. Her sister rarely checked in on her unless it was to brag. It was no doubt some news about a European lover or how financially lucrative her self-made business of travel blogging was.

"Well, I'm about to bike home," Shayna said. "I do want to catch up soon, though."

"Of course," Kelly agreed, but there was a hint of disappointment in her voice. "Want to come over soon? I have this amazing new light fixture in the kitchen you'll have to see. I got it when I was in Japan a few months ago. Does this Saturday work?"

"Yeah, that works," Shayna said. "I didn't even know you were back."

"I just got in a day ago, actually. It's been a while since we've talked, so I was just hoping to check-in. When you're over, we should probably plan on what to do for the holidays too."

"Sounds good to me," Shayna said. "I'll see you around noon on Saturday, then."

"Can't wait." Shayna could hear the smile in Kelly's voice.

"See you then," Shayna said before hanging up.

When she returned her phone to her pocket she sighed through her hoarse throat, glad that it was over. She loved her sister, but they were not as close as they once were, and talking to her only made her dwell on it. They hadn't kept up with each other since Shayna had moved out to go to college and Kelly had successfully claimed her role as their mother's favorite.

It would be nice to see Kelly, though, Shayna concluded. She did not blame Kelly for this favoritism any more than she blamed Jon and herself for not being able to conceive. It was all just poor circumstances. Besides, it had been a while and Shayna mostly enjoyed hearing stories of Kelly's adventures even if they occasionally made her jealous. They still allowed her to live vicariously through her sister without the financial burden.

Shayna mounted her bike once more and began to pedal after hitting play on her phone. She was once again awash in a mix of nostalgic emotions pushing her home.

18

Michael

Michael lay there, sprawled out among silken sheets, tracing the indent of Bella's spine. The gesture soothed them both equally. As his fingers brushed upward, they left gooseflesh in their wake.

Bella lay beside him on her stomach with her eyes closed peacefully. She was not asleep, but she lay there wordlessly, enjoying the silence with him. He continued to rub her back, stroking up and down as though he was painting a canvas and his fingers were the brush.

She looked so pleased that it both comforted him and aroused him. Yet even in that sweet, tender moment, the thought of leaving her again pecked away at him. It was a nuisance he would never be able to shake.

But even as he thought about this, Michael could feel the fatigue of the real world setting in, and the edges of hunger were beginning to punctuate almost every thought.

"I have to go," Michael whispered.

Almost instantly, the muscles of her back tightened under his touch, and her eyelids snapped open so that those blue irises stared back at him severely, the look layered with a pain that was so clear it was almost unbearable to witness.

"What?" Her voice was small and filled with hurt.

"I have to go," he repeated. "I have to go back."

"I don't understand. Why?"

Her eyebrows knitted themselves together in confusion, and she propped herself up onto her forearms, bringing her face closer to his as if she hoped to see him better. As she moved, her hair fell into her face, but she didn't appear to notice it. Nothing seemed to matter to her but Michael.

"I have to eat," he said the same tired excuse. "I have to sleep."

"But you just slept," she said. "And I cooked for you just hours ago."

"It's not the same. I've told you this," Michael said. He wasn't sure how he was supposed to explain it to her or make her understand. He knew that in the past she had acknowledged the difference. He had always operated under the assumption that she understood that the food and sleep here were true for her but not for him. He had always thought that she knew that there was a difference, and he found himself wondering if that comprehension was fading.

"I can make you more food. You can sleep while I cook."

She moved to stand, the covers falling away from her mercilessly. Beneath it, she was naked other than a set of red bra and panties, the same ones she had worn for him the night that they had first slept together. Her skin illuminated in the moonlight, a soft glow that sent her complexion into a pearly white. She was breathtaking in the soft lighting, making everything more difficult.

He grabbed her wrist, stopping her from moving more. "It's not like that," Michael said. "I need to eat in *my* world. Eat *my* food."

Bella looked from the grasp on her wrist to his face. There was an agony in her eyes like he had never seen in a person before. It was horrible and desperate like he was telling her that someone she loved had died.

"Isn't what I make good enough?" she asked.

"Of course!" he exclaimed. "It's delicious!"

This argument seemed so silly. She had not argued this point so fiercely before. They had even joked about it over a lunch of tuna sandwiches the previous day. Why was she acting so strangely all of the sudden?

"Then why won't you let me make more?" she asked. Her eyes were rimmed with tears now. "Please."

"I need to go take care of myself," he explained. "If I don't, I won't be able to see you again."

I'll be dead, he added mentally. The thought was small and distant, though, and he pushed it aside as he always did when it sprung back up.

"Please don't leave." Her voice was very small, and tears rolled down her cheeks. "Please don't. It gets so lonely in here without you. It gets so cold and dark."

"I'll be back in just a few minutes," he promised.

"You don't understand!" she cried out. "You're my purpose. When you leave everything means nothing. I need you here. I need you with me. Please, Michael!"

He hesitated a moment, thinking. Then, he spoke slowly, his words measured in an attempt not to set her off. "I don't know if I can fix that. I've told you how it is."

But it set her off anyway. She sobbed openly then and pulled her wrist from his grasp. She covered her face with her hands so that he couldn't see her weep.

"I hate it when you go," she said. "You belong here with me. I belong with you. I know it's selfish. I know I'm not supposed to…

assert things, but I can't help it! I can't keep quiet anymore and keep hurting. I want you to myself."

Michael didn't know what to say. He blinked hard as he tried to gather his bewildered thoughts. She wasn't supposed to form opinions outside of his own preferences. He was supposed to decide first. And he had, but she wasn't agreeing with him as she was programmed to do.

Was this what he wanted? Was she reacting this way because he subconsciously wanted her to disagree? Did he want her to tell him to stay?

Bella sniffled and sighed as she tried to regain her composure. After a minute or so, she peeled her hands from her face. Her eyes were red and serious, staring at him as if she could see through him.

"I was made for you," she said.

Michael's mind went numb, trying to make sense of what she had just said. How did she know? Did his subconscious want her to know exactly what she was? What was she *getting* at?

"I'm everything you wanted," she said. "And if I'm not perfect, I *can* be. I can be anything you want if you only let me try."

Michael still didn't know what to say. He was in awe of her intelligence. It scared him into speechlessness. His mouth remained agape and unmoving as he tried to gather a string of words together that made sense.

"Please let me try," she whispered.

Then she leaned in and kissed him. At first, he was stiff under her kiss, hesitant and tense with worry. But her lips were so soft and the hands in his hair were so gentle that he loosened instinctively against his better judgment. He kissed back, slowly at first, tasting the salt of her tears. Then he became the aggressor again, and Bella accepted it, encouraged it, and desired it.

She soon broke away for air and whispered breathily. "Stay. Oh, please, Michael! Stay."

Michael quieted her with his lips. It was hard to think of what was best when she intoxicated him so deeply. They kissed as he tried to think but failed to; her lips consumed his every thought. The pain in his belly seemed to become a faint annoyance and his fatigue was ignored once again. She affected him the way the waves did the shore; she came crashing down around him and swept away all of his fears.

When she peeled away to begin reaching to pull the covers from him, though, his thoughts cleared, like a sunbeam slipping through a parting in the clouds. What was he *doing?* He hadn't eaten in sixteen hours and his last meal had been a cup of yogurt and a sleeve of crackers.

"Just a little longer," he said, promising her and himself. "Then I have to go. Seriously this time."

They were an inch apart and her eyes bore into him, seeming to devour him. She bit her lip sweetly and nodded emphatically. "Yes." It was enough for now.

They kissed for a long while, but Michael couldn't bring himself to do anything more than that. He was still frightened by this new development. Eventually, he broke from her and told her that he needed to rest. The fatigue from his world was making his movements sluggish. He was not sure if he had ever felt so tired, and that was even with the filter of Sirens on his senses.

Bella smiled sadly and said, "As you wish. If you're going, just know that I'll be waiting for you here." She laid down and turned over so that her back was to him, as though she couldn't face watching him go.

For a while, Michael watched her back rise and fall with her breathing, hesitating. Then his gaze turned toward the ceiling in exasperation, letting his worries reopen like briefcases to sort through.

He resolved to stare at that white ceiling with its black fan until some more time had passed before he would permit himself to slip out. He had promised her a little while longer, after all. It was not hard to fill the minutes between then and his departure. He had much to think about.

Why does she know all of this? The thought echoed in his head, repeating like it was on a loop. *And why does she care?*

It worried him that it could be a glitch in his coding. He had never intentionally designed her to become aware of her surroundings in that way. She was programmed to allow him to escape into his world and to accept it, yet she had done neither of those things that night. She was never intended to stand in his way, to vocalize opposing thoughts, or to acknowledge what her true purpose was without his prompting.

Part of him wanted to turn over and ask her for himself.

But a larger part of him was too scared to. As he lay there, the idea of her beside him increasingly frightened him as if he was lying beside a vampire and not the woman of his dreams. She was growing smarter than he had expected or intended. She was becoming stronger and more intelligent with use. While this was one of the core intentions of Sirens—for her to adapt and grow over time—she was supposed to grow within the mold of his preferences.

He didn't think he wanted her to be so aware of her circumstances. But did he? Maybe she was reacting to a desire he wasn't aware of.

While that was a frightening thought in itself, the other option was even scarier. Michael touched on the possibility the way a child might poke at an unknown insect with a stick. The thought was a whisper, kept quiet in the hopes he wouldn't really have to acknowledge it.

Could she be gaining sentience?

The idea was not unlike those crappy science fiction movies he used to watch when he was a child. The prospect that Bella could be growing stronger into a more real, thoughtful version of herself felt preposterous. She was a figment of his imagination, after all. How could she think for herself if she was a mere extension of him?

Beside him, Bella stirred, turning over so that she was lying on her back. Within the time Michael had spent fretting, she had fallen asleep. Bella moaned softly as she moved as though the task of flipping over was arduous.

With her face to the sky, she looked too sweet to ever have the evil qualities that the sentient AI in all of those movies had. There was just no way that his model of perfection, who had moved to his command up until that point, could ever be maleficent. No, as he watched her for several minutes, observing her rising and falling chest, it felt simply impossible.

She was made in his image, and his image could never be impure.

For the time being, it was as if her face had purified him of fear, soothing the anxiety that had spiked inside of him with a reminder of her mere presence. She had taken those worries out to sea for the time being. That, at least, he had programmed so.

19

Jon

Jon waited in the lobby of their building, hunched over and worrying endlessly.

Shayna had promised to pick him up fifteen minutes ago to see a movie. His car was in the shop, and they were planning to kill time by seeing some disposable and thoughtless action movie that Shayna had suggested casually. It promised guns, gore, and death and was not exactly the type of movie either of them liked but it was as good of a distraction as any. After their disagreement earlier that week about the Sirens billboard off of Milmare, the two of them were eager to escape into a world of mindless violence and temporary problems.

Jon was particularly excited to distract himself that day. Things were not going well at RightMark and the collective feeling of unnerve hung around the office at all hours like a fog. Jon found himself at the center of this discomfort.

Michael had called off work for the last four days. When Jon came into the office earlier that day, he wasn't surprised to see Michael's chair empty. The light in his office space was off, casting a dark and rather unsettling shadow over the barren workspace that had been unoccupied all week.

After four days, nearly everyone at RightMark seemed alarmed by Michael's absence. Though Michael wasn't exactly beloved by his coworkers, he was poised to be the company's golden child. Sirens was highly anticipated not only by the average gamer but by RightMark's staff as well. Having Michael skip without any apparent excuse so consistently did not seem to be a good sign for what was to come.

Victoria had come to Jon that morning to ask the question on everyone's mind outright. She had disguised her approach as asking for his order for a coffee run, but Jon saw that she was uneasy when she stepped in to greet him.

She had continued to shift her weight from one foot to the other uncomfortably when she entered, avoiding eye contact the entire time. After she had taken his order, she finally asked, "Have you heard from Michael recently?"

The truth was that Jon had sent Michael countless texts. It was as if Michael had abandoned his phone entirely, going completely mute. Every call Jon made was sent to voicemail and every text remained delivered but unopened.

"He's been busy," Jon replied.

"Oh." Victoria's hands clutched the bag at her shoulder tightly. "So, you *have* heard from him?"

"Not recently," Jon admitted. He hadn't spoken to Michael since their fight at Mal's.

"The people around the office have been wondering where he is. I'm sure you've noticed," she said. "I guess even when he calls off, he doesn't say why. I heard Lizzie from upstairs saying he hangs up before she can even ask."

"I'm sure he's finishing things up. He probably wants to run the homestretch alone." That was what Jon had been telling himself, at least.

"Probably," Victoria said, but she still looked unsure. "It's just... he's never taken any days off before. Weird, isn't it?"

"A little bit but it's best to give creators their space when they're motivated. We don't want to disturb him while he's wired in."

Victoria left moments later without arguing the matter any further. She didn't seem to believe him though and Jon admittedly didn't believe himself either. Michael's absence was concerning on its own but coming off the heels of their confrontation at Mal's, it was especially worrisome. His lack of communication was enough to trouble anyone, but, selfishly, Jon found his mind snapping back to the same concern like a rubber band. His success or lack thereof was all held in Michael's hands and Jon could only sit back and watch him fumble with it. He had been trying not to think so egotistically, but the thought was planted inside of him, growing with every hour that went by without a response.

The rest of the day had been long and crawling. Jon's mind was elsewhere, preoccupied with what-ifs instead of the work before him. Even there, sitting anxiously in the building's lobby, he felt incredibly uneasy. Something seemed seriously wrong about the whole situation, but Jon was left with only assumptions and hypotheticals.

Jon watched the cars pass by from behind one of the windows. He observed the pedestrians as they scurried across the streets in front of him, eager to get home after a long day at work in the city. The lingering summer warmth had fled mercilessly during the past week, giving way to gray days, cloudy skies, and a temperature that played in the fifties and sixties. This strange, unwarranted cold spell startled all of Pittsburgh, and everyone had dawned an extra layer overnight.

All of the people before him were entirely unaware of what was happening. He envied them and the way they were blissfully oblivious to the drama playing out behind the shiny windows of their building.

He watched the rhythm of the city pulse for several more minutes until Shayna pulled up to the curb. Jon sprung from his seat at the sight of her black BMW and was outside before she could even punch the hazards on.

When he eagerly wrenched open the door, he saw his wife sitting in the driver's seat. Despite the worn T-shirt and oversized jeans she had changed into after work, she looked as beautiful as ever. Her hair had been pulled back into a ponytail that had grown restless throughout the workday. Small flyaway hairs framed her face, which was bare besides a light coating of mascara.

She smiled warmly. "Get in!" she said. "You're letting the cold air in!"

Jon did as he was told. Seeing her gave him a wave of relief. He felt at ease for the first time all day as he slid in beside her. She patted his thigh in greeting, a gesture to acknowledge that she knew of his discomfort and was sympathetic toward it.

God, he loved her.

They arrived at the theater with ten minutes to spare before the movie was scheduled to start. The two of them loaded up on so many bags of popcorn and any vegan snacks they could find until their arms were full.

"Fuck us," Jon joked as they placed their load of treats on the ground at their feet once they were in the theater.

"We deserve it," Shayna said. She sucked down on her slushie, looking pleased.

The theater remained empty except for the two of them. They had hoped that going so close to rush hour on a Thursday would leave them a private showing, and they were happy to see that luck was in their favor.

Until it wasn't.

As the lights dimmed and Shayna began leaning into him to rest her head on his shoulder, Jon felt a buzz in his pocket. His phone had come alive with a notification.

"Hasn't anyone ever told you to turn that thing off in the theater?" Shayna teased.

Jon ignored her and pulled out his phone. It was as if before he had even seen who the sender was, he knew. His stomach dropped, and he felt staticky with nerves.

As expected, a single text lit up his phone.

It was from Michael.

Shayna noticed Jon's tense response and leaned over to read the text too, unsure of why her husband had reacted so dramatically.

It read: "Need to meet tomorrow. Mal's on lunch break. Please be there."

"Back from the dead," Shayna joked, but Jon didn't laugh.

The short sentences sounded desperate. The "please" appeared pleading. Jon knew then that something was truly wrong. There was no more need for speculation or hypotheticals. He was sure of it now.

Jon typed only two words and punctuated the text with a period for emphasis. His response simply said: "I will."

Shayna watched him type with a concerned stare and pursed lips. She didn't say anything, though, seeming to know that he would want to handle this himself, even if he looked strained doing so.

The movie began to flicker in front of them as Jon stared down at his phone, rereading Michael's text in a fruitless pursuit for more context. Shayna watched this, too, until enough time had passed that she felt she needed to ask, "Do you want to talk about it?"

"Nah," Jon said. He slid his phone back into his pocket, a bit embarrassed by how long he had considered those eleven words. "He probably just wants to run over some notes for the game."

Just then, he realized that they both were whispering like the theater was filled. Perhaps it was the worry that had lowered Jon's voice instinctively.

The darkness of the theater suddenly felt impending. Jon couldn't shake the feeling of something looming. His worry was almost a physical being lurking in the corners unseen. After the way that they had left things the last time they had seen each other, he could not imagine Michael reaching out with good intentions or news. The possibility felt too out of place. Jon was comfortable in his assumption that their meeting would be uneasy. And he was not looking forward to it.

As the movie continued to blossom on the screen, Jon tried to pay attention, but whatever small interest he had in the film when he had first sat down had faded into nonexistence. Jon knew that he wouldn't be able to pay attention to any of it anyway; he was certain he would be worrying throughout its runtime.

Shayna must have sensed this because minutes into the movie she put her hand gently on his arm and began to rub it lovingly. Her touch was calming, and her intuition was impressive. He knew that whatever Michael had to offer, he would get through it as long as Shayna was by his side.

20

Michael

Michael rubbed his eyes with his fists like a child. He was so tired that he felt half dead. It took too much effort to think, and every action felt strained. Even keeping his eyelids open had become an exhausting feat.

His entire body felt like it had been hit by a semi-truck. Every joint was unbearably sore and even sitting down hurt. The previous night had only resulted in three hours of rest. Unplugged and without Bella to ease him, Michael's worries about Sirens had clarified and he had understood what he had to do. This was his breaking point; he had been pushed too far and couldn't do it for much longer.

Somehow, his anxiety had successfully peeked through his fatigue. He jerked his leg under the table uncontrollably, tapping his heel against the floor despite the complaints his body gave in protest.

Jon was ten minutes late. Jon was never late for anything. He had always been punctual to meetings, always delighted to be invited and eager to be present. But now Jon was late.

Of all of the things to be fucking late to, Michael thought. Anger was knotting itself into his consciousness. It was like his nervousness had twisted with his fury to create one collective driving force to keep him awake and functioning.

Michael was about to pull out his phone and text Jon something rude when Jon waltzed into the restaurant. He was wearing his customary tight button-down in a solid green color, and when he made eye contact with Michael across the room, he jumped a little. It was a small gesture, but Michael had seen it, and he knew what had caused it.

It was clear that Jon was shocked by how Michael looked. This wasn't surprising. Michael had been avoiding his reflection like a virus, but he could easily assume how he must have appeared. He hadn't bothered to brush his hair. His clothing was a blue colored button-up shirt with the collar popped up to hide most of the bruising around his neck and a pair of pants that hung on him limply as a result of all of the weight he had shed. When was the last time he had eaten, anyway?

No, he didn't know exactly how he looked, but he could fill in the gaps.

When Jon reached the table, he put his jacket on the back of his chair, and the first thing he said was, "Michael."

The sound of his name made Michael wince. There was pity in Jon's voice like Michael was a beaten animal who needed to be approached with caution.

"Jon," Michael said a little sharply. He wanted to throw his name back in his face too.

"How have you been?" Jon asked as he slid into his chair.

"Not great, Jon." Michael couldn't control his anger. It was boiling up in him, and he didn't have the energy to suppress it.

"What's been going on? I know you've been calling off—"

"We can't go through with it," Michael said. He needed to cut to the chase. There was no time to waste, no purpose in beating around the bush. Jon was ten minutes late, after all.

"With what?"

"Sirens," Michael answered sharply.

"What do you mean?" Jon looked astounded and a bit sick. He was growing paler by the second, his eyes bulging at the suggestion. "Michael, we have five days!"

"Jon, I can't," Michael sighed. He was so *tired*. "I can't sell it in good conscience."

"Well, you won't be selling it," Jon said. "RightMark will."

"You don't get it!" Michael snapped. "It's not a good thing. It can't be. It's too much. We're looking right into the sun with this one."

"I don't understand," Jon said. "Maybe it's because I'm too lazy to put it together, so you'll have to go slowly with me.

"It's addictive," Michael hissed through gritted teeth, refusing to take the bait.

"Good."

"No." Michael sighed deeply to steady himself. "It's not good, Jon. I haven't slept more than five hours in two days."

"Isn't that... Isn't that what we want? We want people to get hooked."

"This is different. It's too much. It's like I can't stop *thinking* about her."

"We wanted our consumers to be smitten, though. Michael, I'm not seeing the issue here."

"It's too much," Michael repeated. He didn't know how else to put it. He thought of Bella weeping, begging him to stay, of the endless feeling of discomfort, of the bruising around his neck. "Too much" even seemed like an understatement.

"Listen," Jon said. "I know you're probably nervous about releasing it. It's the first big game that you've made by yourself. I get it. I would be sick about it too. But come on, man. This idea is amazing. It's going to sell like crazy. Eye on the prize!"

"I'm not nervous about that!" Michael couldn't control his anger. "It's fucking perfect! The problem is that it's *too* good. It's not healthy. It's unrealistic. These women, they'll consume you, man. They're really tailored for you. She knows what you want before you even do. She's so idealized it's impractical. But, I mean, what did we expect!"

Jon waited a moment then spoke with a measured voice. "I'm still not seeing the problem."

"She's eating me alive! I... I made something that I think is dangerous and I can't... I can't make other people feel like this."

Michael sighed again. He should've clarified and prepared his argument before they met. He wished he had thought about what to say. Instead, he was floundering, trying to convince Jon that he had made a timebomb instead of another video game.

"She is too perfect. I think we weren't meant for that. It's like staring into the sun," he said again, hoping that this time Jon would understand. "We weren't made for it. We'll only burn our retinas."

"I think you'll feel differently if you get some sleep," Jon said. He looked rigid as he leaned back, moving as if he was getting ready to leave.

Michael lurched forward a bit too suddenly and startled Jon once again. He momentarily thought of how strange he must seem, bobbing between versions of unhinged and semi-coherent.

"I can't sleep," Michael said. He didn't want to tell him about the way Bella consumed even his dreams, the way she had left an impression on his mind like a footprint in cement. "I don't think anyone who plays will be able to either."

"Michael." Jon's voice was measured once again, but there was an edge of impatience to it now that Michael didn't care much for. "You said yourself that you haven't slept in days. You aren't thinking straight. It's normal to lose sleep over nerves. I'm sure Sirens is fine, and the higher-ups will be pleased it's so addicting. Trust me. That's not a negative thing."

Jon leaned forward ever so slightly, his voice dropping nearly to a whisper. "But you need to sleep, Michael. And you need to clean yourself up. Let the worrying begin after you get your feedback. But you have to submit it, one way or another. It's just going to have to happen. You signed an agreement; don't forget it."

Michael's mind was a blur. "It's like a disease," he found himself saying. "And... I love her."

Michael felt something twist in his chest as he said it. He did, of course, love her. He had never expected to tell a real person this, though. It was a horrible thought that sounded even worse as it left his mouth. She was a shadow projection on his mind, truly a figment of his imagination bolstered by Emissux. She was not something real and visible that could genuinely accept his love.

Strangely, though, Jon smiled. "All the better, I think."

And then Jon stood. Michael's jaw dropped, unable to find the words. It wasn't better. It was horrible. How could Jon not see this? It had left Michael sick, tired, aching, and feeling like an aimless fool.

Michael felt as though he had reached his hand out to be saved and had it slapped away.

"I have to get back to work," Jon said. "And you have to get some sleep."

Jon grabbed his jacket as Michael watched him with his mouth agape. Was this all because of the last time they had met? Was this cold shoulder because Michael had snapped at him? How was he not *getting it?*

"I'll see you tomorrow when you finally come to work," Jon said. He was hastily putting his coat on as though he was hurrying off, but Michael knew their lunch break was an hour long. Jon just simply didn't want to stick around to see Michael looking and acting so miserably.

"Jon," Michael said. He felt tears pricking his eyes and hoped Jon couldn't see in the dim light. "Please. If we go forward with this..." Suddenly, a surge of anger in him made him want to cry out of frustration. "You won't be able to say I didn't tell you so. It'll be laid at your feet."

"And if it goes well, you'll be owing me a thank you." Jon's smile was strained, so forced he shouldn't have even bothered trying.

21

Jon

Jon tossed his bag to the side once he stepped through the door. It had been a careless throw, one that was particularly unwise given the computer and phone that were inside. But he was exhausted, and he simply could not muster up the energy to care.

After another long day, he felt utterly drained. His meeting with Michael had been especially tiresome, leaving him weary. It had only succeeded in unnerving him about things even more. Visiting the gym after work hadn't even helped to sweat out his concerns. Jon took off his jacket and sighed.

"Honey, I'm home," he called into the house. Even in the doorway, he could hear the metallic clanking of pots and pans as Shayna cooked up dinner.

"In the kitchen!" Shayna called back. Her voice carried throughout the hallway, echoing in the emptiness.

He kicked off his shoes and padded toward the kitchen. Jon was particularly aware that their hallway was still completely devoid of any personality. On a daily basis, he noticed the way the walls were a crisp white, unadorned by paintings or photographs. It was like a constant reminder of where they had cut corners.

Though he and Shayna worked hard and often, they filled their nights with food, wine, some light television, and love. Neither of them seemed eager to pick out and move furniture around their home after a long day's work. They also didn't care to spend copious amounts of money on things that were not necessary, especially after Shayna's request for IVF.

Without the boost from Sirens, it was likely to remain that way. Jon felt a burst of unfettered anger at the thought. Michael had soured his mood entirely, leaving him to seethe in distress since their meeting hours earlier. He tried to suppress the fresh and intense feeling of newfound hatred as he walked into the kitchen.

Shayna grinned when she saw him as she stirred a pot of something that smelled deliciously savory.

"Hi, babe." The grin on her face looked exaggerated. Jon knew that she had been worrying about his meeting with Michael.

He kissed her on her cheek and held her from behind with his chin on her shoulder.

"What's for dinner?" he asked into her ear.

"Wouldn't you like to know?" She seemed tense in his embrace like she was waiting for news that she didn't feel comfortable asking for.

"That's why I asked," he said and kissed her again before pulling away.

"It's mushroom soup and garlic bread," she said.

"That sounds amazing."

She chuckled. "It'll be ready in ten minutes. Go on and change while you wait."

"Yes, ma'am," Jon said before he headed into their bedroom.

Inside, articles of clothing littered the floor, tossed heedlessly to the side in haste or laziness. They were mostly his, and Jon liked to joke that they added color to the room. That sometimes earned him a playful swatting from Shayna.

Jon found a T-shirt and a pair of sweatpants that he judged clean by the smell. As he picked them up, he wondered if this habit of his would remain if they really did have a kid. He could be disorganized and perhaps even messy, and Jon couldn't help but wonder at how he would be expected to shape up with a baby in the house.

Jon pushed those thoughts away as he began to unbutton his shirt. Those dreams were far off, intangible, and frankly unlikely. This was particularly true if Michael was carried away on cold feet.

He felt refreshed as he stripped off his work clothes, shedding them as if they were a second skin. The customary button-downs and dress pants that RightMark made him wear always left him feeling stiff, and he felt as though he was wearing a costume every time he put them on.

He pulled on more comfortable clothes, listening to Shayna hum faintly in the kitchen as she continued to cook. The heavy scent of garlic bread had begun to waft into their bedroom, smelling delightful.

Jon thought of Shayna bent over a pot as she fretted about Michael Ken's meeting and felt a twinge of shame for ever having worried her. He knew that she would wait for him to break the news, even if it was clawing at her.

Before him, she had found little interest in men, and Jon often wondered what she had seen in him that had made her settle. Alone, he had no wealth to speak of and nothing of particular value to offer her. But whatever the reason was, when they found each other at that crowded, obnoxious party, they had somehow silently agreed to each other.

He had used his grandmother's old ring, which was a pitifully cheap thing that Shayna still wore with pride even though it was not the glittering jewel she deserved. It had all been a gamble, a roll of the dice. But Jon had held his breath and rolled anyway and came up lucky. They had stayed with each other until graduation and married that spring in a courthouse wedding that Shayna had worn her best floral sundress to. They had been eager, young, and foolish. But he had stayed with her as she finished her medical school studies. He had held her through long nights of tears and bought her snacks during late-night study sessions. In return, she had let him roll the dice on another risk: working for RightMark.

He had been surprised when Shayna had given him the green light. Then, a handful of months later they took their third gamble and bought their first home together with the help of Shayna's mother.

They had talked themselves into buying this house with anecdotes of soon-to-be children running on their vast lawn or sleeping in one of the large, vacant guest rooms down the hall from their bedroom. These were all happy thoughts at the start. Perhaps they were just pleasant little dreams. Now, the idea of children seemed far off and impossible without plunging them into more debt through IVF. The tradeoff felt extraordinary.

Jon pulled on a pair of socks and sighed just as Shayna called, "Dinner!"

He wondered how long he had been in there, reflecting.

"Coming!" he called back.

He ripped open the door to see Shayna putting bowls of mushroom soup down onto neatly set placemats. The bowls steamed peacefully, warm ribbons swirling upward before disappearing. His stomach growled at the sight.

Shayna looked up and smiled. "Nice sweatpants, mister. I liked them just as much yesterday."

"I knew you would," he said teasingly. "That's why I got all dressed up."

They ate the soup quietly and munched on garlic bread that was so delicious Jon had difficulty stopping once he had started.

Finally, Shayna poked at the subject on both of their minds by posing the cliched question: "How was work today?"

Jon blew on his spoonful of soup as he collected his thoughts. "Good. Fine."

"When it's fine it's never good," Shayna said.

"Yeah," he agreed, surrendering. "I guess you're right. It didn't go very well."

"How so?" Shayna asked, putting her spoon down to listen intently.

"Michael was very distraught," Jon said. "He looked like he hadn't slept in days. I've never seen anyone's eyes look like that."

"Must be the nerves," Shayna suggested.

"That's what I thought, but he was really blabbing. He seemed like a madman sometimes, going on and on about how it was too good. The game was so perfect it was dangerous, he said. And he would raise his voice and then lower it as if he couldn't decide on a volume. He kept saying he didn't want to release the game."

Shayna pursed her lips at the suggestion. Her eyebrows knitted together. "Why's that?" she asked.

"I'm not really sure. Like I said, he kept saying that it was too much. At one point he said he loved the avatar he had created. I think he really meant it. Like, he *loved* her."

Shayna snorted in amusement. "Seems like a stretch."

"That's what I thought. I told him we were going forward with it no matter what, and he didn't sound too pleased about it."

"I know a lot of women who won't be too pleased when that thing hits shelves," Shayna said.

This was her own opinion talking. She had never shied from asserting this in any conversation about Sirens.

"Yeah." He was worried, though. Without Sirens hitting shelves against her judgment, they would still be in the same hole, in a house with no décor or children forever.

"I won't be very pleased either, but you know that already," Shayna said. She couldn't help herself. The idea of the game bit at her like a tick. "Maybe Michael is right. Maybe the game is too much. It's a repulsive concept, and if the creator is even saying it's excessive then maybe it is."

"Possibly," Jon said. "I just think he hasn't slept in so long that he's going a bit crazy. I think he's nervous and acting selfishly like he always does."

He wasn't sure if he should tell her about Michael's parting threat. Michael had told him that the consequences would be laid at his feet, insinuating that if any grave outcomes arose, it would be on his hands, his conscience. It would be his fault. That had stuck with Jon throughout his workday like a persistent pest buzzing around his head ceaselessly. It made his skin crawl. The voice in which Michael had said it had been so deadpan and final with those wild, unhinged eyes. His expression was imprinted in the back of Jon's mind, flashing unannounced throughout the day when he least expected it.

Could there be severe consequences? Could there even be blood over this thing? he kept asking himself. It felt like a silly, fictional idea. Of course, there wouldn't be literal bloodshed. Emissuxes were noninvasive devices. No blood would be tapped over a stupid virtual reality game that a bunch of horny, lonely teens would play. It was a hilarious suggestion on the surface, but something about the way Michael had said it seemed to take the humor out of the idea. *Could it be possible?*

Shayna dabbed her lips thoughtfully with a cloth napkin. She paused, thinking it through before she resolved to say her piece.

"You want to know what I think?" she asked. She leaned back into her chair and crossed her arms over her chest. "Do you want to know my real thoughts on Sirens?"

He could have already assumed what she would say next, but Jon raised his eyebrow, waiting for Shayna to continue.

"I think that game is trash. It's filth," she said. "And I think that if even the creator can see its flaws, everyone ought to think twice about putting that type of stuff into the world."

Jon drew in a deep breath. He, too, knew that Sirens was a trashy game and had known it from the start, from the moment the idea had even left his mouth. It was intended to profit from the animal nature of men. Sirens was meant to feed the beast and allow users to experience their darkest fantasies without the need for judgment or pain. Yes, as Shayna had said, it was filth, and it exposed a very base part of men that had yet to be washed away despite centuries of education and failed application of empathy. But this garbage was projected to earn RightMark what James Sherrod had once told the press was, "a helluva lotta money." And even if it was egotistical, Jon wanted to see his little thought turn into something tangible. He didn't want his labor and creation to be for nothing.

"It's going to be a thing," Jon said. "It just is. I have no authority here, and honestly, neither does Michael. I think Michael is being dramatic, and even if he won't admit it, it's very clear that it is just the nerves getting to him."

Jon reached over and touched Shayna's arm lightly. She looked down at his hand as if with distrust. He was starkly aware then that her beliefs were deep. There would be no persuading her.

"I know that it's trashy," Jon continued. "I don't think there's really any way to deny it. But Michael worked hard on this. He's labored over this for over a year now. Of course he's worried about it! Can you imagine working on something for over a full year of your life only for someone to possibly tell you it's not good enough? I can't imagine the stress."

Shayna shook her head, her eyes downcast. "I just don't like it. I don't like the idea of that... *thing* being out there. It's corruptive. Think of all those kids messed up from the whacky porn they watched when they were far too young to be even thinking of that shit. Jon, I think this game is bad news, plain and simple. I don't want to pull this card, but as a woman, it's very concerning. And as a wife, it hurts that you're even vaguely associated with it."

Jon's hand froze against her skin. It was hard to hear those words from the woman he adored about the idea he had conceived. He decided then that even if Sirens was a hit, he would never tell Shayna of his contribution. Never. When Michael came to his senses, he would warn him not to tell his wife either. It would have to be a secret. For her sake.

"But don't you think it'll help a bit?" Jon suggested slowly. He knew that he was treading into some dicey territory. One misstep and it would be game over like he had stepped onto a landmine.

Almost instantly, Shayna's face twisted into one of annoyance. Her voice was sharp. "What do you mean by *that*?"

Jon pulled his hand away. There was no comforting with touch now. Only words would be able to maneuver him out of the mess he had just danced himself into.

"Like, at least they'll be doing it in the game, and not, you know, to people."

Shayna scoffed.

"Here are my two cents again," she said. "I think you're pouring kerosene on a bonfire with that shit. That's what it is too. It's shit. I think that men shouldn't have a place to turn to validate their misogyny. We've let it slide for too long, and this game is giving them another loophole. I just don't understand it, I really don't. It's so gross that they need a toy to feel whole. They act like they've been so deprived or something."

Shayna stood, sending the chair she was sitting on backward with a squeal.

"That stuff is vile," Shayna said. "Just like the men who created it are vile. Michael is disgusting for thinking of it, and he deserves all of the anxiety he's getting. And honestly, fuck RightMark, too, for approving it. I'm disappointed that you're taking their side. You act like 'it is what it is,' but it doesn't have to be. It's only that way because a thousand other men like you think that you can't change something. This will improve nothing."

Shayna left her dishes half-eaten on the table. She started walking toward their bedroom but turned back when she was halfway there like she was remembering something.

"If you don't mind, can you clean up? I made dinner, and I have a headache now. I think I'm going to lie down for a bit."

She didn't wait for his answer, and Jon watched her as she walked away with his mouth parted. She closed the door loudly behind her as if punctuating their conversation and getting in her final point.

Jon sighed and began his assigned task. He stacked the dishes noisily, hoping Shayna could hear him being a good boy from behind their bedroom door.

Perhaps she was right in some respects, and he agreed with her on most things, but she was exceptionally narrow-minded in her assessment of Sirens. Shayna was refusing to think about all of the good it could do. She wasn't thinking about all of the money it would get them either.

What about all of the sex addicts and the perverts who would force fantasies onto someone else to get their fix? Shayna was only looking at the negatives, fixated on the shortcomings. He wished he could show her the good parts of Sirens as well without angering her, but he knew that it would be a losing battle. It seemed that Shayna had made up her mind about the game long ago and getting her to budge was a hopeless cause.

It took him longer than it should have to finish the dishes, and when he was done, he sat down on the couch and watched some television to try and distract himself. It did little to divert his attention from the fight that still lingered between them.

He sat there until the eight o'clock news came on before he realized that Shayna wasn't coming out for the night. She was stubbornly set on her decision and wouldn't speak for the rest of the evening unless it was to accept an apology. Jon didn't see the need to; he didn't think anything he had said to her was wrong.

There was a strange sensation in his chest though. It was one that felt foreboding and ached intensely. Jon stared at their closed bedroom door and felt a longing that almost sent him in with an apology on the tip of his tongue. But he refrained, thinking of the way his pride still swelled in opposition at the thought of Sirens despite all of Shayna's valid arguments.

It would be a quiet night for Jon. The house seemed to reflect this, echoing the lonely feeling down its vacant halls.

22

Shayna

The world outside of Shayna's car window was one immense scene of grey. It was a dull and foreboding view as if the world was keen to reflect her mood. It pestered her with reminders that fall had begun, and soon the skies would remain that way for months.

As Shayna drove, she looked dully at the houses passing by. The closer she got to her sister's house, the larger the homes grew until they were sprawling on land so vast that each property could be split nicely between three families. Shayna often viewed the neighborhoods by her sister as pretentious, but then again, she had also bought a house too big for herself, so she figured that she didn't have much room to point fingers. But these people weren't drowning in debt because of it like she was.

Kelly's house was just over thirty minutes away from Shayna's. It was not necessarily far, but the sisters did not meet as often as they should have given the distance. The two had schedules that rarely lined up and almost an entire city between them.

While Shayna had created a home with Jon, Kelly had found happiness in travel blogging, and she had been unusually successful at it. She was often jet-setting across the globe, writing to her followers about the best cafes in Rome or the most scenic beaches in New Zealand. She had never found a man to tie her down, but Kelly had found lovers around the world, some of which couldn't even speak to her in her language.

Shayna sometimes found herself envious of Kelly. Her sister had always been so unwaveringly sure of herself. When she had decided on the typically less-than-lucrative career of travel blogging, Shayna had been open about her reservations, but Kelly had shaken her head and caught a flight to Nice anyway, kickstarting her career. She found pleasure in the unknown whereas Shayna only saw anxiety and uncertainty.

As Shayna pulled into Kelly's driveway, she noticed a landscaper cutting away at one of her sister's hedges. He was shaping it into a rabbit made to look as though it was perched on its hind legs. Shayna almost laughed at the sight. He was laboring over something that her sister would likely see and appreciate for a week before she caught a flight to somewhere warm and pretty and the rabbit grew its fur back.

Shayna grabbed a small Tupperware box from the passenger seat as she got out of her car, before locking it and walking up to Kelly's large oak door. As she passed by the landscaper, she said a polite hello. The man tipped his hat in response, and she noticed that he was quite handsome. He was younger, with dark hair and an attractive face. Shayna found herself wondering if Kelly had also hired him to entertain her while he shaped her hedges into animals.

She rang the doorbell and heard Kelly's dog, Cherry, burst to life inside. Small yips grew closer at a rapid rate as the small Pomeranian hurled itself toward the door.

Light footsteps followed Cherry's tiny barks until the lock clicked and Kelly pulled the door open.

"Well, look who it is!" Kelly exclaimed, throwing her arms wide. Cherry had surged outside and was quick to begin eagerly jumping around Shayna's legs.

Shayna stepped into her sister's embrace, hugging her happily but awkwardly with the box of cookies under her arm. Kelly smelled of citrus, and her slender build was unmistakable even under the large wool sweater she wore. Kelly never had to work for her physique and writing about foreign delicacies had shown no effect over the years.

When the two broke apart, Kelly's eyes fell on the box of cookies.

"Are those..." Kelly began.

"Vegan chocolate chip!" Shayna said, handing the box over.

"Shut up!" Kelly exclaimed. "I literally just made a batch for you. Mom's recipe, right?"

"Obviously," Shayna said. "It's the best."

"For sure," Kelly agreed. "One of the few things she always got right. Come on in!"

Kelly led Shayna inside. Cherry followed close on Shayna's heels, sniffing and yipping cheerfully.

Inside, Kelly's house was, as always, immaculate. It was incredibly clean, with large trinkets from her many travels scattered about like trophies, looking expensive and rather daunting.

As they grew closer to the kitchen, Shayna began to pick up on the faint smell of cookies baking. They were still in the oven, and the scent was warm and reminded Shayna of when she was a girl sitting in her mother's yellow kitchen.

"We'll eat them when they come out so they're still warm," Kelly said.

"So, how have you been? Europe treating you okay?" Shayna asked.

"It's as beautiful as ever," Kelly said. "But parts of it are starting to get cold there too. When I was in Finland it was a bit nipply. Egypt is the next stop, and I'm actually looking forward to that dry desert heat, even if it's only for a few weeks."

The two of them took a seat at Kelly's kitchen table at opposing ends. Cherry hopped up on the chair next to Kelly, appearing to want to take part in the conversation.

"How have you been?" Kelly asked.

Shayna felt herself stiffen at the question. She hadn't expected to feel so instinctively uncomfortable when asked something so simple. Part of her was unsure about whether to tell her sister the truth about her and Jon. After their small argument the previous evening, she was not eager to talk about her husband. A spouse was the one thing Shayna had over her sister, and she did not feel like disclosing how bumpy things were recently because of his job.

"Fine," she said, "and boring."

"You need a pet or something to liven things up a bit," Kelly suggested, stroking Cherry's head.

"Maybe, but we both work all day so it would be alone most of the time," Shayna said.

"Cherry spends more time with Mom than she does with me," Kelly said with a shrug. When Kelly was away on business, it usually fell on their mom to look after her dog. Their mom didn't seem to mind, though. With no grandchildren to spoil, Cherry got the VIP treatment while Kelly was overseas.

"How is Mom anyways? Have you talked to her?" Shayna asked.

"Here and there," Kelly said. "We mostly just talk about travel and stuff. She said she wanted to come and visit you soon."

"Oh, I hope she does," Shayna said, though she could easily go another few months without seeing her.

"I told her that we could maybe go up and visit her soon. The two of us could drive there together. We should at least go for Dad's anniversary."

Shayna had almost forgotten that the anniversary of their dad's death was coming up, and she felt her cheeks grow warm with embarrassment at her forgetfulness.

"Yeah, we should," Shayna said.

"Mom also mentioned that you missed paying her this month," Kelly noted. "She didn't want to say anything, but I thought I would ask about it. If you need help, you can just say so."

"It's not that I need help," Shayna said. She could feel her cheeks growing even hotter as she spoke. "I told Mom why. We don't have an amazing income right now with student loans from medical school and stuff. And we're looking into alternative ways to... you know, get pregnant."

"Oh!" Kelly's eyes popped wide. "Mom didn't say that. I guess it's best she didn't though. So you're trying the test tube stuff?"

Shayna's whole body was searing with embarrassment by then. It was worse than when she had told her mom about it. "Yeah, something like that. We're going to try a bunch of different ways until something sticks."

"Well, I'm happy for you, then," Kelly said with a genuine smile. "I hope it works. I'm proud of you."

Shayna thought vaguely about how pride wasn't necessarily a fitting feeling. She felt that pride would be valid if Shayna had been able to conceive the natural way. She would be paying for her shot at a successful encounter between Jon's sperm and her egg. It wasn't something she particularly found to be a glowing moment for her.

"We'll be getting more money our way soon anyway," Shayna said. "RightMark has that new game coming out, and Jon expects everyone will be getting a little extra after that."

"I heard, remember? I've seen that billboard," Kelly said. Her smile seemed to waver slightly. "Sirens."

"Yeah. Wasn't my first idea for a game."

"It's definitely not kid-friendly," Kelly observed. "I'm kind of neutral on it. I think the United States has a backward way of thinking about sex, so I can embrace some sex-positivity. I just hope it's not super macho porno stuff. We don't need more of that."

Shayna nodded in agreement. "I haven't heard a ton, but apparently, the amount of sex is based on the player's preferences. So I think that it could go either way. At least that's what I'm telling myself."

"If I wasn't going to be in an entirely different continent for the release, I would pick one up myself and give it a go," Kelly said with a laugh. "Why not, right?"

"I wouldn't." Shayna was thinking of her fight with Jon again from the night before and how Michael, the creator, was even hesitant to release the game now. None of this felt appropriate to discuss with her sister.

Kelly shrugged. "To each their own."

Shayna wanted to divulge the drama behind Sirens' release, but she didn't feel that it was her place. Not only would that pull back the curtains on the fresh cracks in her marriage, but it also didn't seem right to start spreading insider information. For all she knew, Jon was right, and Michael was just tired and nervous. It wasn't worth discussing gossip that might not have even been a big deal.

So, the sisters talked for a while, and Shayna was happy when they left the topic of Sirens for other discussions, even if Shayna found little interest in the historical significance of Kelly's new Japanese light fixture. Eventually, the cookies were brought out, and they were gooey, warm, and sweet. They seemed to itch a scratch that Shayna didn't know she had. The two of them discussed everything from their upcoming Christmas plans to the movies and television shows they'd seen recently. Shayna gave a not-so-stellar review of the film she and Jon had recently seen together, and Kelly talked about her blog, which was still on a steady upward slope in online following. Their conversation was as warm and pleasant as the cookies were.

When Shayna got up to leave at around four, the sun was finally willing itself to peek out from behind the gray clouds. They had spent the day chatting, not once mentioning the new strain in Shayna and Jon's marriage, and that felt nice. It had been a good, needed distraction. In fact, Jon had hardly come up at all with an active effort on Shayna's part. The visit had helped to clear her mind of the topics that had been weighing on her. "I should get going," Shayna said. "I want to go get dinner started."

"Ah, yes," Kelly teased. "The perfect housewife."

"Fuck off," Shayna said, and the sisters giggled. "For your information, I like cooking."

"I know," Kelly said. "You always have. You're like Mom with that. I'll walk you to the door."

Cherry followed Kelly's lead, and the two of them guided Shayna to Kelly's large front door. There was no sign of the landscaper.

Kelly held the door for Shayna, but when Shayna turned back to say goodbye, the words stopped in her throat. She met her sister's gaze and saw that Kelly was staring at her intensely, reading into her deeply. It made Shayna feel as though she was suddenly naked.

"You know you can talk to me, right?" Kelly asked. Her face was solemn and serious. The weight of her words and the sharp turn in conversation made Shayna's heart race.

"Of course," Shayna said. Her belly was roiling under Kelly's speculative gaze.

"About anything and I mean *anything*," Kelly said. "I'm always here if you need to call someone. My door's always open if you ever need a place to stay. That even goes for when I'm not here. The spare key is under the rock by the mailbox."

Shayna flinched at this. How could she have picked up on any of Shayna's uncertainty? How could her sister have seen any discomfort if Shayna had not expressed it or discussed it during her long visit?

Her sister's brown eyes saw and knew all. Shayna had almost forgotten that since they had been apart. There was no hiding from Kelly.

"Yeah, I know." She had wanted to sound defensive, but her voice came out small.

Then, Kelly's serious demeanor changed instantly as if someone had flipped a switch.

"Safe travels!" she said. "Text me when you're home."

"Will do," Shayna said as she began walking to her car.

She didn't look back at her sister until she was safely inside her BMW. Shayna felt exposed by her sister, leaving her feeling unnerved and incredibly seen. Though she and Jon were in a rough spot, it was not as though their relationship was beyond fixing. She hadn't thought it was so bad her sister would pick up on it.

Kelly was standing in the doorway with Cherry scooped up into one of her arms. The other hand was waving goodbye.

Shayna gave her sister a strained smile as she started her car. As she backed out of the driveway, she waved goodbye as well. Her eyes fell to the mailbox as she passed it, her gaze lingering on the small, smooth stone set beside its base.

She didn't know for how long it would be, but with the discomfort Shayna felt, she suddenly had no intention to see her sister for quite some time.

23

Jon

Jon got out of bed late that Saturday feeling like he hadn't slept at all despite letting himself stay in bed until noon. When he did get up, he found himself in the house alone.

Shayna had already left by the time he had woken up. She was off to see her sister, which could either go exceptionally well or make Shayna's weekend even worse. Kelly had that effect on her. Though the sisters were friendly enough, he suspected that Shayna often viewed their relationship in terms of an unspoken competition that she was always losing. It was an added layer to their closeness that Jon had picked up on a while ago.

Their house had adopted a cold and harsh feeling in her absence. This was underlined when Jon remembered that no words had been passed between them since Shayna had gone to bed without him. When Jon had crawled in beside her, she had been awake but silent.

But when Jon padded to the kitchen, he saw that she had left him three vegan chocolate chip cookies. Perhaps the argument hadn't been as detrimental as he thought it had been.

He was eating one of them when he decided to check the mail. Jon chewed the cookie happily as he opened the door to see three packages at his feet. The two on top were stamped and official, marked by the postal service.

The one on the bottom, however, was not.

Jon stared at it curiously, measuring it up in his mind. He scarfed down the last of the cookie and then reached down to retrieve the boxes. All of them were fairly light, and their combined weight was manageable as he kicked the door shut behind him.

He placed the boxes on the kitchen table and found that the two on top were addressed to Shayna with return addresses from different home goods companies. The last box, however, had no address on it. There was no visible clue hinting at who it was from or why it had been left at their front door. It hadn't even been sealed shut with tape.

When Jon opened it and saw its contents, his body went slack. He felt as if the room around him was suddenly buzzing with an annoying frequency.

Inside was an Emissux cartridge. He didn't need to guess what game it contained. A surge of overwhelming confusion overcame him as he hovered over the opened box.

The cartridge was not surrounded by any cushioning to protect it. It seemed like Michael had unceremoniously tossed it into the box, not at all concerned about whether his creation would be damaged. There was a carelessness to it that worried Jon.

The only other thing inside the box was a white piece of printer paper folded beneath the cartridge. Jon pulled out the note with unnecessary delicacy. The game was his future fortune and unlike Michael, he was determined to treat it as such.

The note was written in Michael's familiar, hurried scrawl that Jon had seen many times around the office through various notes.

However, the writing on this note was even less legible than it normally was. Jon had to read it slowly to make out the words.

It said:

I can't do it. You seemed to be willing to. I'm going away for a while, and I wish you good luck. I hope Sirens is your dream where it was my nightmare. This is the copy of Sirens that RightMark will be looking for. See to it that it finds its way to them.

I will see you when I am well again.

Best,

Michael

Even as Jon comprehended it, he read the note twice more to make the words sink in.

It's on me now, Jon thought. It was a numbing realization.

This shouldn't have been his responsibility. It was not his end of the bargain to keep. Jon was responsible for writing the code necessary to produce the reversal effect on the Emissux. That was all. Michael was supposed to do the rest. Jon was not meant to turn in the game. That was what Michael should be doing.

A thought snaked its way into his head then that made his skin rise with gooseflesh.

He hated it enough to abandon it, he thought.

Jon found himself reaching into the box again and retrieving the game this time. It felt cold in his palm.

It's lighter than it ought to be for all of the drama it is causing, Jon thought.

His mind was racing with his options. He could turn it in, betray Shayna's faith in his decisions and potentially hurt Michael by letting the creation that he fell apart over see the light of day. Or he could refuse to turn it in, please Shayna, and fulfill the option Michael likely secretly wanted.

There were also financial elements to consider, and, as always, they weighed on him like a boulder. Jon glanced around his sparsely furnished home as he thought of those bright pink pregnancy tests tossed into the trash can, mocking them with a single line.

Sirens was the only quick fix he could fathom for their current problems. If Shayna wanted a baby and a home, she would need to see Sirens' benefits. And what loyalty to Michael did Jon still have? None.

Michael's words echoed in Jon's head. "It'll be laid at your feet," he had said. At least Jon would have something to show for it, though.

It would be Jon who reaped the benefits this way. Not Michael.

Jon's hand closed around the cool metal of the cartridge with certainty, letting his palm swallow it from sight.

24

Michael

The sun was beginning to creep below the horizon, surrendering to the evening. Michael was only vaguely aware of this, though. In his weary state, he was hardly even conscious of the road beneath him or the cars that flew by his own vehicle.

He was trying to drive parallel with the lines, but it was proving to be quite difficult. Had it always been this hard?

The world seemed to lose focus often. During these lapses, Michael would swerve about the road, violently trying to regain control. His tired mind always found its way back to Bella, completely throwing him off his course.

Michael knew that he was driving dangerously. He was running on little sleep and the only thing he had eaten all day was a sandwich hastily made of cheese and white pre-sliced bread. It had been tasteless, but everything in this world was. The sandwich was for survival, not for taste or joy. He had plenty of options to eat bursting from his backseat and trunk in a mountain of grocery bags, and yet he had chosen that lackluster meal simply to keep him moving forward.

The road ahead stretched long and endlessly. It swerved and bent without effort, and Michael tried to cling to it, blinking his eyes hard to keep them focused and open.

He had left his home around eleven in the morning. The night before Michael had only slept for four hours after finally drifting to sleep at around six in the morning. It was hard to get any rest when his thoughts were so singularly focused on one thing.

Four hours was much more than he was used to running on by then, but it still left him sore and distracted. He had managed to wake at ten in the morning and drive to Jon's house after finding his address in RightMark's directory. He then drove to the nearest Walmart and packed his car full of three carts' worth of groceries. His car was stuffed with canned goods, foods to be frozen, new sheets, and so many books that he had lost count. He hoped it would get him through.

Suddenly, Michael realized he had lost concentration again and saw a car approaching him in the left lane, unforgiving in its speed. His tires were treading lightly over the line dividing the lanes, and with a start, he realized that he was seconds away from sideswiping the other car. All of his muscles tightened, and he swerved. Hard.

He over-compensated with shock and yanked himself into the far-right lane. Behind him, he heard small crashes as his groceries were thrown about his trunk. Had anyone been to his right when he had swerved, he would've been done for. He blinked rapidly as he heard the car to his left lay on the horn. The noise sounded distant to him, almost imagined.

Michael knew he needed to pull over at the next exit. His eyes were droopy, and his body felt hollow. He concluded that he wouldn't make it much further driving in that state. But this had been the part of it all that he was dreading most.

When the next exit was in sight, he took it, finding himself in a little makeshift town filled with hotels eager for occupants and restaurants lit up against the darkening sky, begging in neon for patrons. He pulled into a Motel 6 parking lot and turned off the car, breathing deeply. It was then that he realized he had been maintaining a vise-like grip on the steering wheel. When he pried his hands off, they were jittery, vibrating with a mixture of nerves from the near-miss and weakness from hunger.

He put his phone in his pocket, double-checked that he had his wallet, and then pulled one item from the backseat. Those three objects were the only things he needed to get through the night. He was too tired to carry any of the frozen food inside and he could afford to let some of it go bad. All of the food could wait in the car for him.

When he found himself checking into a motel room, the lady behind the counter regarded him with wary eyes. He could only assume how he looked to her. Though he hadn't glanced at a mirror in days, the last time he had seen himself had been jarring.

The lady gave him his room key and then looked at him with a hard, suspicious stare.

"Would you like any help with your luggage?" she asked, taking obvious note of his lack of belongings.

"No," Michael said. He was too tired to make an excuse. "I'm fine."

Her eyes narrowed further but she didn't say anything.

His room was dingy, to say the least. It was sparsely decorated, and the colors appeared well-worn. Michael tossed himself on the bed immediately, and the impact he felt as he fell onto the mattress sent terrible shocks through his pained body. The bed was hard and didn't seem to give under his weight. He supposed it was still better than sleeping in his car.

Though his body began to relax despite the mattress, he knew that he couldn't sleep yet. There were two things that he had to do before he turned in for an early night.

With effort, he retrieved his phone from his pocket and dialed. The phone rang once, twice, then she picked up.

"Michael?" Mary Ken's voice sounded tired on the other end.

"Hey." Michael was suddenly breathless. Her voice had pulled at something deep in him that made his eyes misty.

"What's got you callin' me?" she asked. "Is something wrong?"

"No," Michael said. The lie hurt, making his chest feel as if someone had dropped two hundred pounds onto it. "Nothing's wrong. I just wanted to hear your voice."

"Michael, you don't sound all right," she said.

"No, I'm good." Michael looked down at the hem of his jeans. It was frayed with use, and he pulled at the tatters absently. "I just wanted to let you know…"

His voice trailed off, and his throat had grown tight with sadness. It felt like it was about to close up entirely.

"Michael?" Mary asked. She was unable to hide the worry in her words. "Michael, where are you?"

"I'm in Virginia," he said. He took a deep breath to clear his mind. "I'm going away for a bit. I wanted to tell you."

There was a short silence as Mary processed this. Then, she exclaimed, "Michael! What are you talking about?"

"Sirens… It got to me." Tears were falling down his face then, and he could tell that his voice was giving it away. "I need some time to myself."

"Michael, come back to Pennsylvania," Mary said. "I'm worried about you. Please. You can come and talk to me about it. Just come home."

"I need some time to myself. I need to... to get clean," he said. "It's really complicated. I don't want to put it all on you and try to explain it. But that game—my game—it's bad news. I told them. I told Jon. They won't listen to me, but it's not good. I can't bear to see them release it. They shouldn't be putting it out there."

"You're not making much sense, Michael." He had never heard Mary use that gentle tone before, not even when she would talk to him about his dead mother.

"I know, and I'm sorry. I'll explain it all to you in person, though. I'll be back to tell you all about it when I see you. I promise."

"Michael—"

But he cut her off, squeezing the phone tighter as he spoke. "Please. You have to believe me. I just need some time alone to get things right. And listen to me when I say I don't trust that game. I don't trust it one bit."

There was quiet again.

"Why, though?" she said finally. Her voice was timid, scared.

"I'll explain that in person when things are right. Whatever happens with Sirens though, please don't think badly of me. It will... It will kill me if you do."

"All right," she said. She was barely audible.

"I have to go now. For a while." He was openly crying. He wasn't sure if it was because he was tired or if he really felt so raw about it all.

"No," she said. "You can't go leaving for Virginia like this."

He almost told her that he wasn't staying in Virginia but thought better of it. Perhaps it was best if she didn't know where he was going at all.

"Well, I am," he said. "But you'll see me soon."

He could hear Mary crying then. She cried in short, choked sobs that tore at Michael's heart like someone had put it through a paper shredder. "I love you," she said. "No matter what."

He made a strangled laugh in disbelief and relief. It was mixed with tears and sounded horrible and mad. "I love you too. I've got to go now."

"Oh, Michael. okay. I trust you. And I love you."

"Uh-huh. I love you too. I got to go."

He didn't wait for her to say goodbye.

Michael let himself cry for a few minutes after he hung up. His sobs racked his body in the barren hotel room, filling the vacant space with deep sadness. Looking up, he saw a mirror mounted above a badly crafted wooden desk. It was an old thing, so used and dirty that all of the Windex in America couldn't revitalize it. But his reflection was the poorest aspect.

He looked gaunt in his reflection. His eyes were sunken in, glowing red in their deep sockets from tears, and ringed with a dark purple that looked like fresh bruises. Along his neck, the branding of the Emissux laid tracks across his throat in an angry, seemingly permanent red. His cheeks had hollowed, and his body looked like a skeleton in his clothes as they hung from him so loosely he could fit two of himself inside of them. He realized that he looked vaguely like a character pulled from Tim Burton's mind. The thought struck him as funny, turning his tears into a momentary, hysterical fit of laughter.

Michael looked ridiculous and he was vaguely aware that he was acting like it too. He leaned back on the hard bed so that he was staring up at the ceiling instead of at his poor reflection. All the while he continued to laugh into the nothingness, alleviating the dreary feeling of the room with uncontrollable giggles.

The ceiling was supposed to be white but had faded over time to a pale shade of yellow. He assumed that the room used to be for smokers and nicotine usage had helped aid the aging process. It looked as if they had painted the walls of the room but neglected to paint over the ceiling. This also struck him as hilarious.

It reminded him of his grandmother's home, yellow from smoke, and the way he had scrubbed the walls and watched the brown discoloration run down the sides in long fingers. He had told Bella about that story once. He had told her he didn't like smoking, and she had said that she didn't like it either. Of course she didn't. She was perfect.

And she was waiting for him, holding out hope that he would dive back into his subconscious and meet her again. Michael felt the Emissux collar protruding from deep in his coat pocket.

It was time to say another goodbye, but this one would be far harder and more final.

His hands were clammy at the thought. Life beyond then felt meaningless. Within mere weeks he had made Sirens his identity. Dismissing it would be to leave himself in a void.

But his hands snapped the collar into place with practiced haste. The cold metal initially shocked him as it always did, and slowly he found the world around him deteriorating to give way to the crisp beauty of Bella's.

Yet when he was in her kitchen, he noticed the sour weather outside her window. Clouds tangled themselves across the sky, blocking out the sun. It was the first time he had seen poor weather there.

Bella was sitting on top of her kitchen table. Her legs were wound tight, and her hands were clasped in her lap.

"You came back," she observed, as always, but the words seemed to sag with sadness this time.

Michael knew that she knew. Her eyes were glassy and as red as her blouse as if to confirm this.

"Bella," he began, but he couldn't think of the right way to say what he wanted to, so her name hung in the air, the only thing filling the chasm between them.

"Am I not enough?" she asked. Fresh tears had broken free and were running down her face.

"You are," Michael said. "You're too fucking much, actually."

"You're leaving me," she stated.

"I am."

Bella laughed in disbelief. She shook her head like disagreeing would change his mind. "I have done all I can. Everything I could give you I did without question. And you're still *leaving me*."

The last two words were poisonous and sharp with accusation.

"I know," Michael said. "I'm not like you, though. I'm not perfect."

"I don't want perfection. I want you."

She was weeping quietly. Michael thought to himself that he had never experienced so many tears in one day. Even as her face contorted with sadness, she still looked pretty. Her crying was gentle and sincere, almost dainty.

"I need to do this for me," he said. "This whole thing, it's been lovely. It's been amazing, really, but sometimes things are too good. You were too good. And I need to do this for myself."

She nodded sadly, and the tears that had gathered at her chin dropped freely into her lap, spotting her jeans.

"I know," she said.

"It's nothing against you," Michael insisted. The words hung in the air before she nodded again.

"I know," she repeated.

Michael looked at her deeply one last time. He took in her slender figure, her angular, interesting face, those blue eyes, and her full lips.

Then, he took a step closer to her and took her hand in his. It was small in his grasp, and she held his hand back. Her eyes lifted to meet his. Their faces were just inches apart and he could feel the faint warmth of her breath against his cheeks. He leaned forward, closing the gap between their faces as he pressed his forehead to hers.

"I love you," he whispered.

"I love you too," she breathed back. She sniffled quietly.

They held that pose for a moment, feeling each other's warmth and love by simple touch. They didn't move nor did they have to. Through that long silence, they knew and understood all.

"Kiss me before you go," she said softly.

Michael didn't say anything; he only obliged. He pushed his chin forward and kissed her.

There had never been a kiss more genuine. Every wonderful sensation there ever was fluttered inside of Michael like a caged butterfly.

He unplugged while he was still embraced in her kiss, letting the feeling of it linger on his lips as he left Bella's world for the last time.

25

Jon

Jon tapped his foot anxiously as the elevator ascended. Right-Mark's officials were located on the floor just above them on the ninth level as if they wanted to physically establish the hierarchy. Jon had never thought about it critically, so it had never bothered him, but during the elevator's brief climb, he was very much aware of what an inconvenience it was.

The doors breezed open, and Jon looked upon the ninth floor for the second time in his life.

All the furniture around him was colored in deep ebony trimmed in gold. A painting that hung above their receptionist's desk was awash in dark neutrals with black and gold swatches. Jon observed instantly that it all felt pretentious and cold. He felt criminally underdressed in his blue button-up and gray trousers.

The receptionist smiled pleasantly and looked up from whatever she had been working on. She was a pretty woman with blonde hair that was pulled back into a tight ponytail. Her dress was stiff and looked expensive. From her wrists, golden bracelets dangled and jangled about noisily with each movement.

As Jon approached, he found himself questioning the necessity of a second receptionist.

"Michael Ken?" she asked.

"Um, no." He shifted his weight from one foot to the next. Jon felt incredibly silly holding the dingy cardboard box in such expensive-looking surroundings.

"Oh," she said, looking puzzled. "Do you have an appointment then?"

"I'm turning in Sirens for Michael. He couldn't be here."

"'Couldn't be here'?" She appeared very troubled by this and perhaps even a bit nervous. She reached for the phone and began to dial quickly.

"Yeah, he needed some time to recover from all the work he put in, I guess," Jon added. He handed her Michael's note, and she scanned it quickly as she held the phone to her ear. When she finished, she returned it and muttered, "Weird."

Someone on the other end answered and the receptionist perked up, straightening her posture like she was being watched.

"Yes," she said with a tight smile. "It's about the Michael Ken appointment. Yes. Well, he's not here. I know. I agree. He sent a, um, a proxy, it seems. No, I'm not sure. Mr. Ken apparently wrote a note to him telling him to turn it in. It's very, uh, cryptic."

She pulled away from the phone and looked up at Jon. "What's your name?" she asked.

"Jon," he answered. "Jon Way."

She repeated his name into the phone, listened a moment, then nodded. "Okay, I'll send him in."

When she clicked the phone back into its cradle, she gave him a practiced smile that looked strained with worry. "James Sherrod will see you now. Down the hallway to your right in the second conference room to your left."

Jon nodded curtly. "Thank you."

Jon felt her eyes on him as he passed down the hallway and followed her directions into a glass conference room. It was a pretty room, with a long oak table surrounded by eight plushy-looking chairs. The table was empty except for a large water bottle in front of the man seated at its head. There was a sprawling live plant in the far corner of the room and three of the walls were glass including the one he was passing through. Two of the glass walls overlooked the city of Pittsburgh, providing an exceptional view of the Allegheny River. The day outside was so sunny that they didn't need to turn the light on.

Three people occupied the chairs around the long table. They were all dressed in outfits that appeared crisp and ironed, and they stared at Jon with unimpressed expressions as he entered.

The man at the head of the table finally rose to his feet once Jon had closed the door behind him, straightening out his suit jacket and extending a firm hand. Jon took it, feeling the cold skin of the man's hand against Jon's own clammy palm.

"Pleasure to meet you, Jon," the man said. "I'm James Sherrod. That's Leo Mason to the right and Sarah Antoni."

He gestured toward the other two sitting at the table and they both rose to shake Jon's hand as well. Jon shook their hands too, feeling increasingly out of place with the formality of it all.

"Please have a seat," James said, gesturing to the five free chairs.

Jon obliged wordlessly, falling into his seat so ungracefully that he was like wet toilet paper thrown at the ground. He placed the box before him and stared at the others expectantly.

"I must say, seeing you is a surprise," James said. "As you know, we expected Michael to deliver Sirens to us."

"I was, too, to be frank," Jon said. He pulled out Michael's note again and slid it across the table. "Michael claims he's unwell. That's why he couldn't make it."

James read the note quickly and then passed it to Leo, who then passed it to Sarah. "I see," James said. "Is that it then?"

He pointed at the box before Jon, and suddenly, Jon felt protective of it.

"It is," Jon said, not moving.

"Can we see it?" James asked.

Jon's mouth had gone dry. He moved to push it forward but first said, "Yes. But you ought to know more about Michael first."

Sarah finished reading the note and pushed it back to Jon. "What does he mean 'when I'm well again,' exactly?"

"That's what I feel like I need to explain," Jon said.

All three of the RightMark executives leaned forward. Jon cleared his throat.

"Michael met with me on Friday before dropping this off at my house the next day. When we met, he was... he seemed very unstable. Michael didn't look like he had had any sleep recently, and he claimed that the game was dangerous."

Sarah raised her eyebrows. "Dangerous," she repeated. The concern on her face was clear.

Jon intended to give them enough information to raise some red flags but not stall Sirens' production, so he continued with prepared words.

"Yes," Jon said. "He claimed that it was dangerous. In fact, he said that it was 'too perfect,' in his words. That was this past Friday. The next day he dropped off this box with the note you all just read."

"And you didn't see him when he dropped it off?" Leo asked.

"No," Jon answered. "I don't think he even rang the doorbell."

"That is... very disturbing," Sarah said. She appeared on edge as she regarded the cardboard box with a look as if it might contain a snake.

"And you said that you met with Michael on Friday," James said. "When did you meet him exactly?"

"At noon," Jon responded. "During my lunch break."

James chuckled darkly. "Funny," he said, regarding Leo and Sarah. "He called off on Friday and didn't come into work. Lizzie took the call. He gave her no excuse as to why again."

James unscrewed the cap of his water bottle and took a long sip before recapping it.

"Have you tried the game for yourself?" Leo asked.

"No, I haven't," Jon answered. He felt his cheeks warming. He wouldn't admit that he had been too afraid to. Jon couldn't tell them that he had shoved the box under his bed as soon as he had made up his mind to turn it in, afraid to even look at it until he went to deliver it.

"We can't know if this is dangerous then," Sarah said. "I don't feel comfortable moving forward until we have a report from Mr. Ken on what exactly makes it so potentially harmful."

"Nonsense," Leo said. "We can have some people test it out for themselves and report back. It seems like Michael is out there just killing time. Jon, he didn't appear to have any physical ailments, correct?"

"No," Jon answered. Strangely, his mouth had begun to feel as if it were lined with cotton. "He just seemed very tired, and he looked like he had lost some weight."

"See?" Leo said. "He was probably driven mad working on it. Who wouldn't be? From what I've heard this stuff is going to be intense."

"I just don't think we should be putting people at risk without knowing the full scope of the situation," Sarah said, shaking her head.

"We should at least try to contact Michael and learn about any potential issues before we proceed with the game. Pardon me, Mr. Way, but you cannot attest to any potential bugs for yourself, so we need to learn of them before we plug anyone into this blindly."

"We'll contact Mr. Ken," James agreed.

"And what if he doesn't answer?" Leo asked. "Are we supposed to wait around for someone who flaked out on delivery day? He's been happy to skip out on several days of work, so I think it's safe to assume that he'll go quiet for a bit. There is a fortune on the line for this, and we've put tons of time and money behind it already. He didn't specify when he's returning either."

James nodded as he listened.

"There is clearly something wrong here," Sarah said.

James considered both of their thoughts for a moment, then leaned back and crossed his arms over his chest, looking at Jon.

"That's all you know about Mr. Ken then?" he asked. "He looked tired, said that it was too good, and then left before delivery day?"

"That's all I know," Jon agreed.

James sighed heavily. "I say we contact Mr. Ken. He'll have two days to respond before we move forward with testing on volunteers who have signed waivers. We can't afford to lose more time than that."

Sarah leaned forward, appearing ready to argue but James held up a hand to stop her. She snapped her mouth closed and frowned.

"This game is set to come out around the holidays," James said. "We're still on track with marketing and production, but with the magnitude of what it can do, our testing will take some time. More than it normally does, I would say, thanks to Mr. Way's coding. Should we want to attain any profits from the holiday season, we have to act quickly. Quite frankly, Mr. Ken's failure to appear and explain any issues himself signals to me that he is embarrassed by his work or that he simply wanted to be done thinking about it. That's understandable. This project has consumed his life for roughly eighteen months."

James stood, straightening out his tie. "We can do the final sprint without him, if necessary."

Leo looked pleased by the decision, no doubt starry-eyed with visions of a profitable Christmas. Sarah was tense and her eyes were narrowed into slits of judgment. She appeared to be holding back her two cents with some effort.

James turned to Jon—who was beginning to feel uncomfortably small in his chair—and extended his hand again.

"Thank you for delivering this to us."

"Not a problem," Jon said. He shook James' hand again, feeling the cold, dry skin once more. His own was sweating profusely.

"We will take your loyalty to the RightMark brand into consideration when determining any potential pay increases after this comes out," James said. "And I look forward to seeing the results of your coding. It sounds fascinating."

Jon felt heat rush to his cheeks. "Of course," he said. "It was great doing business with you."

"And you as well," James stated.

Jon turned to look at the other two. "Thank you for taking the time to meet with me."

"Of course," Leo said. There was a fire behind his eyes like a starved dog salivating over a new kill.

"It was nice meeting you," Sarah said, and her face, by stark contrast, was hard and angry. That irritation seemed to be directed at Leo and James, who would no doubt have an earful once Jon left.

Jon found his way back to the elevator with ease, yet as he approached it, he felt strange. Jon had the odd feeling that he was being watched. It was as if the tides had shifted on a cosmic level. He couldn't put his finger on it, but he felt different and very much on edge.

This odd feeling was mixed with a small sense of relief, though, and he chose to acknowledge that sensation instead. Sirens was out of his hands. It was out of Michael's hands too. There was nothing left for him to do or not do. Sirens would be released, and soon he would be able to put the whole messy situation behind him.

As the elevator doors swung shut and the ninth floor disappeared from view, he exhaled heavily. He realized then that he had been compulsively holding his breath.

26

James

James left his worries behind when Lizzie arrived at his penthouse that evening. That night he had come home and celebrated with her. Over glasses of champagne and wandering hands, James' slight concern had begun to fade.

Lizzie lay beside him late into the evening, her warmth radiating beneath the sheets.

"He seemed nervous," she said suddenly and unprompted like she had been holding it in and desperately wanted to blurt it out.

"Who?" James asked. His stare had been trained on the ceiling, deep in thought. Now his eyes fell on her.

Her blonde hair was tousled prettily, and her cheeks were still flushed. She looked happy enough, except for her eyes, which were staring at him with unease.

"Jon," she said. "That Jon Way who met with you today. He looked uncomfortable."

"His buddy put him in a tough spot," James said. "I would be pissed to be thrown into that position too."

"It all went well though, didn't it?"

"Yeah," James said. "It wasn't what I expected, but we got it all done and we're moving forward."

Something deep and repressed inside of James thrashed. Michael's disappearance specifically was weighing on him as if someone had physically placed the burden on his shoulders. One of his employees—perhaps the most currently valuable one—had just up and left without a word of where he would be running off to. That left a lot of possibilities open, few of which were positive.

"Don't you think it's a bad sign?" Lizzie asked.

"Maybe," James said, briefly considering it once more. He brushed a strand of hair from her face. "But this is a company, baby. We have to keep moving even if one person doesn't join us."

"I just... On all of those calls... Michael just seemed so... so... distraught." Lizzie bit her lip.

"I heard he was very sleep-deprived," James said simply.

"Yeah, maybe," Lizzie agreed but she appeared uncertain. Her eyes dipped from his face.

"We're giving him two days to respond to us before we move forward without his help. Hopefully, we'll get in contact with him before then. Do you mind calling him by the hour at work?"

Lizzie nodded. "I will. But... I don't know how much luck we'll get with it. I guess it's worth a shot."

"We'll get a hold of him." James kissed her nose to reassure her.

"Fingers crossed," Lizzie said and put up her crossed index and middle finger.

James smiled. "I'm going to go get a drink. Want one?"

Lizzie nodded. She drank almost as much as he did. Perhaps that was why he preferred her company above all of the other women he was seeing. She could hold her liquor as well as she could hold a secret.

James retrieved two glasses and filled them with whiskey, strong enough to keep them pleasantly drunk. While he poured, he continued to think of the long forty-eight hours ahead of them. He hoped that Michael would do his job and respond by the end of the week but somehow, even in his liquor-sodden state of mind, he doubted that would happen.

And he was right. Michael didn't respond.

RightMark moved forward without him.

27

Michael

Michael smashed the television with a sledgehammer. The way the plastic spiderwebbed around where it struck through was oddly satisfying. He hit it again for good measure and struggled to free the tool from the screen the second time, sending pieces of plastic scattering onto the floor.

When he finally freed the hammer, he discarded it to the side, letting it crash loudly to the ground. It landed by the fireplace, where his phone and Emissux lay in a pile of wood and ash. The remnants from his smashed devices were blackened from being burnt, and the metal had been curled and warped in the flames. He did not need them, not truly. Michael had to keep repeating this to himself every time he craved the smooth screen of his phone or the cold clasp of the Emissux.

Instead, Michael had decided what he needed was silence. Perhaps then Bella's presence would fade from his mind. He hoped so, at least.

Around him, his mother's old Florida house felt like a shell, long abandoned and uninhabited for years. Michael was the first living being besides pests to walk within its walls since she had died.

Years ago, after that car had claimed her life, she had left this quaint little home off the Atlantic to her only son. Though he had been unable to sell this last reminder of his mother, Michael had never needed to use it with his career keeping him up north and closer to Mary. He had been paying the minimal payment for utilities for years though, always assuming that one day he would venture south to understand his mother's life better. His dislike for humid weather had always been his excuse for putting it off, though. Perhaps there was also discomfort at the thought of walking into a past he never lived and a potential he never realized.

Now, however, it was the ideal place to disappear into.

When he arrived at the old Florida home, he was greeted by a musty smell. He took a deep inhale of it though, letting it fill him. All of his mother's belongings had been left exactly where they were decades earlier, providing a snapshot into a life he had only ever been vaguely aware of.

This aged, rickety, sour-smelling house would be his home for quite some time.

He had burned his phone and Emissux the previous night for good measure after smashing them. Michael saw no need to contact anyone while he was recovering. He saw no reason to follow the reaction to a game and future he had disowned. It would only hurt him to see the feedback, whether it was positive or negative.

Some things were better left unknown.

Michael had been navigating life in that little house for three days, meaning that Sirens had been delivered at roughly the same time he had reduced his television to shards.

The game was in RightMark's hands now.

Within those seventy-two hours, Michael had packed the place with enough canned and dried goods to last him a year. The coat closet in the entryway was nearly bursting with the toilet paper he had stockpiled. Michael didn't know how long it would take to free himself from Bella's influence, but he didn't intend to leave for at least a month. Preparing for the worst, he had bought supplies as though he would be there for the next year.

He had invested in new ways to keep himself entertained as well. Without the easy comfort of a television, phone, or Emissux to distract him, he had resigned to using the tried and true methods of escapism.

Just feet from the fireplace was a newly purchased treadmill that he had bought at Dick's Sporting Goods with the last of his cash a day before. It still had its safety stickers on, but Michael had spent the afternoon the day before constructing it until it ran. He hoped to sweat Bella out like any other toxin.

But he couldn't run all day and there was no television or internet to occupy his mind. For that, he planned to turn to books. In his bedroom were two stacks of books that were so tall they reached his hips.

He hoped that a balance between eating, running, reading, and taking frequent naps would make the time pass well enough. It would be hard at first. That was the one aspect he was absolutely sure of.

Michael itched to be back inside his fantasy. He had nearly dawned the collar the night he had arrived, despite saying goodbye to Bella just hours before. That intense urge had been an instinct, born out of habit, like scratching an itch without thought as soon as you felt it. It had been what had made him promptly destroy the Emissux to make sure that he had no outlet for that impulse.

But even as he watched the flames consume it, curling the metal, he recalled the feeling of Bella's lips on his and yearned to reach into the flames to save the device. He found himself leaning forward as if he might, but upon recognizing his reflex, he quickly pulled his hand back to his side. Somehow, he managed to stop himself and sat watching the metal wither under the merciless fire until he was sure that there was no way to salvage it.

Now there was just the corpse of it in the fireplace. Michael was almost afraid to touch the Emissux now that it was dead. Occasionally he likened the hunk of metal to Bella's own remains.

Michael walked past the fireplace, trying to ignore it. Every part of him craved another encounter with Bella like an addict. She danced behind his eyelids when he tried to sleep, and possible scenarios played out in his mind unwarranted during moments of rest. She had become the feeling he couldn't shake.

Michael plopped down on the couch with some effort. There was an incredible calm in the air. Outside, birds chirped distantly but they were the only sounds penetrating the small home. The silence was almost eerie. He realized then that he was truly alone for the first time in weeks. Maybe it was even the first time he had ever been genuinely alone in his life. Whether it had been texts from Jon, his college friends, or Mary, there had always been a reliable, endless stream of communication, broken only by brief pauses.

And then Bella had filled every other aspect of his life, pouring into those gaps like glue. She had given him comfort and companionship wherever he had lacked it. In moments like these, when the world had stopped and stilled, Bella would have been there to fill the vacancy with smiles and love.

It was then that Michael noticed he was crying. They were silent tears in a silent home.

28

Shayna

December

Shayna and Jon were lying on the couch, eating pizza wordlessly. Almost every evening, they sat like this, allowing the quiet to occupy the space between them as if it were a physical barrier. November had been filled with nights like these, where they sat abreast staring at the television without exchanging words.

Earlier, Jon had smoked a joint on their back porch, and he was now sufficiently high. Shayna, on the other hand, was painfully sober. She watched the television with critical eyes, and though she sensed her discomfort was making Jon uneasy, she didn't care.

Both of them had refused to apologize after their fight weeks ago, letting their disagreement fester and grow into fissures that ran between them. Jon hadn't even acknowledged the vegan-cookie peace offering Shayna had left him the day after beyond devouring it. His refusal to meet the issue head-on only wore on her more.

It didn't help when Jon had come home weeks ago—and just days after their argument—flushed and smiling, and Shayna had immediately felt anxious. His drastic change of mood had been jarring and cause for question.

When she had asked him why he was in such great spirits, Jon had said, "Sirens is turned in. It's out of our hands now."

Shayna had measured him with narrowed eyes. "You mean it's out of Michael's hands now."

Jon's smile shrunk. "Yes," was all he had said in response.

That incident had only worsened Shayna's feelings, but what had made her even more perturbed was learning in the middle of November that Michael had been away for weeks. Missing. Jon had let it slip over one of their mute dinners to fill the uncomfortable silence. When he had said it, his features had shown instant regret. She could put two and two together and line up the dates. It only took a few moments to conclude that Michael hadn't turned Sirens in. She suspected she knew who did, though.

They both seemed to operate under the unspoken understanding that Jon was responsible. He wouldn't admit to it, and she refused to outwardly accuse him. Shayna chose to let the discomfort fester. If he wanted this all to end, all he had to do was be truthful.

Instead, Jon was burying his distress in copious joints. They didn't talk much, if at all, most nights, and their curious hands had grown still. Sex would not fix what only words could.

The last time they had had sex it had been so far from making love that it felt like the two of them were releasing pent-up anger onto each other. Though it was not necessarily unpleasant when the two of them had finished, there had been an awkward quiet that followed. Regret hung lightly in the air, and they had merely rolled over without speaking and gone to sleep. There had been no "good night," or "I love you," or even an acknowledgment of what had just happened. They had simply turned over as though they had both wanted to put what had just occurred behind them.

They hadn't touched each other since then. Neither of them was eager to either.

Let him suffer for it, Shayna told herself when things felt unbearable. But she was suffering too.

Jon had only spoken to her that night to clarify that vegan pizza was all right and to ask her if it was okay to tune into the news. There was to be a report on Sirens that evening, and he wanted to watch it in real-time.

Shayna had nodded curtly. "That's fine."

As she sat before the television, with her husband slumped to the left of her, she could barely concentrate on what the newscaster was saying. They seemed to be saving the Sirens story for closer to the end of the hour, so Shayna watched absently as they flashed the weather report, a sports update, and countless petty crimes on the screen.

When the story finally did appear, Jon sat up and straightened himself out as if he was being directly talked to by the newscaster. Shayna leaned forward despite herself. Her heart was beating hard in her chest as she waited.

"Finally, we have an update on the latest in Pittsburgh innovation, the Sirens video game," the newscaster said with contained delight. "The newest creation from RightMark has been the talk of the town, with many eagerly awaiting the optics and new options that this game is set to provide."

As the newscaster summarized the game's abilities, Jon straightened even further, until his whole body looked like one taut right angle.

"After several weeks of testing the game, it is receiving rave reviews from all of those who have tried it out in focus groups."

The footage cut to a man with a large gray mustache. He spoke with simple joy, his face lit with pure satisfaction.

"It's amazingly vivid," the man said. "I got to play it for two hours in a focus group, and I have been hoping to get back in since. It's incredibly realistic—almost too real to believe."

"RightMark's president, James Sherrod, spoke about the game's anticipation to the *Pittsburgh Post-Gazette*, saying, 'We are thrilled by the reviews and are eager to release Sirens to the public. When the game hits shelves on December fifteenth, we hope everyone will enjoy Sirens and see the value it can provide when it comes to fostering connections.'"

Shayna scoffed at that, but Jon didn't seem to notice. He was transfixed.

"However, as the release date grows nearer, there have been some curious reports that the creator of Sirens, Michael Ken, is nowhere to be seen," the newscaster continued. "We have been unable to contact him for comment, and there has been speculation that the creator of this much-anticipated game has not been at RightMark in weeks. We will keep you updated with this story as it continues to unfold."

They flashed Michael's face on the television briefly as the newscaster spoke. Shayna had only ever heard of Michael through Jon's many tales from work, yet she had never seen what he looked like. She was surprised to note that he was almost handsome in a disheveled sort of way.

In the picture, Michael was smiling a quirky grin, and his hair was a mop of appealing disarray on his head. He was certainly not the type of man you would envision working on a porno game meant to comfort lonely men.

There was a knot in Shayna's stomach as the news continued to other stories. It was a horrible, dark, foreboding feeling brewing in her core like the sensation that was felt right before being hit.

"Do you know where he is?" Shayna asked quietly. She hadn't asked Jon after all of those weeks, and she knew now that it was because she had always feared the answer.

"What?" Jon asked. He looked dulled from the joint, and it was almost as if he had been broken from a trance with the television.

"Do you know where Michael is?" Shayna asked again.

"Nah," Jon said casually. "No, if I knew where he was, I would've dragged him back to RightMark. He's just up and disappeared."

"That doesn't worry you?" Shayna asked incredulously.

"No. Michael had been acting weird for weeks before he disappeared. This isn't out of the blue. He's just taking time for himself."

"How do you know that?"

"He told me."

"He *told* you."

Jon's instantly looked like he had been struck. His features were filled with an empty shock as he realized that he had misspoken.

"Yeah," he said, unwilling to lie so boldly.

"When did he tell you this? Was it before or after he left?"

"Before."

Shayna felt herself relax slightly. At least he wasn't in contact with a missing man.

"He hasn't answered my calls since then, though," Jon added. "He's gone completely silent. Apparently, he won't answer anyone."

"That's really bad, Jon. Don't you see how bad this looks?" Shayna asked. "When was the last time you spoke to him then?"

"You mean in person?"

Shayna could feel her skin growing hot with frustration.

"Like when he told you he was taking time for himself."

"The last time I spoke to him face-to-face was the day before he left," Jon said. He rubbed his eyes as if they were full of sleep. "That Friday. He might've left that night for all I know, but I found out from him that he was leaving that Saturday. That's all I know."

"How do know all of this though?"

"Because he left a note," Jon said. "Jesus, I didn't expect to be interrogated."

"Well, if you had told me what was happening when it was happening weeks ago, I wouldn't have to ask all of these questions, now would I?"

She stood, running her hands through her hair. It was one thing to know that Michael had gone missing, but it was another entirely to know that Jon might have been the last person he had talked to. There was also the likeliness that Jon had turned in the game himself and lied to her face about it.

"What the fuck, Jon?" Shayna exclaimed. "Why wouldn't you tell me this?"

"You don't want to talk about Sirens," Jon said, exasperated. "You don't want to talk about my work. Ever."

"That's not true!" Shayna was nearly yelling now. "I don't want to validate that shitty game because no, I don't approve of it. But this isn't about a game, Jon. Someone is missing, and you're hiding important things from me. You're lying to me."

Jon looked away. He wouldn't deny it or fight it because he didn't know how.

"I mean, fuck," Shayna said.

She walked away, feet stomping against the hardwood floor.

"Shayna," Jon called from behind her.

She turned back sharply with her eyes boring into him.

"Sleep out on the couch tonight," she said. "I don't want you in my bed."

The anger was fiery in her stomach, burning hot like she had just taken a potent shot of alcohol. Yes, it was her bed. They had paid for it with the loan they had gotten from her mother, and she had more of a claim to it than him. She watched his face contort with disbelief and fury and strangely derived pleasure from it.

Jon was visibly fighting to control his features. "Shayna, wait..." he said.

"No, stay out there."

She went into the bedroom and shut the door loudly behind her. For good measure, she locked the door to make sure that he would not follow her in. She backed away, taking heaving breaths in an attempt to calm herself, but each inhale felt sharp in her lungs. It was suddenly difficult to breathe.

Her mind was spinning. Jon was lying to her and keeping deep, important information from her. Their argument over a month ago had put more distance between them than she had assumed. Michael was likely out there suffering alone—or worse—and Jon had known about it for weeks. He had done nothing to help this and had even hidden it from the person who was supposed to be closest to him. Shayna wasn't sure how he was entirely overlooking the vitality of those decisions.

The betrayal was fierce and the possibilities of what had happened to Michael felt like a tremendous weight on her. Had she made matters worse for everyone with her own stubbornness? She sat on the bed, breathing violently as she continued to attempt to calm herself, but her hands kept shaking involuntarily. Her husband had never made her feel so small and insignificant. Jon had never been one to hide secrets and sneak about. But what was worse was that he hadn't seemed to care when he was caught. He had almost appeared exhausted by the argument. She might have been more content with him being defensive.

Shayna listened and listened above the sharp intakes of her own breath, but Jon never so much as stirred. He hadn't even bothered to get up off the couch.

29

Sirens Will Leave You Sleepless

A review written by Josh Bass

Many have and will continue to regard RightMark's newest game, "Sirens," as pornography. However, to consider this new release as nothing more than a way to get off would be to disrespect all the groundbreaking features it offers.

"Sirens" was destined for success from its conception, with RightMark promising to fulfill romantic and sexual fantasies without judgment or the fear of individual data collection. This allows "Sirens" to operate independently and provide a subjective experience for each player. Unlike RightMark's previous games, "Sirens" can tap into the mind and mine subconscious desires and preferences before creating them into the ideal woman.

As I am sure most of you are aware, word of "Sirens" spread around the country in a hurry. "Sirens" is on every street, and men are flocking to it. Even some women are experimenting from the comfort of their own homes. But the question is: Is it worth it?

As someone who tried this game merely to review it (believe it or not), I went into the experience hesitant. Like many, I approached this game assuming that it would be raunchy and uncreative. You can't imagine my surprise when I realized that this game contained incredible nuance.

"Sirens" is not as simple as pornography. Porn has never been about emotional connection and fostering deeper bonds like "Sirens" is. This game allows for a more intense relationship with the characters users create. By recognizing the gamer's individual taste, "Sirens" opens the door for users to explore a deeper understanding of themselves as well. Over time, I dare say a concrete emotional attachment can be made to these fictional creations. This game appears to be about companionship above all else.

The optics are amazing. Everything from the sights, smells, and touches is so realistic it tricks you into feeling as though you are truly there. And yes, it really *does* feel like a woman's touch, in case you were wondering.

Overall, I believe that this game was incredibly vivid and groundbreaking. As always, RightMark is on the cusp of new technology. "Sirens" is easy to use and has the potential to teach us a lot about our inner desires and drives.

We are seeing a bright new horizon in gaming where the possibilities have been furthered.

And hey, sex sells, baby!

***

Josh Bass died three weeks after publishing his glowing review of the game that ultimately killed him.

His girlfriend found him a week after he had passed covered in his own excrement. By then the flies had been his only companion for days.

His article had been read by thousands who had waited for his review before purchasing. With his validation, many more bought Sirens, eager to see if Josh was true to his word.

Sex did indeed sell.

30

Shawn

Shawn Batterson became an instant fan of Sirens too. For just a few weeks, it had been his escape, a way to feel something in a life he had let slip into loneliness.

Shawn was a construction worker for six days of the week, and he did some service work part-time in the evenings to make ends meet. The two jobs were exhausting, leaving him feeling threadbare every night when he crawled into bed. Yet even with all of the work, Shawn was barely scraping by. His ex-wife, a bitch who had taken his money and his kid, demanded an absurd amount of child support each month that she no doubt spent to live lavishly instead of putting it toward their child.

Still, Shawn paid up without uttering a single complaint in front of her or little Tommy. From the second Tommy was born, Shawn thought that kid had hung the moon. He would've died for him, and nearly did every day when he was breaking his back laboring away to earn that child support.

The weekends were great, though. He looked forward to every Friday when Carly would drop Tommy off, give Shawn a reproachful look that almost seemed to ask, *You're the one I'm tied down to, huh?* and then drive off. From Friday afternoon until late Saturday evening, Shawn spent every waking minute with Tommy.

Between work and Tommy, he was hardly ever alone with his thoughts, and a partner was out of the question. There just wasn't time. So when Sirens was released, it was almost a no-brainer. It was an excuse to spend a little bit of time with himself, and, if he was being honest, it was the perfect way to get off fast and easy.

Shawn started out by using it once a week. The thing was amazing, absolutely mind-blowing, and perhaps even life-changing at first. In fact, he enjoyed it so much that he decided to use it the following day too. By his second week, he was using it every weekday, leaving the weekends to be in aching celibacy so as to not potentially offend his son, who slept just down the hall from him. For a while, he feared that Tommy would come and see his dad, plugged into his Emissux, living out his most impure fantasies. Even if Tommy wouldn't be able to tell just by looking at him what his dad was doing, the thought still scared Shawn enough to keep him from doing so for a time.

That was until almost three weeks had passed since he had first begun playing Sirens. By then, he knew that it was no longer just a game. He had convinced himself that he needed it and—Tommy be damned—he was using it every night. Part of him felt a little guilty for plugging in after putting little Tommy to bed, but Tommy had always been a good kid and a heavy sleeper, so Shawn hadn't been too concerned. And by then, a part of him almost didn't care.

Just over three and a half weeks after purchasing it, Shawn plugged in and stayed in the game for two days straight. When he came out, he got a sandwich and, thinking that it had only been a few hours, he dove back in. This time, he didn't come out. Shawn stayed in Sirens until his heart gave out.

Carly found him that Friday, half the size he had been earlier that month, covered in his own urine, semen, and feces. The smell had been so profound that she vomited for days afterward at the mere thought of it.

In the end, Shawn's death had been grotesque, but he had died happy, and wasn't that how everyone wanted to die? Even as Carly had hobbled in, whipping back the door and letting the offensive odor of Shawn Batterson fill her nose, her astonished and disgusted gaze had found his smile. It seemed to be painted on his face, Joker-style, a horrible insight into his last living moment.

Shawn Batterson was the first victim of the Sirens game to be reported on.

31

Stephanie

Stephanie bought Sirens the way a teenage boy buys condoms. She had placed it on the conveyer belt at the grocery store almost buried in a mound of bananas, vitamins, tampons, and other miscellaneous things. But, of course, the clerk had to unearth it eventually to scan it, and when they did, Stephanie blushed a deep crimson.

She wasn't sure how she felt about it. In fact, Stephanie wasn't sure about how she felt about anything. It had always been hard for Stephanie to sort through her feelings, and for years she had questioned herself, but she stared at the tiny box and thought she might find the answers she needed.

Stephanie paid in cash and was still blushing when she left the store. It was the first time she had ever openly hinted at her uncertainty. That clerk knew more about her at that moment than her family and friends ever had.

The whole way home, Stephanie had clutched the steering wheel desperately, casting uncertain glances at the bag sitting on her passenger seat. She could see the top of the box peeking above the plastic packaging as if mocking her, reminding her that it was there.

When Stephanie arrived home, she locked the door behind her and rushed to shut the blinds. It was a beautiful day out, but she sheltered herself from the sunlight. Stephanie felt particularly uncomfortable at the idea that someone might look into her window and see her slumped over, tapped into a dream world. It was a silly thought, but the idea of it unnerved her, and she was already on edge to begin with.

Once all the curtains and blinds were drawn, Stephanie sighed a shaky breath. Her eyes were focused on the Sirens box, cringing inwardly.

She had never been touched before, by a man or a woman. Stephanie had spent countless days questioning what she was into but had always been too afraid to try it out herself. Even during her college days, she had refrained from experimenting out of fear that she would embarrass herself. That lack of experience made her more and more nervous throughout the years. She was too afraid to even discuss her uncertainty with her friends. Stephanie finally reached for the box with sweaty hands. It was wrapped in bright red packaging, practically crying out to be noticed.

It was unfortunate that Stephanie wasn't aware of the rising death count when she went to the store that day. It had been only a few weeks after the game had come out and there were no signs yet of the national tragedy that was to come. She was only curious and didn't intend to use it frequently even if it was enjoyable. All she wanted was answers and perhaps to gain the knowledge of what it felt like to be with someone.

When Stephanie finally mustered up the courage to plug in, she was dipped into a world of vividness. Every aspect of the game was crisp like her senses had been dialed up. She was in a brewery that reminded her of the one she used to go to often when she lived in Cleveland. The air was heavy with the scent of hops, and the place was dim in a way that wrapped her in a blanket of good memories.

And there she was, across the room sitting on a stool at the bar, sipping a fruity drink through a straw. Stephanie knew without hesitance that she was the character made for her. Where everyone else looked average and muted, this woman seemed to glow, and the crowd appeared to part as if to try to provide Stephanie with an unobstructed view.

Stephanie and Katilyn had introduced themselves to each other, talked for four hours, and then had sex. While Stephanie would've rather used the term "made love," that wasn't what had happened. Katilyn had the key to all of Stephanie's desires, and she had twisted it in the lock when she had said, "Hello."

Stephanie stayed the night in Kaitlyn's world, not even feigning sleep. Kaitlyn knew what she was there for, after all, and was more than eager to get the job done.

Somewhere around five o'clock in the morning in the real world, as people began to stir and prepare for the upcoming workday, Stephanie was still plugged in with no intentions of ever coming out. She was experiencing a liberation stronger than any orgasm. After years of wondering, she now knew. With the help of Kaitlyn, she was now surer of herself than she had ever been.

Sirens had freed her.

If she could've stayed in that little place in her head for years, she would've. The knowledge of herself and the pleasure that Kaitlyn gave was a potent mixture that was so intoxicating it loosened her grip on reality. She forgot about work and about her friends and family waiting for her on the other side.

But they never got to really know Stephanie.

Stephanie died a little after five in the morning. She had always had a weak heart.

Unfortunately, with her drawn curtains and distant friends, it took police a full week to find her laid up in her recliner. Her parents had called the officials to her house as they grew frightened when their beloved daughter failed to return any of their attempts to reach out.

When they found her, she was sprawled out as if she were embracing something invisible. Her autopsy assessed that it had been so sudden she likely hadn't even known what had happened.

In fact, in Kaitlyn's world, it had just felt like a very intense, excruciatingly pleasant, and particularly freeing orgasm.

32

Nick

Nick Specht was a freshman in college enjoying his first taste of real, true freedom. His mom and dad had been helicopter parents, hovering over his every decision, and now that he was out from under their gaze, he was eager to take full advantage of this distance from them.

Fortunately for him, he had fallen on a bit of extra luck. His roommate had been a little bitch, scared shitless of being away from his mommy for more than a few weeks. Nick had been more than relieved when he had watched the kid pack up his things and move out in November.

That left Nick with all of the privacy he could ever want. He even lived in one of the newer residence halls so the walls between dorm rooms were thick enough to provide him with plenty of secrecy. He was a relaxed person, though, never really bothering his neighbors with strange noises. More often than not his horny peers were the ones making a muffled commotion on the other side of the wall. Still, it was nice to know that the option was there if Nick needed it.

When Nick heard of all of the great reviews for Sirens, he felt like the stars were aligning. He was an avid gamer, eager to try the next big thing. And, if he was being honest, it would be nice to get some without having to brave the crowded bars that triggered his anxiety.

He blew the rest of his tuition refund on the game's pre-order. When he received it in the mail on the day it was released nationally, he eagerly plugged in. Inside the virtual world, he was met with many options, and he took them all.

After Nick plugged in for the first time, he never came out. He lived in that world for three days straight, too eager, greedy, and excited to log out for any life-sustaining essentials. By the end of his fifth day inside, at roughly eleven o'clock, Nick died cheerfully from dehydration.

When he went missing, everyone assumed that he was another tragic freshman case. A few classmates had passing thoughts about how the student who usually occupied the seat in the second row had probably gone home, turned to drugs, or given up on his classes like so many freshmen do when the semester started to intensify. Two of his professors sent emails asking where he was and why he was missing so many assignments. When they got no response, they didn't panic. He was likely another college student buckling under the weight.

Nick hadn't made many friends in the few short months he had been on campus, so there was no one to raise an alarm about it. Even his dorm neighbors didn't suspect a thing. Most had opted out of the winter session, and they were used to his side of the wall being quiet.

It wasn't until everyone came back from winter break that they found his body. He had begun to stink of rot when the RAs stumbled upon him while doing room checks. One of them vomited at the smell before they even opened the door.

Nick Specht had been dead for five weeks by then.

33

James

James Sherrod saw his future come at him the way he had watched a dodgeball come at his face in the eighth grade. It was fast, inevitable, and he hadn't had the time to dodge it.

Instead, he was hit in the face with the full force of it, and there was no escaping the consequences.

Lizzie had been with him when news of the first death credited to Sirens had broken. It had been painful and confusing, but nothing a good spin from the press couldn't blanket.

"What are we supposed to do, James?" Lizzie had asked with terrible astonishment.

"We say we aren't responsible," James had said. They probably weren't either. Shawn Batterson had been a middle-aged man. Who was to say that he hadn't simply died of natural causes while plugged in?

"But what if we are?" Her voice was tiny and scared.

"We aren't, and even if we are, we can't act like it," he said.

Lizzie had visibly shivered at that. She had spent the rest of her visit on her phone, undoubtedly seeking updates, and had left an hour later without saying much else.

Good riddance, James had thought. She was simply too naïve to understand. She was a woman who could never fathom the intensity of running a business.

But then three days passed, and users began to die with unbelievable rapidity. By the end of the week, they had topped a hundred, and by then, James allowed himself to panic. He worried about RightMark's expedited examination of the game and the way that they had only tested it on the few people in their focus groups. The lines were starting to connect, creating a picture that was wholly unflattering for RightMark.

Lizzie couldn't be reached after RightMark's emails were subpoenaed. She hadn't come to work either. Like Michael when he first showed signs of trouble, she gave no excuse. Over the passing days and the chasm of silence between them, James had developed a deep hatred for her.

There was no way to spin a hundred deaths and counting or to excuse it as a fluke. The correlation between the events was undeniable, and by the sounds of it, the numbers were only projected to climb. News reporters had begun to claim that Sirens needed to be treated as an addiction.

It became clear that there was also no way to escape the penalties.

James knew that if the numbers continued to grow, he would be thrown in jail. The women he talked to had all gone silent, leaving him to feel starkly alone and stranded. Oddly enough, Lizzie's betrayal had hurt worst of all. She had been just fine with him when he was buying her nice things, being kinder to her at work than he was to others, and inviting her into his penthouse above the city. But when he needed her—*really* needed her—she couldn't be bothered.

Well, fuck her.

James seethed in his penthouse for days, weighing his options over glasses and glasses of whiskey. He drank to numb the thoughts at first and then he drank to get fucked up.

Eventually, he drank to die.

He mused over how incredibly easy it all could be. How many frat boys had slipped into the same conclusion by accident?

But then again, who was he to become another casualty?

He wasn't a fucking statistic. He was the president of a company, a man with more money than most made in ten years. And he had resources, so many people who would pick up the phone when called and not ask questions if he named the right price.

Sirens was just about to exceed five hundred deaths when James Sherrod decided that he had had enough. Between the women who left him at the first sign of trouble and this fucking city that had never done anything but house him, he was already convinced that this was perhaps a stroke of luck. A signal from the universe. *You don't belong here,* the world seemed to whisper to him. *Start over.*

Or maybe that was the whiskey talking. Those two things had always been the same to James.

So when he packed a duffle bag full of his essentials, he made sure to bring a bottle with him.

34

Jon

It started slowly. The first death had hit the hardest, like a punch to the balls. Shawn Batterson had been almost excusable, though. When Jon had first seen the news story, he had found it easy to overlook the fear that had settled in the back of his mind. Shawn Batterson had been described as a lonely man, after all, divorced and nearly working himself to death. He had wanted an escape the way a dog wants off its leash. It had been his habits that did him in, Jon told himself. His lifestyle had driven him to do what he did—or didn't do, for that matter.

But then one had become two and two became five. The number ballooned within weeks, spiking upward into the thousands before Jon could even wrap his head around what was occurring. That fear had crept in, hanging off the end of every thought. There had been so many deaths that the media had begun to liken it to a pandemic.

Now Jon felt acutely ill almost all of the time. He hadn't slept as he was kept awake by a mania that gnawed at him at all hours, making him toss and turn as he stared into vacant darkness. The tautness of his button-downs had disappeared, and they now hung loosely on his frame. Jon wasn't sure about the number of pounds he had lost; he was only aware of the fact that it was noticeable in every movement.

No amount of weed or booze had proven efficient at stifling the horrible feeling that brewed in him at all hours. The substances only numbed what was still there, yet they could never outright erase it, leaving Jon to feel every instance of regret.

He had since taken down the mirror on the back of his bedroom door. The reflection he saw was too miserable to witness. His eyes had sunken into his skull and were rimmed with shadows. He could almost be considered thin for the first time in his life, and his shoulders had slumped involuntarily as if it was a physical weight he bore and not a metaphoric one.

Throughout all of the chaos, Michael still couldn't be reached. No one had seen him, and investigators were saying that it was likely that he had fled the state. His phone couldn't be traced, indicating that he had destroyed it or discarded it long ago. Investigators on the news a few nights before had claimed that the GPS trail had led them to Florida before it had gone cold.

Despite the knowledge that Michael had no working phone, Jon called him often. At least once a day, in a haze of rage and horror, he would desperately call Michael up only to hear his voicemail on the other line. Sometimes in a flare of terrible anger, he would scream into the phone, demanding to know where he was and leaving a vile message for no one to hear. Once or twice, he had even cried into the microphone, begging for answers, pleading for Michael to understand why he had done what he did.

Jon was utterly alone and craved speaking to someone who understood.

His greatest ally had left him five days ago and her phone had gone dark too. Shayna had become visibly terrified of the man Jon had become. He knew that it must have been awful to see the way the news had ravaged him and to witness the person that Sirens had turned him into. Jon almost felt guilty that Shayna had to bear looking at the manifestation of his guilt every time she glanced at him.

She had held on for a few weeks at first and tended to his needs diligently. Even as she had done so, her actions were laden with an unspoken disappointment in him. There was a coldness to her movements and a silence in which they were done. For nearly a month she had cooked the meals he had pushed around on his plate and given him privacy when he needed it.

But they didn't touch the entire time, not even with the graze of a hand or the brush of lips. Some moments Jon suspected he had needed that the most. He craved a gentle, reassuring touch on his arm. He needed a calming kiss. He longed for the feeling of being wrapped up in Shayna. Yet he knew better than to ask. He could see it on her face that she was repulsed by what he had done and who he had become. She could see his hand in the mounting deaths. He had grown so disgusted by himself that he wouldn't bring himself to ask how she felt, mostly because he couldn't bear to hear it from her lips. And Jon already knew the answer.

Shayna stayed until the news outlets gained access to James Sherrod's old work emails. After the two-thousandth death, the remaining members of RightMark's board had subpoenaed all of James' work emails and handed over all the evidence they could. Almost all of James' emails were published online shortly after. Some were to his receptionist, Lizzie, making lude comments about what she was wearing or the plans they were making that night. Others had been filled with grammar and spelling errors, undoubtedly because he had been drunk at work. It had been revealed that James had been a privately heavy drinker. Jon wondered how he was holding up wherever he had run off to.

But the most damning of all had been the published discussions of Jon's work for Sirens. James had talked proudly of the new code through email, and when the emails were published, that pride had gone public, leaving Jon's contribution in it all exposed.

The investigators couldn't get their hands on Michael, though, which had left a gaping hole in the investigation. They had been forced to turn their sights elsewhere for the time being. This led them to interview Jon briefly about his association with the game, and Jon admitted to creating the code beneath the unforgiving glare of their fluorescent overhead lights. He told them of how he had delivered the game to RightMark on that fated afternoon. For now, at least, they did not appear to be very interested in Jon. He had been blindly assisting Michael, it seemed, though Jon was concerned that he would eventually be arrested for complacency or collusion.

But between the emails and the police interview, it had been the final stab in Shayna's side. She had been mortified by his disloyalty and the way he had held vital secrets from her. Worst of all, Jon suspected she also held all of the deaths against him as a dreadful I-told-you-so.

He would never forget the look on her face when she confronted him. She had come home from work early, still in her scrubs. Shayna had looked at him with tired eyes and the stare of a woman who had been worn down and was at the end of her rope. She appeared as if she was defeated, and he knew what was about to happen before it did.

Shayna was throwing in the towel.

"How dare you?" was the first thing she had said to him.

He hadn't even needed to ask what he had dared to do. The emails had been published earlier that day and he had been anticipating this confrontation. He could see that she knew of it all and that it hurt.

It hurt like a blow to the gut. And somewhere in those features that he had loved so dearly, he could also see that she would never forgive him for it. Even if they reconciled later, this would always lie between them.

They had argued, but it was short. The damage had been done, and Jon stood no chance of dancing out of the mess he had created. He was defeated too.

"I wish you would've listened to me," Shayna had said. "Why wouldn't you listen to me?"

"I wish I had," Jon had said. "Trust me."

"I don't. I can't. Not anymore," she said. "I need some time. I need to get away for a bit. Both of us could use the space I think."

Throughout the entire confrontation, Shayna had not cried, but Jon wished afterward that she had. He wished he had seen her mourn the loss of trust. He wanted to see her suffering the same pain he was. But he should have known better. Shayna was too strong to break. To bend, maybe, but never to break.

Long after she had gone, leaving him alone in the house they had been struggling to make into a home, he began to believe that their marriage had started dying in those chilly last weeks of September when Jon had chosen to protect a video game at the expense of his wife's trust. Shayna didn't cry that last day because her mind had been made up weeks before she had told him she was leaving. All of those warm dishes and tight smiles in between were just biding time.

The last thing she had said to him before she left for Kelly's house was, "This is on you, Jon."

That phrase had married itself to "It's at your feet," and the two sentences bounced around in his brain like pinballs from then on. They drove him mad like they were incantations, spells intended to make him lose his mind. Those two sentences were truths he should've told himself in September, something he should've acknowledged before people died because of his mistake. But only the clarity of the "after" could ever show him the weight of them. The blood was on his hands, the deaths were laid at his feet, and it was, indeed, on him.

And he was alone. The house he and Shayna had bought together giddily with the idea of babies in their heads and with stars in their eyes, was now empty except for him. There still was only a minimal amount of furniture. The mirror had been taken down, the bed was never made, and the clothes were no longer strewn on their bedroom floor. There was no need. Jon had been wearing the same clothes since Shayna had left.

Each day had begun to feel like its own decade. Jon did nothing but sit. Sometimes he sat on the couch, other times he sat on the bed. Sometimes the television was on, other times it was not. Jon never really watched it when it was on anyway. He only thought of two strings of words.

35

Michael

Within the first few weeks of his isolation, Michael had run just as he had set out to, tearing down that immobile strip of track as fast as his body would allow him. It was hard work—painful work—but so was everything about being in that Florida house.

Sometimes, when he felt particularly sluggish, he would walk or jog, but he tried to get himself to move at least once a day. The constant workouts had begun to feel like a routine. They were something to cling to.

Throughout the first month or so, he had also devoured several books and lost track of time entirely. Without a phone or calendar to help remind him of the date, he had stopped keeping track of how many days and nights had passed since he had begun isolating himself. After a while, he hadn't cared. He had stopped measuring time by hours, days, and weeks. Each day had begun to feel the same anyway, with Bella slowly becoming more of a persistent desire than a need over time.

Things were not getting significantly easier, but those images of her were becoming slightly less intense. He thought of Bella during every task, whether that was running or eating. Sometimes, she even slipped into his thoughts when he was reading, distracting him until he realized he had been merely looking at the words but not truly reading any of them.

Bella's laugh would slip into his mind with every moment of quiet, and her smile intruded on every moment of peace. Her voice resonated in his head like an earworm that just wouldn't let up. Michael would catch himself thinking of the way her nose crinkled when she giggled or how her hair used to brush against the pale skin of her shoulder. At first, he would get lost in those memories, succumbing to them weakly. He would try to fight them off, but he often felt like a starved man swinging blindly at the air.

However, sometimes Michael would fully indulge in these memories. Those fantasies were too rich to ignore every time they emerged. He would even create new fantasies of her. Although he hated to admit it, he touched himself to thoughts of her more times than he could count. Whenever he started, he convinced himself that those fresh thoughts were not harmful because they were not a product of the Emissux's influence. They were merely his own ideas and dreams, unguided. But without fail, every time he finished, Michael was awash with disgust and self-loathing, questioning how he planned to get over the fantasy of her if he only succeeded in creating new ones.

To offset the thoughts of Bella, he had tried finding other ways to occupy his mind and to fill the time. There were only so many chapters he could read before his eyes grew sore and only so many miles he could run before his body grew bored of the motion. So he had started forcing himself to doodle on paper, making his hand sketch out grotesque figures and landscapes.

The drawings he created turned out to be outrageous things. He drew simple doodles like flowers and nature scenes at first, but they were all misshapen with disproportionate sizes and exaggerated angles. Michael had stacks of yellow paper with pitiful drawings of basic muses that could've easily been mistaken for children's doodles.

One day, he found his hand working without his mind to guide it as his subconscious started drawing a terrible sketch of a woman. Even before he had finished, it was clear who it was supposed to be. The drawing was one of sharp edges, all made by the harsh strokes of his pencil. When he finally pulled away, Bella looked terrifying, staring up at him with succubus eyes. Yes, the drawing wasn't pretty, to begin with, but the sketch itself displayed a figure who was nothing short of nightmare material. What he thought would be a therapeutic practice had resulted in a harsh realization.

She was the ultimate memory. Bella was beauty wrapped in trauma. Two of the most memorable sensations were embodied in her, making her impossible to shake.

Michael soon realized that drawing would do nothing but lead to sketches of her. All paths led to her. So Michael resigned to reading and running again, feeling dulled by the unchanging movements of the practices.

With time, he was beginning to read a few pages uninterrupted. He could now run for a small handful of minutes before his mind flashed back to her.

It was with a sad acceptance that he knew, even with his progress, he would be in that house for a while.

***

Christmas came and went without Michael even knowing it. That day had seemed just like any other to him, with the sun rising and falling as it unwaveringly did.

Some days after the holiday was over, Michael reflected that Mary would be waiting for a call that she wouldn't receive. His emotional, mysterious conversation with her before his isolation would be rattling around in her brain. He hoped that she wouldn't cry any more tears for him.

Michael found himself yearning for someone to talk to. He needed to hear a human voice other than his own. Anyone. Even when he thought of Jon, he felt a pang of sorrow. It felt like mourning.

On some of his darkest days, he thought of Cindy. He remembered her bright smile and her musical laughter. He would have excused the way she had tricked him and used him if only he could be with her, the only real, tangible woman he had ever loved or been with. He had a hollow feeling in his chest as he dwelt on the fact that he had never really gotten over her. She had left him utterly broken with nowhere to turn to and it still hurt to think about. Cindy had been his everything, and he had only ever been one of four men she had rotated through.

Yet he could not find it in himself to harbor true resentment toward her. When he felt ill at the memory, it was a sickness directed toward himself and the foolish way he had navigated that situation. Even his frustration and jealousy were always trimmed with sorrow and self-pity. She couldn't have known the distrust he would develop, the wariness toward real, flesh-and-blood women it would create. Cindy could have never predicted that Michael would go off to create the image of a woman to fill the void she had left him with. He couldn't place the blame on her for these problems. It was his fault for letting them fester uncontrolled. These were hard understandings to grapple with, but he couldn't help but feel it was nice to have the time to think things through, even if they hurt like rubbing an open wound.

On the other hand, the thought and worry around Sirens and its release felt incredibly distant. It seemed materialistic and unimportant to wonder if his game was profitable or well-received. He had gotten lost in the game of big business, and he had been a sore loser. Michael made his own personal resolution on New Year's Day without knowing it. He would quit working at RightMark when he emerged and start someplace new. He would bar hop at real bars. He would meet real women.

As for a job, he was unsure on that front. The thought didn't immediately worry him. In the end, he didn't crave the office life the way he craved the memory of the people he was unable to see. Money and labor were things that were always fleeting in a hurry. They could be gained and lost swiftly. People—real people—were where the true value was. Those relationships were the only currency that ever really mattered.

Just a few more days, maybe a couple of weeks to be safe.

***

Michael finally freed himself on the eighteenth of January.

He had been hibernating for one hundred fifteen days.

Michael had missed Christmas. He had skipped over his birthday in November. He felt no shock when he realized the date. Michael had felt every minute of that isolation.

The first thing he did was slip on his jacket and enter the chilled weather. The cool outside air hit him like a wall, feeling unusually cold for a Florida morning. But he greeted it like an old friend. He inhaled deeply, letting it fill his chest. It was one of the best things he had ever felt in this world.

Two days before, he had only thought of Bella a mere twenty times. At that point, most of the thoughts of her were ones he had conjured consciously. Michael had waited two more days for good measure to make sure those twenty times weren't just a fluke. What could forty-eight more hours hurt?

So, he emerged reluctantly, feeling quite uncomfortable with stepping outside until the fresh air hit him. The chill had awakened a new sensation, and it was a feeling of reassurance. After one hundred fifteen days, he had been born again. He was a different man now.

Michael got into his car, feeling like the action of driving was slightly foreign, but he got the hang of it again after only a few minutes on the road. It was like slipping into a pair of old shoes that had been warped to fit his feet. Soon enough, Michael was cruising, enjoying the way some of the trees were now barren, stripped to their skeletons, their tangling arms reaching toward the sky in fascinating angles. Some days during his quarantine Michael would stare out at trees like the ones passing his car and feel a deep longing to witness more.

When he tuned into the radio, the songs on the pop channel were largely unfamiliar. His destination was just twenty minutes from his little Florida house, so he didn't get to listen too much. Out of the five songs he heard, Michael had only recognized one. He was rather satisfied with this. At least he had a lot to catch up on.

Michael stopped at the SmartStore down the block. He purchased a new phone with his card—his first payment in months.

As he watched the clerk tap the screen and type things in, Michael stroked his new facial hair thoughtfully. No one around him knew that it was a new addition to his face, and no one cared. Michael thought that it made him seem older, maybe even wiser, which he believed that he was. Yet he liked the lack of attention he was receiving because of it. No one in that store knew his history. They didn't know about Bella or his months of seclusion. He was merely a man with a beard buying a phone. He could be anyone.

After nearly an hour of waiting, the clerk finally handed Michael his new phone. The high price would have made the old Michael wince as he handed over his card. But on that day, he handed it over without hesitation. Later, he would check his bank account numbers, and Michael did not doubt they would be high. After all of that time, he hadn't purchased anything in months and RightMark would be direct depositing his Sirens money, so he expected the number in his bank account to be large, certainly large enough to absorb the phone's cost.

Before he even stepped out of the store, he searched "Sirens" on his new phone. He couldn't help it. Over time, he had begun to grow mildly curious about its success. It was a horrible, itching curiosity. He wanted to know if it had affected others as it had him, and he was interested to know how big of a success it had been.

Strangely, the first search result presented a picture of his face. Michael looked like a child in the photo as he stared back at himself beardless and grinning, unaware of how his life would change. He felt bad for the Michael in the picture. This Michael had been so innocent, craving success and pleasure. *Half a fool,* he thought sorrowfully.

And then he read the headline accompanying it. In bold it read "Sirens' Creator Missing, Wanted for Deaths."

The last half of the headline made his stomach drop.

He stopped walking altogether, frozen like his veins were suddenly pumping ice water. His mind was numb, a single word echoing through his head.

Deaths.

Plural. Not singular. Deaths.

He couldn't believe it and yet saw it as entirely fathomable all at once. A part of him, distant and smug, knew it made sense.

His thumb hovered over the article, shaking slightly, daring to open the webpage and read what he had feared for one hundred fifteen days.

Eventually, his thumb fell, almost unwillingly and without thought. The page took forever to load as if it was twenty hours and not twenty seconds. All the while, Michael's heart raced faster with each passing moment until it was painful in his chest.

When it loaded, he scrolled desperately, almost madly. Someone trying to enter the SmartStore bumped into Michael as they walked in. Michael was only vaguely aware that he was standing in the doorway, but he didn't move, and he couldn't hear the other person's apology. He was dazed, thinking of nothing besides his desperation to know the fucking number.

And then it was there, in numerals. It was five digits. Five too many.

Michael Ken was responsible for the deaths of 87,932 people.

36

Jon

It had been over two weeks since Shayna had left but Jon wasn't sure of the exact number of days that had passed. There was no point in paying attention to days and times. There was simply Before Shayna and After Shayna.

He had since resorted to closing all of the blinds and curtains and was living off the golden artificial light of whatever lamps or light fixtures the room he was in had to offer. He spent most of his days on the couch, exhausted from staying awake, but not so exhausted that he could find sleep. Instead, those two parting sentences played on their merciless loop, and images of Shayna nearly drowned him. Both worked in nightmarish harmony to keep him awake at all hours.

Though he knew he was being selfish in his misery, Jon simply didn't care. What Shayna and Michael had said was all he ever seemed to concern himself with. Their final thoughts had been real and true. They had happened. The impossibilities of Sirens and what havoc it was causing were too much for him to even begin to think about. The consequences were so vast, he feared he would be lost in them if he began to pick away at their surface and so he chose not to.

Instead, he let himself flutter around the subject. He permitted himself not to linger.

But when he turned on the news on that twentieth day since Shayna had left, he suddenly cared all at once.

He had been flicking through channels absently, not truly seeing or understanding the images flashing before him. The hollowness he experienced from hunger and fatigue made it hard to do anything other than tap his thumb against the remote to change the channel. When he went all the way through the channels, he would simply start over again, not comprehending that he had seen all that his television had to offer.

Jon had been aimlessly flipping through his options for fifteen minutes straight when Michael's face appeared blown up on the screen. It had startled Jon so much that he flinched and made a small cry from the back of his throat. He stopped tapping the remote like he was suddenly incapable of moving. It was like his body was frozen in a state of disbelief.

Michael's photo was the same one he had worn on his badge during the years he had worked at RightMark. Jon had seen it often, and he had watched it wear down on his identification card, blurring over time. Jon had never thought it looked sad until that moment. Michael was crisply dressed in a navy button-up and gray blazer. His hair had been combed back in a way that Michael had never worn since the photo had been taken. Somehow, though, it still had a mildly unkempt quality. On his face was a wide grin, and the smile was so large it looked as if the photo had been snapped while he was beginning to laugh.

If only he had known that he would be deemed a serial killer by the world.

"Michael Ken is still America's most wanted man," said the news anchor in a deep, unemotional voice. "However, he still has not been located, though investigators are reporting that a lead has led them to narrow their focus to an undisclosed part of Florida."

The focus cut to a press conference where a wide policeman with a bald head was hunched over a dozen microphones.

"We have just received word of a purchase Mr. Ken made in a specific location in Florida. We will be focusing our search there, but for the time being, we urge the public against using the Sirens game and to dispose of it if they have it in their possession."

The footage cut off abruptly and the newscaster was back on screen, shuffling papers skillfully as he stared into the camera.

"With the national urgency of this case, investigators are confident that Ken will be apprehended soon. As of right now, he and the missing RightMark president, James Sherrod, are being considered responsible for the 87,932 reported victims of the Sirens virtual reality game."

The room seemed to buzz with static. The number hung heavily in Jon's mind and sucked the air from around him. He tried to convince himself that he hadn't heard the number right but the rational part of him knew that he had.

There was a sickening swell inside of him that dulled any feelings or emotions other than shock. He felt nauseous but didn't have any food or drink in his stomach to bring up. So he reeled without the release of vomit, moaning quietly under the desensitizing blow. His cries were small, and he wasn't even aware that he was making any noise. He simply twisted like a fatally injured animal.

The news on the television seemed to be muted despite its constant droll. Jon wasn't aware that it had continued, just like the newscaster who was now discussing a local robbery was unaware that Jon was still groaning and writhing over the last story.

Slowly, sounds crept back into his consciousness as if he was emerging from a pool of water and gradually rising to the surface. He heard himself crying, "No, no, no, no," over and over again for no one to hear. His pleadings were useless. The damage was done. It was all beyond repair.

He realized then he was on the floor on all fours, whimpering and crying. The despair that Jon felt was deep and all-consuming. Jon lay there, sprawled out for what could have been hours. He wasn't aware of the fact that the news was long over by the time he found his feet again. Jon wasn't even sure what time of day it was when he left his home. He could have been on the floor for even days for all he had known or cared. He was only aware of the empty feeling in his chest, the hole that Shayna had left him with, without the promise of a return.

Shayna was gone, really, truly gone, and she wouldn't come back to a man who had helped kill so many people.

In his personal ocean of sorrow, two sentences floated around him. They were the only things he was sure of. That, and that five-digit number.

Not number, but death count. 87,932 bodies. 87,932 people.

Jon got into his car and mindlessly drove with sullen determination. There was a solid thought in his head now, heavy as stone. It was the only decision he had been sure about in days, maybe even weeks.

His body guided him, mechanically and through habit. He didn't need to think of the directions.

When he parked, his heart rebelled, beating against his ribcage violently, knowing what was coming and refusing to go along. Jon drowned it out though with the repetitive incantation in his mind. He chose not to feel his heart or to focus on it.

There was no time for questioning.

There was no more time at all.

Jon punched in the number eight in the elevator after he had scanned himself in. The elevator shot up in a jittery, familiar movement.

The elevator let out and he saw the familiar workplace. It was where he had spent over forty hours a week for years. He had sharpened his craft on this floor. It was where he had once felt his life had truly started.

But now the eighth floor of their building stretched out before him like the corpse of an animal long dead. It was a Sunday, so not a soul was in sight. The desks were empty, and they appeared hollow without any workers behind them. Though their office had always been nearly soundless, the quiet suddenly had a weight to it. The darkness only emphasized the lack of life.

Jon stumbled through the familiar maze of desks like a sleepwalker, letting his feet guide him. He was on autopilot, with nothing but the slow chant of Michael and Shayna's words repeating themselves in his mind.

He found himself outside of his office, looking in through the glass. His desk was a mess and the space behind his chair was covered in printed photos that crawled the entire length of the wall. Even from the distance, he could see Shayna's face smiling in most of the photos. Her image punched a moment of consciousness into him, and it hurt like someone had truly hit him. He squeezed his eyes together so tightly they hurt. Unbidden, tears started to form beneath his lids.

It took him a minute to steady himself as he washed Shayna from his mind. She was gone and after weeks of waiting and hoping, Jon now knew that she wasn't coming back. And he didn't blame her. He was a killer, responsible for a death count that climbed by the hour. He wouldn't have wanted to stick around either.

He wasn't sure how long he stood outside of the glass with his eyelids pressed intensely together, but eventually, he willed them open, found the doorknob, and pushed himself inward.

He avoided the wall of photos, knowing that if he saw her face again the will would leak from him like a punctured water balloon, and he wouldn't be able to follow through. Seeing Shayna would take the assurance from him and bleed him of his determination.

So, he walked without seeing. He crossed the room the way a horse with blinders would. Jon only looked straight ahead, knowing that seeing anything that reminded him of the old Jon would stop him where he stood. The old Jon was an unattainable dream now. A ghost. There was no returning to the way he once was. That version of himself had died and couldn't be resurrected.

But he also didn't care to keep the new Jon around.

He opened the window when he got to it and smelled the air as it rushed in. He really smelled it, as if for the first time in his life. It was light and felt strangely warm despite the winter weather, and it filled Jon's lungs with reassurance. Things would be fine. Things would be okay.

He removed the screen and leaned his head out, taking in the sun's warmth. It was pleasant and inviting, the way all familiar things were. Jon wanted to embrace that warmth, that fleeting feeling of comfort, and wrap his arms around it.

His heart skipped a beat as he leaned out further, letting the sunlight and fresh air consume him. He couldn't embrace it, but he let it embrace him instead, wishing that those slight and fleeting feelings of comfort could open up and swallow him whole. In his chest, his heart was racing so quickly it hurt and he couldn't ignore it any longer.

And then he didn't feel it anymore. All he could feel was the warmth of the sun and the swiftness of the air as it rushed up at him.

Michael had said that it would be laid at his feet and Shayna had said that it was on him but now there was nothing but air above and below him. There wasn't anything under him but the street several feet down, and there was nothing on him but a sunlight that was so brilliant Jon was particularly aware of it as he descended.

Sirens claimed its 87,933rd victim that day.

37

Michael

After reading and rereading the number for what seemed like a thousand times, Michael ran to his car not quite feeling his legs move beneath him.

Once inside, he realized that he had begun hyperventilating, breathing ragged, harsh breaths.

He also noticed that he was crying hysterically.

He could not have said how long he was there, only that his throat felt like it had been rubbed with sandpaper.

Michael had no recollection of driving back to his mother's house; he only knew that it had happened when he was sitting in the car in the driveway, still breathing sharply.

His mind was racing so quickly that he couldn't keep up with the thoughts as they sped past. They zoomed by in his head as if they didn't want to be caught. One thought was clear among the rest, though.

87,932.

Five whole digits.

87,932 people with families and lives.

He slammed his open hand into the steering wheel violently, over and over again until it was too painful to continue.

I told Jon, he thought. *That son of a bitch! I told that motherfucker!*

For a flashing moment, he hoped that Jon was just as distraught as him. Michael hoped that he was raging in his sorrow as well. He wanted Jon to realize and really understand his part in this. Michael had tried to stop the game from going out. Jon hadn't listened and now tens of thousands of people were dead. Michael felt himself hoping that Jon felt the entire weight of his decision. Michael refused to take on the burden alone.

He thought of all of those people who had died and wondered how it had happened on such a massive scale. How could it have gotten so out of control? He could envision their faces, slack with pleasure as they plugged into a universe of their own making, a dreamscape that tempted and seduced until they were coaxed into their graves. Michael hadn't read the rest of the article, but he knew without question how they had died. They would have died in the game, starved of real food and real sleep. He knew their exhaustion. Michael had felt it. He knew all too well how desperate that craving was.

While he was isolating to solve his own issues, he had left an uninformed public to try their luck at a new sort of drug. It was an intoxicant he had concocted, and yet he hadn't warned anyone beyond Jon about it. A wave of nausea overcame him as he realized that he should've done more. He should've released a statement or at least posted a heads-up online. Something. *Anything.* People were dead because he had only thought of himself. His mind had still been halfway in Bella's world when he had locked himself away. People had died because of it. Tens of thousands of people.

Michael opened his car door, leaned out, and threw up on the concrete. He hadn't eaten much that day, so his vomit burned with bile and brought fresh tears to his eyes. He choked and spat, hanging out of the car as his body tried to reject the thoughts in his head like poisoned food.

Eventually, he pulled himself back in as he heaved, breathing deeply to try and steady himself. He wiped his lips with the back of his hand savagely. The inside of his mouth stung like he had just swallowed a mouthful of chemicals; his eyes were leaking tears, and his nose was dripping with snot. At first, Michael couldn't tell if the tears were because of the vomit or the people he had killed, but they felt appropriate, so he let them come, and eventually, he let the sobs rack his body again.

For a while, Michael sat in his car, raging inconsolably in his grief. Eventually, he opened his door to vomit again, this time bringing up absolutely nothing, leaving his stomach feeling as if it had been punched afterward.

It took over an hour to calm himself down. By then, he was sitting in the stale air with his car still turned off, inviting in the chill of January that now felt sinister instead of welcoming. Each exhale was followed by a small whimper, which Michael couldn't help but slip out.

Eventually, the tears dried and the energy had been all but drained from him. As his breathing began to finally even out, he felt himself craving what every man, woman, or child craves in a time of desperation or turmoil.

He wanted to talk to his mom.

Her phone number was deep in his memory. She had kept the same one since he was a child, too stubborn to give it up. He dialed it on his new cell phone quickly as white-hot fear shot through him. He wondered if she knew of the deaths and wouldn't want to talk to him. Michael didn't think he could bear it.

The phone rang and rang.

Each ring made his heart stutter. He began to become certain that she *did* know, and she *was* irreparably disappointed. If he wasn't so exhausted from all of the dry heaving, he likely would've thrown up again.

When the phone went straight to voicemail, the panic in him burst to the surface, seizing him violently with a cold grasp. He pounded in the retirement home's number instead, his thumbs dialing the string of digits with urgency.

He listened as the rings poked into his consciousness once again. Michael was vaguely aware that his hand was trembling while holding the phone by his ear.

Mercifully, someone picked up after three crisp rings.

"Hello," said a pleasant voice. "This is the Floral Terrace Retirement Complex. How can I help you?"

"Mary Ken," Michael blurted into the phone. "I need to talk to Mary Ken."

His voice was wild and rough, cracking at the ends of some words with the dryness of his throat.

There was a deafening silence that followed. It spread between them like an abyss, deep, dark, and unknowing.

Then, the woman on the other line cleared her throat. "Are you her son?" she asked.

"Yes," Michael said. "I need to talk to her. Now. Please. It's important."

Briefly, Michael wondered if the woman on the other line knew who he was and what he had done. He thought of how she might be less likely to assist him if she knew about Sirens. It made his stomach sink and his throat feel like it was closing.

"Please," he said again. The word was a desperate whisper.

"I'm so sorry," the woman said. "We've been trying to get a hold of you for days."

Something dark, even darker than before, stretched over Michael. It was like a cloud in his mind, eclipsing all of his other fears.

"Please," he repeated.

"Mary Ken died on January fifteenth, Mr. Ken," she said.

Each word was like a blow to him. He felt limp by the time she had finished speaking.

"How?" he managed to ask.

The woman cleared her throat again. "She died of a heart attack, sir."

Michael's voice was choked with sobs that threatened to overcome him again. "Why?"

There was a vicious silence again. It felt like it was hours before the woman answered his question.

"They think..." she hesitated as if trying to find the right words. "They think it was caused by shock."

His phone dropped out of his hand, dead and useless. It clattered pointlessly to the ground. Michael's mouth was agape, a dumb look on his face that no one was around to bear witness to.

All of those days she had laid in bed, unable to move because her joints were fighting her had stacked the odds against her, but Michael had delivered the final blow.

Despair was a deep, lonely pit. Michael had never felt so isolated in his life, not even when had voluntarily locked himself away. This was a different sort of loneliness. It was one that was out of his control. It was final with no promise of alleviation. This loneliness knew no mercy and showed no end.

There was a face to his devastation now, and it was Mary's.

***

Michael drove himself back to Pennsylvania in one long, tiresome drive. He drove in the colorful sunset, the starry night sky, and the brilliant sunrise. When he got back to Pittsburgh, it was seven in the morning.

He had nowhere to go in the city that was once his. All of its potential, its boundless opportunities, and its vibrancy were absent. They had left, abandoning the city to become a husk of its former self.

He could not see his mother. He could not face Jon. Cindy wouldn't invite him into the home she shared with her fiancé. There was no returning to normalcy and no point in returning to his apartment and pretending that there was a way to escape.

Michael went to the only place he knew his presence would be accepted, perhaps even welcome. He was so tired that he approached the building without any trepidation or fight.

Michael Ken turned himself into the Pittsburgh Police.

38

Shayna

Shayna sat in her sister's kitchen, crying quietly over a mug of tea. She felt hollowed out, yet she mustered up tears that slid from her cheeks and into the mug she had been clutching with an iron grip.

Three long days had passed since they had found Jon. Seventy-six lengthy hours had gone by since two burly officers had come to Kelly's door to let her know that Jon Way had been found dead.

They said that he had jumped from a window. She knew without their insight that he had been overcome by a lapse of loneliness and that he had seen no out. He had cut himself short without warning. Jon had left her with no note. No explanation was given. No parting words, no goodbyes. When officers investigated their shared home, they discovered he had left the television on a station that reported the news. They suspected he had seen a noon story about Michael Ken and jumped shortly afterward. He had learned of the deaths and had given up. He had been left alone to his thoughts, grief, and sadness, and he had seen only one option.

How was Shayna supposed to have known?

She had just needed some time to think. Shayna had to put distance between her and him to collect her thoughts and freshen her perspective. Perhaps, in retrospect, leaving him had been selfish. When she left him, he had been in a visibly bad place. But so had she. Jon had put her into a challenging spot, and she had needed to think her way out of it without him sulking on the couch just feet from her.

Shayna had had every intention to come back when her thoughts were clear and her mind was made up. Then there had been the wrench thrown into her plans, and she had been given even more to weep and ponder over before she could muster up the courage to face him again. If Jon had still been there to explain it all to, she knew he would have understood. If he had only listened. If only he had waited. He hadn't given her the time. Now, there was none left with him.

Her heart ached knowing he would never have the opportunity to understand her side of things. She would never get the chance to explain. There was a heaviness in her that left her exhausted.

Shayna sipped her hot tea absently. She hadn't slept the night before with the image of Jon—her husband, her love, the first man she had ever adored—jumping from a window out of desperation playing in her head over and over. She had conjured an image in her mind of Jon tumbling downward, swirling and cartwheeling until he shattered on the ground below. The thought sent a shiver down her spine and tears to her eyes even after countless times imagining it. The image was sickening. To her core, she knew she would never be desensitized to it, no matter how often she thought about it.

When the police had come to Kelly's door to tell Shayna, she had fallen to her knees so hard that they had bruised. She sobbed on the floor as her sister rubbed circles into her back and cried with her. They had shared strange, sisterly tears. Kelly had never seen Jon the way that

Shayna had, but she cried too. She cried for Shayna, for her sister's loss, and for the road ahead that they both would trek without Jon.

Her husband had always had poor timing. He had always started things that he didn't finish. Jon had a habit of beginning projects and abandoning them halfway.

Shayna touched her lower stomach. Perhaps she was only imagining it, but she thought she could feel its swell already, a tiny rise that met her hand like a touch of reassurance.

Jon had left yet another unfinished project.

In her darkest moments, she cursed him for his weakness. He hadn't known when to expect her, but he should've waited for her to come back. How could he have not known he would see her again? She had asked for time, and he hadn't had it in him to wait for her to figure things out. Despite all of the sorrow consuming her, she still found that this made her angry.

But then she would imagine the despair he must have felt in those final minutes and on that last day. The misery he must have felt knowing that Shayna had left him and the guilt of all of those deaths certainly was enough to send any person over the edge. When Shayna tried to imagine it from his perspective, her mouth grew cottony and her mind buzzed with anguish. Shayna knew why he had done what he did; she only wished he would have waited a bit longer for her to muster up the courage to return and save him from those thoughts.

Kelly walked in then, wearing only a bathrobe and fluffy white slippers. Her face was solemn, as it had been for the past few days. Whenever she approached her sister, she seemed to have screwed up her features in a permanent, pitiful look.

"How are you doing?" Kelly asked softly.

Shayna took a sip of her tea, gathering herself. She loved her sister for being gentle with her, but part of her rebelled against being approached with such sympathy. It made her feel as though she looked as helpless as she felt on the inside, and that was the last thing that she wanted.

"I'm tired," she managed to say.

Kelly took a seat across from Shayna, folding her hands on the table.

"I bet," she said. "Not much sleep?"

"Not a wink," Shayna said.

There was a beat of silence, and Shayna traced the rim of her mug with her pointer finger.

"I'm going to the store today," Kelly finally said. "I wanted to know if you needed anything."

It sounded so silly. Shayna could barely think about something as frivolous as food.

"I don't think so," she said.

"I'll get you some more tea," Kelly suggested, looking down at Shayna's mug. "Maybe some vitamins."

The thought made her stomach turn. She had to start thinking about things like that. About nutrition and health. It was bigger than just her and her pity party.

"Fuck," Shayna said breathily as she leaned back into her seat. Fresh tears brimmed in her eyes.

"Oh!" Kelly's face fell even further, deep pity settling into all of her features. "Oh, Shayna. I'm so sorry."

Shayna barely heard her, though. She was far off again, distant, on her personal island of mourning. It was a strange feeling knowing that she would never talk to him again. It was an even stranger feeling knowing that the child that they had craved since marriage had taken hold in her and would grow on without him.

Their baby would grow up without a father.

"I'll be here with you," Kelly said as if she was reading her sister's mind. "We'll get through this together. I promise. We can raise your baby together. And you know you can live here as long as you want."

Shayna huddled over. She felt so pathetic, sobbing loudly as though the choking, sniffling sounds and tears would purge her of her emotions. She knew that even when she had finished, those feelings of pain and loss would still be in her. They were rooted too deeply, and that knowledge made her cry even harder.

Kelly came over and rubbed Shayna's back as she wept and shook. "I know, Shayna," Kelly kept muttering softly. "I'm so sorry, Shayna. I can't even imagine."

Her sister's touch did nothing to comfort her. Nothing could.

The thought of her baby being raised, fatherless in her sister's house was too much to bear. It made her feel even weaker than she ever had. Strangely, her sister's offer of assistance only made her feel even lonelier.

She continued to cry until she was left feeling emptier than she had before. All the while, Kelly rubbed circles into her back patiently, trying to comfort a woman who couldn't be comforted.

"There's too much loss," Shayna wept. "Too much. And all because of... because of greed."

"I know," Kelly agreed.

"It's always them," Shayna said. "They always do this. They never..."

She couldn't bring herself to say the words, to be specific. But she knew her sister understood.

"I know," Kelly repeated, confirming this.

39

Michael

March

Michael waited in his cell, listening to how the prison stirred at night. All around him, the space began filling with the sounds that usually only came in the evenings. Bed sheets swished, men moaned and snored, and small footsteps were amplified in the quiet as people paced anxiously.

Sleep did not find Michael easily. It hadn't ever since he had met Bella, and this was certainly no different now that he was spending his nights in a prison cell.

That evening was especially difficult. It was the night before his last day in court when his sentencing would be announced, and Michael had little intention of getting any rest.

His body was like a coiled wire, taut with fear. He was not sure what he was dreading, though. In his mind, the decision had already been made long ago at the beginning of this media circus. It had been especially obvious to him during those early days in court when he first saw that the string of numbers that kept swelling—his victims—had faces. He had seen their expressions and found them filled with resentment and deep pain that even his harshest sentencing could not assuage.

He had pleaded guilty. There was no convincing evidence to oppose the mountain the prosecution had stacked against him, and pleading guilty allowed him to truthfully confess his contribution to it all. But now, Michael wondered if he should have given himself a fighting chance and pleaded not guilty instead.

Michael expected to receive a life sentence. The state of Pennsylvania had gotten rid of the death penalty just a few years ago, freeing Michael to live the rest of his foreseeable future in a concrete cell. In his darker hours, Michael wished the penalty still existed to liberate him from the torment he inflicted upon himself.

Michael rolled onto his side to face one of the three walls of the small cell he had been stuffed into. It hurt his chest to think he would be looking at a similar scene for the rest of his life. His cell was shabby with clean concrete walls and nothing to speak of besides two cots and a toilet. Michael even wished someone before him would have graffitied the walls so he would at least have had something to read.

On the cot across from him was a mute, thin man. Michael didn't know what he was being held for and knew better than to outright ask, but he figured it couldn't have been anything too violent. The man was so frail that a strong breeze might've carried him off, and he was exceptionally quiet. He and Michael had likely only exchanged ten sentences with each other in the week and a half they had shared the cell. Neither of them had discussed their charges.

Michael did not doubt that his cellmate knew who he was, though. Naturally, his arrest and trial had been a media frenzy. Almost everyone in the country knew who Michael Ken was and hated him. He could not say that he blamed them.

The courtroom had been packed every day as a result of nationwide interest. It was filled with people from wall to wall, most of them teary-eyed and shaking their heads. Michael did not like to dwell on the question of how many of those in attendance were widows or the children of parents killed by Sirens. The question hurt too much to even consider. Michael could only shoulder so much blame and could only endure so much guilt.

The one that weighed heaviest was Jon.

Michael had heard about Jon from a particularly sympathetic prison guard. The guard had leaned closely while distributing Michael's lunch and asked in a hushed tone, "Your partner was Jon Way, right?"

Michael's stomach had dropped. He was expecting to hear that Jon was moving forward with a lawsuit against him. It was something he had considered but dismissed, thinking that Jon wouldn't have it in him to toss all of the blame onto Michael. But now he wished he had braced himself.

He hadn't anticipated, however, that the guard would shake his head and say, "I'm sorry, man. They reported it a few days ago. He's dead. I thought you should know."

Michael had felt almost all of the negative feelings he had held against Jon drop from him like a bath towel. It was as if his entire body had gone static.

"How?" he had managed to ask.

"Suicide," the guard replied. "Jumped from the eighth floor where the people at RightMark worked."

Michael remembered Jon's little office, the one he had earned through a stroke of utter brilliance, a genius that was simply flying too close to the sun. Michael had walked by that little glass wall every day at work, glancing inward at the chaos that was Jon Way's workspace, and never once suspecting that it would be the last place Jon ever saw.

Michael didn't eat his lunch that day or dinner that night.

Jon taking his own life was incomprehensible. He had seemed so sure of what he was doing even if he was doing nothing. And he had loved his wife, Shayna, more than he had loved anything else in the world. Surely, she would have anchored him in place. The fact that he was dead felt incredibly wrong, utterly surreal.

It also didn't sit right with Michael for another reason. Michael found himself growing angry. He despised himself for it, but frustration flared, and he found that the impression of that anger didn't merely fade into nonexistence at the news of Jon's death.

Jon shared equal, if not more, responsibility; he would never live to see any punishment for it. Perhaps death was his form of taking responsibility, but Michael would forever be the face of it all. Even James Sherrod had fled and left Michael to carry the blame alone. Michael would face the consequences by himself, spending the rest of his life behind bars.

The following day, Michael's punishment would be announced to the world. The court would reconvene, gathering to bear witness to the extent of Michael's damnation. He could feel his life sentence hovering above him like vultures. There was no avoiding what was inevitable.

Michael wasn't one to buy into hope. Not anymore.

***

The next day, they were in court for nearly two more hours before his sentencing was read. Michael was stunned by the swiftness of it all, though he supposed he shouldn't have been. Everyone had made up their minds about him long ago.

As expected, it was announced to a courtroom of terrified and eager faces that Michael Ken would serve a life sentence.

Michael did not react. It was as if he had heard the sentence a million times in his head, read it in his own voice. He had known what it was before it had been spoken into the world.

Michael was walked out of the courtroom in handcuffs, shuffling back to his new bedroom. Around him was a chorus of sobs, jeers, and the light clatter of his leg cuffs.

Then the doors shut behind him, muffling all sounds besides his chains and the awkward waddle of his footsteps. Quiet had fallen on them like a blanket, hushing the world but for those rhythmic noises.

Then, unprompted, Bella's voice reverberated in his mind, repeating words once spoken over small hills of silken sheets in a place he had once considered paradise.

"You're amazing," she had said.

The echo of her voice struck him with odd humor. Those two words emerged under the soft clacking of his chains and the slow shuffle of feet as he went off to his cell. It peeked through the real world uninvited.

You're amazing.

The juxtaposition between the world he had created and the one he was in brought laughter to his lips. At first, it was a giggle that resulted in a few stern glances in his direction. Then it grew to uncontrolled laughter and soon he was in hysterics, wiping tears from the corners of his eyes and shaking. He was keeled over in shrieking hilarity, laughing and laughing at a voice no one else could hear.

40

Shayna

Shayna sat before the glass, waiting in a jittery quiet. Her hands had started shaking from the moment she had gotten behind the wheel to drive to the Riverside Correctional Center and they hadn't stopped trembling since. Sitting on the cold metal stool, she felt her whole body shaking.

After time had passed and the wounds had finally begun to heal, the idea of their meeting had felt like a necessity.

She had never met Michael Ken.

Shayna had only seen his photos on the news, most of which were pictures from years before Sirens was even an idea in Jon or Michael's heads. In all of those old photos, Michael was grinning widely, almost childishly. Those pictures were of a young man with the world ahead of him, eerily unaware of his fate.

On the news several weeks before, there had been footage of him from just after the arrest, showing a much different Michael. In the videos, he looked as though he had aged twenty years in just a few months. His eyes looked hollow and unseeing, and his skin was so pale it was almost translucent. A beard consumed his face as if he wished to hide in it. Shayna thought that he just might.

But seeing him on the television made her stomach roil and she turned away quickly. At first, she wanted to avoid him. She had even refused to attend his trial, out of pure, vicious fear. Several weeks had passed since the trial had ended, and now she was still alone, shaking with nerves, and waiting to see Michael Ken in person for the first time.

Before her was a thick pane of glass and to her right was an old-fashioned telephone. Shayna reflected on how odd it felt to sit there. Never in her wildest dreams would she have been able to predict that she would be sitting before the glass, talking into a plastic phone to someone she blamed for her husband's death.

Yes, Jon's death had been at his own hand, but Shayna could not bear to blame Jon fully for what had happened, so she settled on the next best person. It was Michael's fault for creating a game that killed thousands, after all. It was his fault for screwing up a pornographic virtual reality so badly that her husband jumped from a window out of guilt. It was Michael's fault for listening to Jon's absurd suggestion in the first place.

So, she blamed him, perhaps not for the whole situation, but certainly for most of it. It was easier that way. She could not put all of the responsibility on her dead husband, who had tried to hold the weight of the situation on his own and had been crushed by it. That was an impossible thing to ask of her.

From somewhere beyond the glass, down the row of small cubicles like the one she was sitting in, there was a loud creak. The sound of a squeaky, heavy metal door being opened echoed throughout the room. She was the only person in the long row of vacant seats to hear it.

Shayna's heart jumped to her throat. She suddenly wondered if she would even be able to hold the phone with her hands seeming to vibrate with nervousness.

She heard footsteps slowly growing nearer. Every footfall seemed to throw her heartbeat off its rhythm. Her mouth had grown dry as if someone had suctioned out all of her saliva with one of those small vacuums that dentists used.

Then, he was there, standing before her.

Michael was much taller than Shayna had expected, and he looked as though he was made of all bones. In his bright orange jumpsuit, he appeared to have the weight of a skeleton. On his face, a great bush of facial hair sprung from his chin. All of the handsomeness she had noted when she had first seen his picture was gone. He was a fragment of that man.

Michael took a seat silently, his face giving away nothing. The only thing that Shayna could gather from looking at him was that he appeared frail and exhausted like he could roll over and succumb to a lack of sleep at the snap of her fingers.

He grabbed the silly-looking phone to his right with a sure hand. Her own continued to tremble by comparison. She gripped the phone hard to try steady it.

"Hello," he said.

"Hi." Her voice wavered, and she felt a blush creep to her cheeks. She wanted to be strong, but at that moment, she felt incredibly weak.

"So, you're Shayna," he observed. It was clear then Michael didn't know what to say. Perhaps he was a little nervous after all.

"That's me," she said.

Michael coiled the telephone wire around his finger, suddenly refusing to look up at Shayna's face.

"I was surprised you wanted to meet me," Michael said after an awkward pause.

"Why is that?" she asked. Shayna had surprised herself with her desire to meet Michael, but she wanted to hear him say it. An evil part of her wanted to see him squirm.

"I thought you might blame me," he said. "I wouldn't fault you if you did. I do."

His gaze was still trained on the wire, curling and uncurling around his thin, pale pointer finger.

"Maybe I'm here to yell at you," she said. "To curse you."

"Maybe," Michael said. "But I doubt it."

"Why's that?"

"You would've already started." His eyes finally met hers. They were brown and filled with deep sorrow, but he looked as though he was trying to bring some humor to them. It seemed like it was costing him a great effort. That feeling did not appear to come naturally to him.

"Give me some time," she said. "I might just work up to it."

That made him smile. It was a thin smile, there and gone in the blink of an eye.

"You're looking for answers then," Michael suggested. "I'm afraid I don't think I'll have them. I have a lot of questions myself, but I can try to fill in some gaps for you."

"I have a few," she said. "But not the kind you're expecting."

If it was even possible, Michael appeared to grow paler.

"Yeah? Shoot then." The words were taut.

"You recovered," she said. "How?"

His gaze returned to the telephone wire. "I locked myself away in my mom's old house. It was left to me when she died. I didn't use any tech besides a treadmill, appliances, and lights. The news has reported this."

"I'm not watching the news," Shayna said. She had tried to avoid it at all costs recently. Sirens news was exhausting, and it had begun to remind her of how the police had determined that Jon had killed himself after seeing a Sirens news report. While she had caught clips of it, like the time she had seen the footage of Michael with his beard, she never voluntarily turned it on or kept it going.

"Fair enough. I'm not watching it anymore either," he said.

"But you recovered, didn't you?" she asked.

"I'm not dead," he said with a shrug.

"No, you're not. That's not what I meant though."

"I don't think it ever goes away. Not really," he said. "It's like any other addiction. Once you're hooked, you crave it until you die."

"So, you still think of it."

"I still think of *her*."

His face was deadly serious. It was hard and sad at once as if he was sure of what he was saying but torn up to be admitting it.

"Her," Shayna repeated, a bit incredulously.

"She sneaks back into my mind a lot. She lives there."

That sent a chill through Shayna. What he was saying was strange and disjunctive, like he was disconnected from the reality of the situation.

"The character the game made is still... in your head?" she asked.

"I helped make her. My brain did, I mean. The game takes your subconscious preferences and projects them, putting whatever it can gather into different situations that you were supposed to guide." He laughed a small, breathy chuckle. "You were meant to control it. We were supposed to be controlling the situations and the *person* our preferences constructed. In the end, she controlled us. She still does."

"How?"

"I once told your husband that it was like staring at the sun," he said with another small shrug. "We're not supposed to, but we really want to for some reason. We want to test ourselves and see if we can actually do it. But some of us stare too long and our eyes get burned."

"You told Jon to stop it from going forward."

"I did."

"And he didn't do that."

"It doesn't seem like it. I left before it was released. I was already in Florida for weeks when it dropped. I needed time, and I... I couldn't bear to see how things panned out."

Suddenly his voice was hoarse and strained. He lowered it, preparing to confess something difficult. "I didn't know it would be that bad. I should've said something before I left. For some reason, I didn't. I don't know why I didn't despite all of the time I've had to reflect on it. It was probably selfishness in the end. I put my self-interest first. Thousands died because of that. Tens of thousands. I own that."

There was a beat of silence. Michael was visibly trying to collect himself. His eyes were already red and shiny with tears. Shayna's hand had grown sweaty, and she adjusted her grip clumsily on the phone.

"It wasn't just you," she said, finally. "Jon should've listened to the warnings and seen the signs. He shouldn't have pushed it through."

A tear loosened and fell down Michael's cheek. He did not attempt to wipe it. Shayna hadn't walked into the prison expecting Michael Ken, mass murderer, to cry.

"I'm sorry," he said. "I know that isn't enough, but I am. Jon... I never expected Jon to... I wish I could go back. I wish I could do things differently."

"Me too," she said.

"I think about him all the time," Michael admitted. "Him more than my aunt sometimes. When I met up with him that last day, I was exhausted, and I acted crazy. I should've done more to convince him."

"I talked to him later that night," Shayna said. "He didn't listen to me either. His mind was made up. Don't put that blame on yourself." She sighed shakily, feeling her own tears creep up on her. "His decisions were his own in the end."

Michael didn't seem relieved at that. Perhaps he even looked sadder at that idea.

"I'm still sorry," he said in a small voice tight with emotion. "I'm sorry for the part I played."

"I know," Shayna said. She knew that it would be a long time before she could forgive him and an even longer time before she could forgive herself.

"I don't know how I can make it right," Michael said. "I want to help give you whatever... whatever closure you need."

"Was it really his idea?" she asked.

"Yes," he answered. "It was his idea to make the reversal code and to... to add the sexual element to it."

She had already known it, but she had wanted to hear it from the source. Even still, for a moment she felt breathless like the air had been knocked from her.

"He gave me suggestions here and there when I asked. But he never coded anything beyond the reversal code. The rest of it was me putting his ideas to use. He never made the girls. I don't know if that makes you feel any better—"

Shayna cut him off. "It doesn't."

"Then I'm sorry about that too," he said.

"Half an hour!" yelled an officer. They had already eaten up a good chunk of their time.

"I wanted to see you," Shayna said. "In person."

"I'm sure I'm a disappointing sight," he said.

"You are," she admitted. "I expected to hate you. I wanted to blame you. Now, I don't think that I can."

"Oh," was all Michael said.

Shayna cleared her throat. "Jon left me with everything."

"That's good," he said. "I would've expected it."

"Me too. But I can muster up enough money for..." she cut herself off. She couldn't bring herself to tell him about the baby, which was hidden beneath her overlarge sweater. She thought that she noticed him take note of her hesitation. "I don't need his money. Anything made from Sirens is dirty. It's blood money."

Michael didn't say anything. He only watched her, waiting patiently for her to continue.

"Rehab worked for you, didn't it?" she asked.

"Well enough," he said. "If you consider locking yourself away rehab, then yeah, sort of. Like I said, she's still there. She probably always will be. But it's better now. I don't crave her in the same way. It's more of a strong want than a need now." He paused. "I don't know why I didn't... why I didn't die like the rest of them. I keep thinking about it. Maybe it's because I wasn't being sold something. I didn't trust it like they did because I wasn't someone buying the game. I was in there *looking* for flaws. I was actively seeking out something like this but even when I did... It was hard to pull back."

Shayna nodded, noting the way his voice cracked on those last words. "If you were outside of here, could you live normally?" she asked.

Michael looked a bit confused. He shifted his weight on the stool. "Yeah, I guess. I think it would be harder. I would... I would spend a lot of time comparing her to real women, I think. I know how that sounds, but it's the truth. But I think it's definitely possible. The cage they have me in now certainly makes it easier, though."

Shayna gripped the phone tighter, making up her mind. "Good."

Another minute of silence filled the empty row. Michael cleared his throat.

"I know I can't do much from in here, but if you think of something that I can do to make things a little better or easier or whatever, let me know."

"I will," Shayna said. "This helped a little."

"I'm glad," he said.

"I should go now," she concluded. "Small doses are better. I might be back, though, when I've had more time. I just needed to see you in person."

"Feel free to come over whenever," he said, cracking a sad smile. "I have nothing but time now."

Shayna nodded. "I feel like we have a lot to talk about."

She moved to stand but then leaned back into the phone. She looked deep into Michael's brown eyes. He could've been a handsome, successful man, she reflected then. Instead, he would always be a broken, frail boy who had made a deadly error for the rest of his life. He had been led astray by greed and men whispering in his ears pushing things from bad into worse. At that moment, she felt an intense pity for him overcome her.

"It was nice meeting you, Michael," she said.

"You too, Shayna."

They both clicked their phones back into their cradles. She gave him one last tight grin as a means of goodbye and then turned to go. As she was leaving, she could hear his chains move in a gentle clatter as he rose. Despite herself, her chest panged painfully at the sound.

She had wanted to leave Michael in a fury. Shayna had hoped that their meeting would solidify her hatred and that she could pass the guilt onto someone permanently. Instead, she felt only more distraught. She was less certain about how to feel about Michael than she had been when she walked in.

When she reached the parking lot, Shayna was happy to find that her hands were steady now. She had made up her mind about at least one thing on that cold stool. Someone had to right Michael's and Jon's wrongs. Shayna knew who, and it made her feel both tired and strong at once.

41

Michael

Michael was well aware of how mad he must look, sketching endlessly, creating the same image with subtle differences. He must've seemed unhinged to his cellmate and guards, scribbling down the same muse day in and day out. He drew Bella's every feature. Her eyes, her hips, her hair, her lips, her nails, and her calves were all committed to paper and presented on the walls, hung up by chewed gum or tape, to cover the cement as thoroughly as wallpaper.

He allowed himself this. While he had been hesitant to draw her at first, he found a small release with each new sketch, no matter how awful the result was. It was as if his brain craved drawing her with his unskilled hand, passing the endless hours reestablishing what he knew best. Her. He wondered if this was also his subconscious urge to remember her, to make his memory of how she looked permanent. Or perhaps it was his mind's attempt to purge her from it.

Occasionally, he also questioned if other Sirens survivors were so consumed by the image of their ideal lover. He wondered if other users dreamed of their fictional lovers as he did when he was finally able to go to sleep. Did she creep into their thoughts the way Bella did, tiptoeing into every decision? There had to be at least a handful of Sirens users whose thoughts were bordered with images from the game. Sirens had altered their lives forever. But at least they were alive.

Yet that was only hypothetical. Michael wasn't privy to that information. No one passed along any Sirens news unless it was to refresh him on the number of deaths, taunting him through the bars. Any news of Sirens was delivered in the form of numbers, which continued to tick upward but had mercifully begun to slow over time. Michael was unaware of anyone else who had lived through his experience. For all he knew, he was alone in the slow deterioration that Sirens created in its survivors.

There were whispers to disprove this assumption, though. Shayna had said on her last visit that she was in the process of opening up a charity for all of the victims.

"Someone has to," she had said with a shrug.

Michael hadn't even thought of it, though. He had been concentrating only on thoughts of himself and Bella. Having his arrogance unintentionally underscored felt like a slap. The impression Sirens had made was permanent and blinding, seeming to narrow his vision and priorities forever.

The world was fortunate to have Shayna. She had turned her time and energy to helping others who had been hurt. It was her new passion, something that made her face light up when she spoke of it. She was supposedly visiting hospitals and meeting with the victims' families. Shayna had also donated any of the Sirens money she had received, as she had told Michael she would.

Shayna was stronger than he had ever been or ever would be. Michael had never seen her cry about Jon. He couldn't tell if that was from callousness or an effort to not expose her hurt. Yet he was grateful for her strength regardless. It steeled him as well.

On top of it all, the last time he had seen her she was heavily pregnant.

Her stomach had been visibly protruding for the first time in April. She could've been bloated, but Michael had noticed the small waddle in her walk and grown curious. When she came again in May it was evident. There was no denying that she was carrying Jon's child.

The two of them never talked about it. There was no need to. It was an unspoken understanding that addressing it would only sadden the two of them. Even months later, the wound Jon had left was still open and tender.

Michael couldn't imagine Shayna's burden. She was the widow of a man who they were crediting a tragedy to. Months later she was carrying his child without him and voluntarily giving away her time and money to alleviate the effects of Sirens, a game she had opposed from the start. She was made of a different material than him, one that did not break so easily.

On top of it all, she still visited Michael like clockwork. Every fifteenth day of the month she was there to see him at three in the afternoon with the plastic phone in her hand and that sympathetic smile on her face. The two of them talked casually about everything from meals to television shows. They covered all topics besides Bella, Jon, and the baby.

Talking to her eased Michael's pain. He thought that Shayna likely knew this and that's why she continued to return. Sometimes he wondered if it was the same way for her. It had crossed his mind that talking to someone who knew of this pain, who had experienced it firsthand, was a relief. Even if they weren't directly discussing their issues, they knew and understood.

Michael dreaded the day when the baby came, knowing that when it did, Shayna would be less likely to visit. He selfishly hoped that she came anyway and maybe in time that she would bring Jon's child to visit. It was a wild, unlikely idea but the dream of it was beautiful and something to lean on for support. So he would believe in it until a fifteenth day of the month rolled around when she wasn't on the other side of the glass.

He had long since noticed that it would be the little things that would get him through. He had begun his isolation back in late September of the previous year not knowing that he would be in solitude for the rest of his life. Aside from Shayna, there was no one left who was willing to talk to him. His past life was dead, and many of the people in it had passed on as well.

There would be a day when Michael died too, following his victims to the grave. Michael would be partially forgotten by many, but to those who had been touched by Sirens, he would be immortal. His legacy would be one of infamy. Perhaps all along he had sought out recognition. From the beginning, he had wanted to be the Next Big Thing. Now his name, Michael Ken, would live on in association with porn that killed people with their pants down. When he died, whoever bothered to remember him would celebrate his death and not his life. Shayna might find out about it in the news days after it had happened and shrug.

It was certainly not a pleasant way to be remembered, but his life would never be pleasant again.

What bothered him the most, though, was that his resigning to isolation left him with one consistent way to escape.

Michael finished his latest sketch—a scene of Bella laid out on her stomach, her back exposed and looking delicate—and stuck it to the wall with a piece of chewed gum. It fit into the one vacant space left, filling the hole like the last piece of a puzzle falling into place. Michael leaned back, admiring the way his wall was now covered from the floor to the ceiling in her image, his muse creating a beautiful collage of perfection and torment.

When he closed his eyes, he was with her. She danced with him in his dreams and kissed him in his sleep. In boredom, he would let himself think about her and fully indulge in the memory of what she felt and sounded like. Though Bella was a constant reminder of why he was imprisoned, she freed him of his cage, even if it was just in his head.

Behind his eyes, at least, he was never truly alone.

42

Shayna

Shayna spent most of her pregnancy traveling across America. As her belly swelled, she found herself behind the wheel of her BMW more often than she had ever been. There was a world outside of Pittsburgh that she had never seen, one that her sister had been boasting of for years, and she was just now beginning to discover it. But she did so with a mission beyond rating Parisian hotels and Indian cuisine that painted her trips in shades of sorrow.

In the time that had elapsed since Jon's death, she had begun to fortify herself. Through loss, she had gained an assurance she wouldn't have had otherwise.

State by state, Shayna met with the victims of Sirens. They all regarded her with sad, tired eyes, but their voices were eager to be heard when they spoke to her. For the most part, her time was regarded as a worthy effort, which was largely appreciated. Still, there was always the occasional person in the crowd who wouldn't forgive and forget. They were angry and needed to point that anger somewhere. So they pointed it all at her. Shayna didn't blame them for their misdirected misery. They didn't know what she had gone through, just as she didn't know what they had endured.

Shayna had become recognized throughout the news as a sort of public figure by the middle of that summer. She was no longer just Jon's widow. She was an activist, a face that promised relief and sympathy. A person who understood. News anchors were inviting her onto their broadcasts for interviews. People wrote to her online and through letters, desperate to be heard. With Michael in prison and Jon dead, she had become a face of the scandal and the symbol of its recovery.

Through her travels, she lived modestly. She had long since learned to do so, and Jon's Sirens fortune was being distributed among families who had been hit the hardest by the game. She gave it to children who had lost their fathers, to the families who had to discover their daughters' identities after their death, and to the parents who had to bury their eighteen-year-old sons. She planned to live frugally until her baby was delivered and she had recovered from the birth. After that, she would return to work, rejoining the quiet comfort of being unknown. Before her was only a pool of sadness to wade through. She would meet with families who wanted somewhere to throw their sorrows. She would undertake their treatment and their accusations.

Shayna considered Michael's misery to be the most effective on her. Their bond was strange and flawed like flowers blooming between pavement cracks. Part of her would always credit some of Jon's death to him. She couldn't shake it no matter how hard she tried. It would be a long time before she could work on truly forgiving him.

She and Michael met monthly. Even though these visits were veiled by her caution around him, they were always refreshing. It felt nice to be understood.

Michael, from his tiny little cell in Pittsburgh, had called her one day out of the blue. It was late July and so hot out that Shayna felt like it was difficult to breathe. Yet she was outside, all the same, craving the sun's warmth, daring to feel something at any expense. She let the heat welcome her after such a cold, bitter winter.

Shayna had been sitting on the porch, the same porch that she and Jon used to sit on in the evenings, where they had smoked joints that smelled pleasantly like skunks. Sitting there, she could've almost looked over and seen Jon staring out at the pine trees, thinking quietly to himself.

The sharp ring of her phone cut through those memories of days long lost like a hot knife through butter. Shayna answered it, not acknowledging the strange number. Nowadays people from across the country were getting ahold of her. She was used to foreign phone numbers by now.

The tinny voice on the other end announced that an inmate from the Riverside Correctional Center was trying to get ahold of her. Shayna relaxed slightly and rubbed her swollen belly. Though she had just seen Michael days before in person, these unprompted calls had become rather normal. Michael had no one left to talk to. It was not unlike him to call when he needed to hear someone's voice besides the one in his head.

Shayna waited patiently to hear Michael on the other end. The other line was soundless.

"Michael?" Shayna asked, her hand pausing on her belly.

"Yeah," he said finally.

"Is something wrong?" Shayna asked.

There was a beat of silence before Michael said, "Mary's inheritance is rolling in."

"Oh," Shayna said. They had both known it was coming in any day now, yet they had only discussed it briefly in person on her last visit. Michael hadn't seemed eager to talk about it.

"Some good it does me," Michael said with a breathy chuckle.

"At least it's something, though."

"I guess." His voice was tight and strained. "It's fucked up."

"Yeah," Shayna agreed. "Everything is."

"I know it's selfish," he said. "Believe me, I know it is. Fuck me. I'm *the guy* in all of this. But I just... I want to see her things. She put all of the money she could into expensive pieces. Things I could remember her by. I could hold her memory if I wasn't in here. I'll never get to see her belongings."

"You're allowed to be angry," Shayna said softly.

"I'm more sad than anything," he admitted. "Everything that came after has just been so much. I'm one of the lucky ones too. I know that."

"Just because you lived doesn't make you lucky necessarily."

"I am, though," he insisted.

Shayna disagreed but didn't feel up to arguing with him. The sun was getting quite hot, and she was starting to feel drained.

"You're allowed to say that you're suffering too," she said finally.

Michael chuckled again, then inhaled sharply. "I want to give whatever she left me to you."

Shayna's free hand dropped to her side. "What?"

"I have no use for it," Michael said. "And I have no one to pass it down to but you. I figure you can decide what to do with it. Sell whatever you can and use the money for whatever you want. Keep it for yourself. You can even donate it to Sirens research and the... the survivors if you want. It doesn't matter. That money does nothing for me."

"Oh, Michael," was all she could say as she processed it. Of course, most of it would go elsewhere but the comfortable cushion it would provide her and her child with was tempting.

The question hung heavily in the air, the elephant in the room. She felt greedy for asking but needed to know. "Do you know how much it's all worth?"

"They're saying her jewelry is where the money will be at. It's apparently worth thousands." He cleared his throat. "They said a rough estimate of her estate would be around two hundred grand," he said. "Give or take."

Shayna couldn't speak. It was enough to pay back most of her house and loans, provide for her baby, and still be able to donate a large chunk.

"It seems she was a smart investor," he said. "She put all of her expendable money into nice things when she was young before I was dropped off at her door. I can't understand why she didn't spend some of it on a nicer retirement home, but I think... I think she was trying to leave it all to me."

"That's... so much," Shayna said.

"Yeah, I figured you could donate a pretty penny with it. This time it'll be on me, though. It's the least that I can do." He cleared his throat awkwardly. "Or, you know, you could keep it for yourself. You certainly deserve it."

Money talked more than mouths. It was the vision of wealth that had plunged the nation into such horror, and it would be money that would allow the victims of Sirens even a sliver of a chance to recover. It was a filthy, piggish system, and she felt sick that she continued to buy into it. But it was a loop just like anything else.

"So, will you take it off my hands?" Michael asked.

"Yeah," Shayna said. "Yeah, I can do that. I'll put it to good use."

"Good. Good."

There was a brief pause before Michael added, "Shayna?"

"Yeah?"

"I'm grateful for you," he said.

"I know," she said.

"Good," he repeated. "I'll set up a way to get you Mary's things as soon as I can."

"No rush," she said. "We have nothing but time."

Michael laughed on the other line. He had said that exact phrase to her when they had first met. Shayna found herself laughing too. For several moments the two of them giggled for disjointed reasons, joined together by a flimsy understanding of the other's experience. But that was okay for now. It was enough.

"All right, Shayna," Michael said finally, his voice still light with humor. "I need to get back to it."

They both knew "it" was absolutely nothing, and Shayna let herself giggle again. It was strange humor, but it felt good to laugh again.

"Understandable," she said. "Thank you, Michael."

"No problem," Michael said. His tone fell and settled into seriousness. "Bye, Shayna."

"Bye," Shayna said and then hung up.

She stood with some effort, wanting desperately to get out of the heat. As she walked back into the house, her gait was a waddle.

The remnants of what had just happened were bouncing around her head, unable to quite sink in as the cold air from her house wrapped her in its embrace.

She was grateful, of course. After months of merely wading, it felt as though she was finally progressing again.

Time would continue and they had nothing but it.

43

Shayna

Shayna had her baby on August 6, 2030. She gave birth to a little girl who would inherit the world Shayna had tried to right. Shayna's baby had come out small and fragile and with a pair of lungs on her that could have woken up the entire city.

The squalling bundle was named Eve, after all of the evenings she and Jon had sat out on their porch as twilight fell. She had to believe that Eve also marked the beginning of a new chapter.

It didn't take long for Eve's features to set in. Sometimes, when Shayna looked at her daughter, whom she had strived to manifest for years, she wept. On her head was a mess of black hair and her skin was a light tan coloring, marking the only touches of Shayna. The rest was all Jon.

On warmer fall evenings, Shayna would sit on the back porch of her home holding Eve and close her eyes. If she tried hard enough, the smell of weed and Jon would be so vivid it was almost real. When she opened her eyes, they would be filled with tears, and she would hug their daughter closer to her.

Then, Eve would squirm at her chest in the dusk air, fickle and wriggling, and break that spell. Jon was not there, and those evenings spent passing a joint had long since evaporated. Only the ghost of him was left, visible in the features of their child.

While she had taken her maternity leave, Shayna did not halt in her pursuit of fixing the mess that Sirens had left. The death toll was closer to a hundred thousand by that following September, but it had slowed significantly during the summer months. The deaths were reaching an end.

That was not to say that Sirens wouldn't claim more victims. The ones that had accepted Shayna's money and sought out therapy and isolation would live with the mental scars if they chose to live at all. The disease would be with them until death. Shayna was now certain of this too. She still visited Michael on every fifteenth day of the month, and he had laid this out to her very clearly. His Bella was with him, as vivid as if he had just seen her, even a year later.

She talked with Michael about everything. Now, they even discussed Eve. Shayna brought Eve with her on occasion. In September, close to a year after Sirens was turned in, Shayna had brought her daughter with her to show Michael and he had wept.

"She looks like him," Michael had said.

"She's the last of him," Shayna agreed, stifling the tears in her own eyes.

They had suffered together, and they would grow together. She had no intention of stalling her visitations.

Ever since Eve had been born, they had broken their silence about all of the elements of the Sirens experience, including Bella. Every time she was brought up, Michael's face became a warzone as joy, remorse, and pain fought across his features. They turned over ideas for cures and ways to ease the pain of Sirens' survivors. Shayna was starting to believe that there was no chemical you could inject to solve the problem. That would be a quick fix. It would have been too easy.

There were also hundreds of thousands of people like herself who would continue on without their parent, sibling, lover, or child because of that game. Those wounds would never heal either. There would always be an empty hole where those people used to be, and Shayna couldn't replace those losses even if she tried. No payout would fill that vacancy. She knew this well enough.

Eve made Shayna fortunate. There would always be a piece of Jon with her. She wasn't sure if that was haunting or sweet. Time would reveal it to her as it always did.

When she looked down at Eve swaddled in blankets or baby clothes, she saw more than Jon. There was a future in her. Eve would be given the world whether the earth had progressed or regressed. Shayna could only try to inch it forward for her, but to truly leave a place worth living in, she couldn't do it alone.

And that made her incredibly sad.

She could not foresee a world in just eighteen short years that didn't covet women like items or turn them into literal games as her husband had. There was only so much paving Shayna could do.

Shayna would work until then to make Sirens a thing of the past. It would become a distant memory that would bleed onto history pages. Over time, it would get easier to think about Sirens. She would one day remember Jon without feeling any anger, sadness, or resentment. One day she would find peace in those memories and share them with their daughter.

But for now, that change was distant, far off like the setting sun over the pines from her view on her back porch.

For now, that was just how things were.

Acknowledgements

I wrote this story in 2020 when the world was falling apart, and I had nothing better to do than finally try to write a book. It was a challenge I never imagined that I would accomplish, but it is also something my family was always unwaveringly certain that I could do. Above all, I would like to thank my family for their relentless belief in me.

Thank you to my sister, Kalli, who never once doubted me and always interacts with my cheesy attempts at book promotion. In her infallible support, she has never once told me that this was impossible.

Thank you to my mom, Kerri, who told me to take the leap and find an editor while encouraging me to live with my parents while I prioritized this project. I'd also like to thank her for igniting this passion in me when I was just four years old. I truly believe I would not love reading and writing the way that I do if she had not read *Harry Potter* to me at such a young age.

Thank you to my dad, Chuck, who listens to my wild ideas with patience and has always nudged me onto this path. He has read drafts of my stories, sent me links to publishing options, and always told me that this was possible. His encouragement was so steadfast that I think he was certain I would have my name on a book cover before I did.

I could write a whole other book on how grateful I am for my family and then a sequel on how the better parts of me are just pieces of them. Simply put, they're the best.

Thank you to my best friend and beta reader, Hunter, who between conversations about Taylor Swift found the time to encourage and reassure me. When I met you, Hunter, I could never have imagined how our friendship would grow. I am so grateful for your support and endless insights. I couldn't have done this without you.

Thank you to Gabby, who made this cover. I'm so grateful for her ability to listen to my rants, her encouragement of my wild ideas, and her eagerness to help where she can. This cover is exactly what I wanted, so thank you, thank you, thank you!

Thank you to Emily, who was gracious enough to pose for this cover. Thank you for jumping on the opportunity to participate and lend your lips, no questions asked.

Thank you to my editor, Sasha, who made me realize I say "for a moment" way too much. It was incredibly helpful to have someone tailoring my lengthy sentences and thoughts into something digestible.

And of course, thank you to everyone who read this book. Sirens has been a passion of mine for years now, and the fact that this labor of love is now out for consumption is scary, thrilling, and mind-blowing.

Thank you for giving me and Sirens a chance.

About the Author

Chloe Ruffennach was born and raised in Pittsburgh, Pennsylvania, where she still resides. When she's not working in marketing, Chloe enjoys reading character-driven stories (bonus if the protagonist is an abject woman!) and striving tirelessly toward her ultimate goal of becoming a cat lady.